STRAW GIRL

Brigid Barry

Thank you to Katie, Patti, Fran, and the folks at Absolute Write for your relentless support. Heather, you inspired me to pick the pen back up. And my wonderful and patient husband, thank you for answering all of my writing related questions without any context. You really are my favorite. This book is dedicated to Bri, because without you, this never would have happened.

Dear Reader,

Once upon a time, I didn't believe in ghosts. Then I did a favor for a friend and ended up sleeping overnight in a haunted house for three nights. I still don't know how I stayed in the house after the first night, but the experience changed me from skeptic to believer.

I had more or less forgotten those events when I ended up in a brand-new house, later pronounced "the most haunted location" the paranormal investigators had ever been to.

Decades later, by random chance, I found the collection of EVPs (Electronic Voice Phenomena) and photos from the investigations, as well as my diary entry from the first haunted house.

"Straw Girl" is based on those materials. I hope you enjoy reading it as much as I enjoyed writing it.

Very truly yours,
Brigid

Prologue

In bed with the covers pulled up to my chin, I squeezed my eyes closed. The power had gone out, the air conditioner dying with a loud *beep*. Had it been a few minutes, or hours? Despite the late August heat and humidity outside, the temperature in the room had continued to plummet without it. My breath would have been visible if the room wasn't pitch dark.

The hoarse whisper from an audio recording echoed in my head.

Let me in.

I tucked myself into a tighter ball, missing Ryan. Would tonight have been different if he'd been here? I wouldn't wish this experience on anyone, but the last thing I wanted was to be alone. Spectral fingers clawed along the vinyl siding, inches away from my head. More tapped on the window next to my bed. I kept my back to it, which somehow made it better.

Let me in.

Hiding under a blanket, I didn't feel like a thirty-four-year-old woman with two college degrees. It was more like being six years old again on my mother's couch, terrified because, in the dark, a hanging plant resembled a witch. I did now what I'd done then: pulled the covers over my head and squeezed my eyes shut. Just like a rabbit, if I can't see it, then I don't need to be afraid because it's not really there.

Tap. Tap. Tap.

Let me in.

Three were in the house with me, but how many were outside, pleading to be let in? Five? A hundred? There was no way to know. Shivering, I pressed my hands to my forehead and tucked my chin against my chest. My harsh breathing almost covered the sounds of tapping and scratching on the exterior of the house.

Almost.

Nothing could block the words reverberating in my mind: *Let me in.*

An old coping mechanism took over and my mind wandered away from what it couldn't handle. I went back through my memories to unravel how I ended up here. This wasn't the first time I'd been in a haunted house alone. Dread it wouldn't be the last time lodged in the pit of my stomach.

I considered when I first thought about spirits. They'd become such a huge part of my life lately that I struggled to remember when they weren't. I'd picked up tarot cards when I'd converted to Paganism, if one can convert from non-practicing, non-denominational Protestantism. Were tarot cards fortune telling or communicating with spirits?

What came before that? Was this a delayed response to using a Ouija board as a teen, and not taking the dire warnings seriously enough? I couldn't think of anything earlier than those years in high school, moving the plastic indicator over the board covered in letters. Laughing at the warnings about it being a gateway for spirits and the demonic.

Everything before that seemed vague. Hazy. I'd grown up in Southern Maine, not thinking very much about ghosts at all.

Tap. Tap. Tap.

I huddled farther under the blankets. The idea of wandering spirits had popped up now and again, probably when my raised-but-not-practicing Catholic mother had said something about the dearly departed. More than once, I'd been worried about undressing before a shower. All my dead relatives might be in there with me. It had creeped me out, but I never shared the worry with anyone. Who would I have shared it with? Then the idea of ghosts would go away as quickly as it had appeared. But now they wouldn't go away, no matter how hard I tried.

I fought to control my breathing and take myself somewhere else. Anywhere else. I kept sorting through memories, trying to find the time in my life I could identify as "this moment is when I started to believe."

But something had definitely shoved me in that direction.

Chapter 1

March 18, 2003

Linoleum that may have been white once upon a time, now yellowed and curling around the edges, surrounded me as I stood in the kitchen of my one-bedroom apartment. Paint bubbled on the walls, most likely a result of the leaking roof the landlord didn't care much about. "Shabby" was a generous description given the condition and location, but beggars can't be choosers. I'd reached out to the realtor-slash-property manager from a payphone in Texas, trying to find a place to live before my discharge went through. The agency had a reputation for low-quality properties—for sale, too, not just for rent—but was the only place to call about a place to live. With no such thing as Wi-Fi in the dorm of my squadron, I'd had no way of getting pictures, so I didn't bother. If I hadn't been too afraid of running into people I didn't want to see, I could've gone to the base's library to use the internet there. Instead, I told him my price point and got what I got. No use crying over it now.

I hung up the phone, disappointed once again to find out I hadn't gotten a job. My last Air Force deposit from the DoD would last me two more rent payments, assuming I didn't need food. If I did want food, then one month's rent, and maybe enough of a second to not get evicted for a while. I'd taken care of the place well enough—maybe it would earn me a reprieve.

When the phone rang again, I picked up immediately. Hoping for a job offer, I used my most professional voice to answer. "Hello, this is Melisandre Roberts."

Silence for a moment, then a familiar laugh came over the line.

"You know, I've worked in a hotel for three years and never has my customer service voice been that customer servicey. Congratulations!"

I sat back, disappointed again. "Hey, Alexandra, what's up?" My best friend, Alexandra Narvaez. Never Alex. I could have asked her to scope the place out for me, but I hated asking anyone for help out of fear of having it used against me later.

Without seeing her do it, I knew she rolled her eyes at my tone. "Don't sound so happy to hear from me. Since when do you go by Melisandre?"

My finger wound itself in the curls of the phone cord. "I have to put my legal name on job applications. It's easier to tell people later that I go by Melissa or Mel." I pulled my finger free. "I could change it with the probate court, but a mean part of me likes to snub the pretentious name my mother gave me."

"Ah." I could practically hear her nod over the phone. "I have two things for you. First, you remember Rebecca James?"

The energy in her voice had me exhausted already. Not perky, but forceful in a positive way. "Do you mean the psychic who's been on the radio a few times?"

"Yeah, that's her."

"What about her?" Alexandra never asked idle questions. They always led somewhere.

"Well, she and her family are on vacation and I'm house-sitting for her. She has a dog and a small menagerie outside. My coworker had her baby two weeks early, and they need someone to do her overnights." She paused. "I'm going to pick the shifts up, but that means I can't be at Rebecca's overnight."

Silence weighed on the line like a wet quilt. I poked at a paint bubble and it ripped, revealing several layers of color. My fingernail left an indentation in the soggy drywall.

She exhaled. "I know you've been looking for work, so I have a weird, odd job for you. I could give you a hundred and twenty bucks if you're able to go over for three nights."

Mentally, I went over the bills I could pay. My phone bill for one. "Three nights?"

"Yeah. I don't have to be there twenty-four-seven, but she wants someone there overnight because of some break-ins in the area. If you could get there at, like, eight and stay until six or seven in the morning, that would be awesome."

I choked back my laugh. What else was I going to do with my time? "Sure, no problem."

Relief came through in her voice, even if she hadn't sighed. "Awesome, thanks. So, this is tomorrow, Thursday, and Friday. They're coming back Saturday morning, but not until ten or so. Rebecca told me to outsource if I needed, so no worries there, but I need to meet you there to go over a few things."

I frowned. "I'm pretty sure I can manage house sitting and a dog."

"Well, it's the dog, a couple of horses, and some chickens." She could tell I was gearing up to interrupt because she rushed to add, "I know you know about the horses, but it's really the house. It's this weird old farmhouse that's been added to about a thousand times and it's hard to explain, but I'm not—we're not—allowed to go in certain areas."

With my thumb, I smoothed the piece of paint, trying to line the ragged edges up. "Yeah, whatever. Just let me know."

"Cool." She hesitated, and I waited her out again. "So, the second thing. How are you doing?"

Closing my eyes, I took a deep breath. "I'm fine." I stretched the phone cord as far as it would go around the wall and into the living room to sit in my desk chair

"Are you actually fine, or are you saying you're fine and just trying to get me to not ask you how you're doing?"

"Anything stopping it from being both?" I closed my eyes, leaned back, and pressed the heel of my palm to my forehead. "I'm actually fine, but I want you to not ask me anymore?"

"Hey, you know I'm here for you and I'm always on your side. Are you going to the funeral?"

"I think you already know the answer to that." I released a breath in a gush. "I'm really fine, just like the last four times you asked."

"Just making sure. Anyway, I have to be at the house at ten this morning. Can you meet me there?"

I agreed, and she gave me the address, which I jotted down. We hung up, and I tucked my pencil over my ear, unfolding the newspaper to read the classifieds. The phone rang again, and I let the caller ID catch up before I answered.

"Alexandra, what did you forget?"

She paused so long, maybe she'd pocket dialed me.

"Hello?"

"Mel." She paused. "There's something else."

My sigh probably sounded as exasperated as I felt. She knew I didn't want to talk about my parents. I had a therapist for that. There was only so much time I wanted to spend on them. "Alexandra, I said I'm fine."

"I know you're not, but that's not what I wanted to talk to you about." She paused. "It's about the house."

"Rebecca's?"

"Yeah. It's not just the break-ins that Rebecca wants someone there." Alexandra took a deep breath and let it out. "You know she's a psychic, right?"

I wanted her to get to the point. I pinched the bridge of my nose. "Yeah, she's been on the radio a couple of times." The repetitiveness of the conversation gave me déjà vu. "What about it?"

"Well, she's not a read-your-mind psychic. She's a talk-to-ghosts psychic."

My eyes rolled.

"Don't roll your eyes at me, Mel. I'm being serious." Her voice lowered. "The house is actually haunted."

I shook my head. She didn't need to see me to know about the head shaking any more than the eye rolling, but she didn't comment. "That's fine."

She couldn't hide the surprise in her voice. "Really?"

"Yeah. Have to be honest, I could use the money. Wait. Is this because you don't want to be there overnight?"

A nervous laugh. "Yeah, kind of. I hadn't actually confirmed I'd be taking the overnights at the hotel yet, but I wanted to. Being at Rebecca's after dark freaks me out."

I raked my fingers through my hair and knocked the pencil off my ear. It bounced on the floor and rolled across the worn carpet and under my desk. "Yeah, no problem. It's all good. I can be there for overnights."

Alexandra apologized a few times and assured me everything would be fine, and I let her. Ghosts were stories and not real. She'd said it was an old house, and old houses made noise. Regardless of whether the place had a ghost infestation, I needed the money.

Chapter 2

March 19, 2003

The house looked different from earlier in the day with Alexandra. It wasn't just that the sun had gone down and the motion sensor lights made the shadows play strangely over the clapboard. I couldn't pinpoint what had changed.

As I grabbed my pillow and my overnight bag—a fancy number: a plastic Shop'n'Save bag with something for me to sleep in, a book, and my toothbrush—I couldn't take my eyes away from the house. A cute farm house during the day, but tonight, it loomed over me in the semi-dark. Darkness swallowed everything outside the circle of light like a black hole. I shivered and blamed the chill in the air.

A slightly overweight yellow lab greeted me at the door, obviously starved for affection, but still disappointed I wasn't his family.

"Hey, Bailey." I pushed the door closed with my foot so I could pat him. I locked the door behind me, my hand automatically sliding up the door, seeking the deadbolt on my apartment door that didn't exist here. The house smelled clean, with faint tones of old wood, and a hint of dog, which could have been Bailey. I paused. We weren't supposed to go to my right—a no-go zone, Alexandra had called it—Rebecca's office and supposedly the most haunted part of the whole house. Remembering the expression on her pale face—and not just her usual shade of fair skin—made me shake my head. It was always weird being in someone else's house alone. Rebecca must have told Alexandra some crazy stories to scare her so badly.

Straight ahead, a flight of stairs rose into the space above the office, and I went to the left, through the biggest kitchen I'd ever seen and into the living room. I set my grocery bag on the couch—my bed for the next three nights. Most of the farmhouses I'd been in had a room like this, a long and narrow rectangle, approximately half the width of the house and the full depth. The cracked-open bathroom door allowed golden light to spill out across the wide pine boards. Alexandra must have left the overhead on so I wouldn't be fumbling around in the dark trying to orient myself. This particular room had something resembling but wasn't a wood stove sitting in the middle. What had Alexandra called it? I couldn't remember. She'd said it would go off and on by itself. Flames flickered behind the glass, illuminating and warming the room.

"Don't worry about it and don't touch it," she'd said. I flopped onto the couch and the kitchen—part of a renovation to the house where the attached barn had been converted to living space—opened in front of me. To my right, a blue door hid a three-season porch being used for storage. Alexandra had warned me repeatedly not to go out there—why I would eluded me—because the door was stuck shut, had piles of stuff behind it anyway, and wouldn't open. From the looks of the long crack running down the center of the door, it might break from a stern look or strong sneeze.

There was another no-go zone over my right shoulder, directly across from the off-limits porch. We weren't allowed to go upstairs, either. Was Rebecca trying to preserve some privacy, which I assumed could be tough for a local celebrity, or a control freak? It didn't really matter to me either way. I sank into the couch, spreading my arms and patting the cushions on either side of me. The house's cozy warmth wrapped around me like a blanket and I should have been ready for sleep. Instead, I pulled a thick paperback out of my grocery bag, and Bailey sat at my feet, staring up at me, his tail swishing across the floor behind him.

"Oh, right." We went back to the front door, and I let him out. He trotted in front of my car and disappeared into the night.

The deep darkness threatened to swallow me. My apartment in Sanford—right on Main Street—had streetlights and giant signs for businesses that had already closed up shop glaring through my thin curtains all night. Even the house where I'd grown up in an old subdivision had lights from neighbors' porches, or the streetlight from the road above ours filtering through the woods and down the hill. And on base, there had been lights on everywhere, from dusk until dawn. This unsettling darkness filled me with awe.

I could shut the porch light off, just to see the stars, but Bailey came trotting back, tongue lolling, clearly proud of himself.

We went back inside, and, after I locked the door, I also shut the outside light off. After spending the last nine months with a light glaring outside my bedroom window all night, I eagerly anticipated sleeping in the dark. I looked at the fire. Well, mostly dark.

After changing in the living room, I settled on the couch, pulling up one of the blankets Alexandra had left out for me. I fluffed my pillow, glad I'd brought it. The couch and blanket both had the same clean but unfamiliar smell as the rest of the house. Without my own pillow, I might not have been able to sleep. Bailey hopped up and settled on my feet, releasing a long groan on a sigh. I read by the light of the fire, very comfortable there with one arm up over my head.

Before long, I couldn't keep my eyes open anymore. I made a note of the page number and let it fall to the floor. My eyes drifted closed.

I startled awake, not sure what pulled me out of sleep. The fire had gone out, and a faint bluish light glowed in the kitchen. Holding my breath, I stiffened on the couch, my eyes wide as if it would somehow help me hear better in the dark. My heart thudded in my chest as I waited. The seconds ticked by, and my body relaxed.

Waking up in a panic wasn't new, I reminded myself.

Then, heavy work boots walked across the wood floor above me, from the top of the stairs toward the bedrooms. One, two, three, four steps and then they reached the carpet. I kept listening, waiting for the sound of a door opening that never came.

"God, Mel, don't be stupid," I said, needing to hear anything other than the heavy silence of the house. "You seriously think that someone snuck past you and the dog? Then they got up the bare wooden stairs, and we didn't hear them until they walked across the landing? Right."

At my feet, Bailey dozed through my monologue.

Closing my eyes, I folded my hands across my chest and released a deep breath. My eyes popped back open. *Unless someone has been upstairs the whole time*, my mind suggested helpfully. I pressed my feet against Bailey, hoping his deep, even breathing would help calm me. My lungs wouldn't cooperate, only allow-ing shallow breaths. I lay in the dark, waiting for something else to happen. A door opening, more footsteps, anything.

Nothing.

I couldn't take it anymore. In my stockinged feet, I crept to the bottom of the stairs and strained to hear. When Bailey brushed my leg, I about jumped out of my skin. My hand gripped the top of the newel post so hard, the edges of the flat top dug into my fingers, grounding me. I wasn't sure if I wanted to go up the stairs—a clearly identified no-go zone—or not. I swallowed hard and licked my lips, trying to get some moisture into my suddenly dry mouth.

My mind argued with me. The whole reason I was here was because of break-ins in the area. I was also less than comfortable with the idea of being asleep when a potential burglar came down the stairs to leave the house.

"Stay," I whispered, giving Bailey my sternest expression.

He wagged his tail and sat.

With one hand firmly on the railing, I made my way up the stairs, pausing on each step to listen. On the stair just below the landing, I flicked the switch for the light. Pot lights in the ceiling completely illuminated the walkway.

The empty walkway.

I was alone on the stairs.

Someone wasn't creeping through the house. Some of the tension drained out of my shoulders and I sagged against the smooth wooden railing. But I couldn't dismiss the very distinct footsteps. I shook my head and turned the light off before returning to the couch.

I tucked the blankets around my legs and beckoned Bailey up to sleep on my feet. He happily obliged. I settled down, taking a few deep breaths to relax. My eyes fell closed again, and I began to drift off to sleep.

Bailey leaped off the couch, and I jerked into a sitting position, one leg on the floor before my eyes opened. He ran to the front door. Every time his feet touched the floor, he barked, and I jolted at the noise. I jumped to my feet and jogged after him, my heart pounding. My hand fumbled on the wall, searching for the outside light switch.

A Maine Coon cat sat on the step, tail flicking behind him, amber eyes narrowed in the sudden brightness.

Not sure whether to laugh or cry, I felt ridiculous for being this scared. There were plenty of reasons to freak out by myself in the dark, but I still chastised myself for it. I let the cat in, and he immediately wrapped himself around my ankles. After I locked the door and shut the lights off again, Bailey and I resumed our previous positions on the couch.

My heart still thudded in my chest, and sleep wasn't going to come any time soon. I tried to take deep breaths, the song "My Favorite Things" running through my head as I counted on my fingers. My therapist approved of this coping mechanism when things that went bump in the night reminded me of things I'd rather not think about.

Eventually, my heart slowed, and I got my breathing back to normal. I shifted to my side and tucked my feet between Bailey and the back of the couch. The cat crunched food somewhere in the kitchen, and my book summoned me like a siren.

This time, when the dog bounded off the couch and I jumped, I nearly fell on my face on the floor. I caught myself on my palms and knees, and I envisioned my TI from basic training screaming "push-up position!", the image so brief, it barely registered before I was on my feet after the dog. My heart had resumed its pounding, but I didn't run.

Peering through the glass into the darkness, I flicked on the light. A face stared back at me, and I jumped. My reflection in the glass of the storm door.

"Breathe," I said.

A shrub near the outer door of the enclosed porch swayed with the breeze that had picked up, the still bare branches brushing against the clapboard. I stood there for several minutes with my arms crossed over my chest, trying to see into the darkness beyond the limits of the porch light.

If something had been out there, the motion sensor light would have been on. The dog probably heard the shrub touching the house. I flipped the light off and went back toward the couch, glancing into the dark kitchen. The glowing blue light from the stove clock told me it had only been ten minutes since I'd let the cat in, even though it seemed like longer.

Bailey and I settled back onto the couch. The cat joined us, crouching on the arm near my head, purring so loudly, I swore I could feel it in my teeth. I reached over my head and stroked his silky fur, and the volume increased.

The fire extinguished itself with a *whoomph*, and I jumped. I wracked my brain, but couldn't remember the name of the stupid thing.

The dog jumped up again, getting to a sitting position before running for the front door. My heart stayed in my chest this time instead of leaping into my throat.

I followed. The clock said 9:30. Exactly ten minutes from the last time.

Once again, the motion sensor hadn't tripped, so I only waited a minute before turning on the outside light. Even the shrub remained motionless, as if holding its breath, and I had no idea what the dog had lost his mind over.

Bailey and I returned to the living room. The cat—I'd have to ask Alexandra his name—hadn't moved from his perch on the arm of the couch, indifferent to the dog's antics.

Chapter 3

March 20, 2003

"Alexandra, it was freaking ridiculous. Every ten minutes, Bailey ran off the couch to go bark at the front door. He did it until midnight. By the time he stopped, I was so wound up, I didn't get any sleep at all."

Silence from her end of the line. I couldn't wait her out. "What?"

The phone creaked in her hand as she fidgeted. "Mel, it was the ghosts."

My shoulders slumped, and I pressed my palm over my closed eyes. I needed a nap, not this crap. "Oh, for crying out loud. You have got to be kidding me."

"I wasn't kidding when I said the place was haunted. I told you it was."

I threw my free hand up in the air. "Fine, let's assume for a moment it was ghosts, and that's why the dog was losing his marbles all night." I tucked my hand under my elbow at my waist. "Why didn't the cat freak out? I thought they were guardians of the underworld or something. Only the dog did anything."

"First off, that wasn't the home run you wanted it to be. Winston is a super chill cat. Unless you're turning the faucet on in the kitchen, he doesn't care about much."

"They named their cat Winston?" I wiped my face. My bed beckoned like a siren.

"Yes, his name is Winston. Second, I think you're quoting *The Mummy*. Ancient Egyptians saw cats as representatives of the divine and protectors against evil." She yawned. "I doubt the ghosts at Rebecca's are evil."

Shaking my head in defeat, I leaned my shoulder against the wall. "Okay, fine. It was ghosts keeping the dog up all night. How do I get to sleep before midnight?"

She could hear the air quotes in my voice, but she didn't comment. "Tell them to stop bothering the dog because you need to go to sleep."

"Right. Okay. I'll do that." I shifted so my shoulder blades pressed into the wall. Tucked between the basement door and my desk, I sank to the floor.

"How's the job search coming?" She was grasping for something else to talk about. Her way of gauging how upset I was.

"Good." It wasn't good. It was bad. I had finally gotten the gumption to call a couple of places I'd applied to and never heard back. They'd passed because of lack of experience.

A long pause. I waited, not knowing what to say.

"Are you okay with going back tonight?"

I needed the money. I wanted the sleep, but the money I needed. "Yeah, of course."

"Okay, call me tomorrow morning and let me know how it went."

We settled on the couch a little before nine. The fire had already gone out, but I left the bathroom light on. I didn't want to admit to myself that the dark frightened me, but I was definitely freaked out. The wind outside howled around the house, and I pulled up an extra blanket to ward off the chill. Dreading another night like last night, I couldn't pretend to be anywhere near sleep.

After the sixth time the dog had jumped off the couch, my body finally stopped reacting like I was going to die. Sometime around eleven o'clock, I'd stopped getting off the couch at all. Maybe that had motivated Bailey to give up on his barking. The most unsettling thing was it happening every ten minutes, like a timer had been set somewhere.

TV would be a good distraction, assuming I could find a remote.

I jumped when Bailey charged for the front door. I sat up, but waited to see what would happen next before I followed him.

"It's probably the cat," I said, not completely convinced.

My hesitant footsteps didn't make any sound on the pine floor, and my shoulders screamed with tension. I had to remind myself to breathe. I flicked on the porch light. Just like last night, Winston sat on the concrete pad, tail flicking and the porch light reflecting in his eyes, and somewhat offended I hadn't been there to open the door sooner. I shook my head and let him in.

The flames had reappeared, so I pulled out my book—a Stephen King novel about ghosts was probably not the ideal choice under the circumstances—and lay down on the couch. As I pulled the blankets up to my chest, Bailey took his spot on my feet and Winston settled on my hips. Chilled even with my snuggle buddies, I huddled under my two blankets and pondered pulling up the last one. I opened my book, holding it from the top with one hand, my thumb in the crease, and let it rest on my chest as I read. With my free hand, I stroked Winston's back. His purring competed with the sound of the fire.

When Bailey jumped off the couch again, I didn't move except to close my eyes and take a deep breath. I felt like an idiot, but at least no one was here to witness my humiliation.

"Listen, guys." I opened my eyes and scanned the room. "I'm trying to get some sleep tonight and would really appreciate it if you would let the dog settle down for bed."

Bailey returned, tail wagging, and his eyes gleamed in the faint light of the bathroom.

I stayed awake for quite a while, tense and waiting. After rereading the same page four times and not remembering any of it, I put the book on the floor beside me. The fire went out with a *whoomph*, taking my reading light with it. Bailey snored. Winston stopped purring and went to sleep with his head resting on my hand.

Eventually my eyelids got heavy, and I fell asleep, too. When the fire started back up, I didn't even notice.

The dream started the way it always started: in the squadron laundry room. One of the fluorescent bulbs in the back corner flickered, threatening to go out. Washers and dryers hummed with unattended laundry. I've always been a rule follower, and the rules said stay with your laundry. I'd bring my study materials and sit in the row of plastic chairs outside of the laundry room while I washed and dried. Occasionally, someone would pop into the laundry room to collect or deposit something, but for the most part, it was quiet on weekdays and I'd be left alone to study.

This particular day, I stood on the end row of the machines, near the doorway, switching my stuff from the washing machine into the dryer. A hallway door opened. Someone laughed in the dayroom, on the other end of the long corridor, near the female hallway. The sound distorted on its way past the offices, so I couldn't tell who it was.

An airman walked through the doorway. I looked up from my notes and gave him a polite smile. I knew him, or at least, I'd seen him around. He was part of another squadron using the first-floor hallway near the laundry. I'd spoken to him a few times in passing and got a kick out of his Louisiana accent. The first time he'd asked me for a "pee-en," I was at least as confused as the non-New Englanders were when I slipped up and said "cah."

He smiled and nodded. The same height as me, but built like a gorilla, his muscles strained the navy-blue t-shirt. Why did all the guys insist on wearing their shirts two sizes too small? "Louisiana" flowed in bold yellow cursive across the front, underlined by the horizontal line of the L. He went to the row of washing machines behind me, and I went back to my own laundry. Suddenly self-conscious about reaching down into the washer, I hurried.

As soon as I closed the dryer door, the hairs on the back of my neck rose. He stood there, still smiling. He invaded my personal space, but I had nowhere to go. With the stack of dryers in front of me and a cinderblock wall next to me, the only open route was between the maze of washing machines. Unfortunately, a dead end unless I wanted to climb over the rows of washers.

"How's it going?" he asked.

A shiver ran up my spine and my instincts told me to get out of there. I peeked through the door, hoping to see someone, but the hallway was as deserted as it always was at this time of day. On the opposite side of the hallway, the row of chairs sat empty except for my open notebook.

"I'm good, just finishing up here," I said.

His smile widened a bit. "So, we're all alone in here, huh?"

The bad feeling worsened, and I tried to tamp it down, accusing myself of being paranoid. "One of my roommates is on her way down," I lied. "We're meeting to study."

"You're pretty cute." He stepped forward.

If I breathed in too deep, I'd touch him. I backed up and inched sideways. If I could somehow squeeze between him and the wall, the doorway beckoned only a few feet away.

"Thanks. Listen, nice to see you, but I have to run. I have a test tomorrow and left my flashcards in my room." I didn't even try to be subtle about moving toward the door. He stepped in front of me. My eyes widened and I couldn't breathe as my heart slammed inside my chest.

"You know what you need for your test tomorrow? A little stress relief."

Everything in me screamed to run, get the hell out of there as fast I could and not look back, but I tried to stay calm. "Oh, I'm not stressed at all, but thanks."

He put his left arm up next to my head, resting his palm on the dryer door behind me and leaning toward me. His breath washed over my face. He'd had something with maple syrup recently. I backed into the dryer, and he followed. When I stepped sideways, the sleeve of my shirt brushed the cinderblock.

"We can fool around if you want." With his right hand, he grabbed my wrist and pressed it against the fly of his jeans.

I struggled against him, but his grip tightened, holding me firm. "Let me go."

"Come on, let's fool around. It'll be fun."

"Dammit, I said let me go."

My free hand came up to slap him, but he swatted it away.

He hit the side of the head with the heel of his hand, and I went sideways into the wall. In a heartbeat, he had a beefy hand around my throat, underneath my jaw. He lifted me up off the floor as I kicked, my heels hitting the cinderblock. I kicked out at him, but the soft toes of my sneakers were no match for his shins. I clawed at his wrist, desperate for him to release me. He grabbed my hand again to put it back on his crotch and rubbed it up and down against a prominent erection. I tried to scream, shout, make any kind of noise, but all that came out was a gargle. Stars danced around the edges of my vision and I struggled to breathe.

"Oh, shit, dude, sorry!"

My assailant and I both turned to the doorway. Another airman had walked in and stood with his hands in the air like he was being held up. My vision darkened and my eyes bulged. Couldn't he see I needed help? Why wasn't he doing anything? With one hand pressed into my assailant's crotch and the other trying to pry his sausage fingers off of my throat, I couldn't make the gesture I desperately needed to.

The airman, my potential rescuer, didn't say anything else. He disappeared back into the hallway. Without saying anything or doing a damn thing to help me.

More haze clouded my vision and all I could think about was if I passed out, I'd be in even more trouble than I was now. I folded my knees up as high as I could and kicked out with both legs. Whatever I hit, he released his grip on my throat and the air rushing into my lungs whistled. I fell to the floor, my knee folding awkwardly beneath me. Every nerve tingled and my knee burned as I got back to my feet, and he lurched toward me again.

With as much force as I could muster, I brought my knee up between his legs. Then I balled my fist and punch him as hard as I could in the face. There was a satisfying *crunch*, and my hand exploded in pain. Without waiting to see what would happen, I shoved myself away from the wall with all of my strength and fell into the hallway.

I tumbled off of the couch and landed on the floor on my hands and knees. My heart raced so hard in my chest, I might have a heart attack. I put my hand over my throat where his beefy hand choked the life out of me, forcing the back of my skull into the cinderblock. During the day, I could press the memory back, put it away and pretend like it hadn't happened. But at night, as I lay sleeping and vulnerable, my brain insisted on poking me with a sharp stick to remind me it had happened when all I wanted to do was forget.

I stayed on the floor where I'd fallen, fighting to not cry and nearly choking on the tears clogging my throat. Bailey nudged me in the side with his nose, and I pushed myself to press my back against the couch. I put my arm over his shoulders and pulled him close. The tears flowed then, soaking Bailey's fur. We sat like that for nearly an hour until the tears stopped and my breathing settled down.

After I put the blankets and my pillow back on the couch, I glanced at the clock in the kitchen. At barely one a.m., dawn was a long way away.

"My Favorite Things" running through my head, I counted on my fingers over and over until sleep came back to claim me.

A bloodcurdling scream pulled me out of a sound sleep. I sat bolt upright, my hands grabbing the cushions to stop me from leaping to my feet.

Bailey launched himself toward the blue door. Even in the dim light, I could see his hackles up. His growling intruded over the rushing in my ears. When he made it about five feet away from the door, it swung outward onto the porch without making a sound. My heart tried to escape through my mouth. Bailey barked but my thundering heart drowned it out.

He came back to me, constantly looking over his shoulder to keep his gaze on the now open door. I didn't want to, but I padded across the room. Total darkness blanketed the interior of the porch, and I would never get back to sleep with the door hanging open. Alexandra's warning the door wouldn't budge echoed in my head as my hand touched the knob. It registered in my brain that the door and hardware may have been original as I pulled it shut. The edge of the door caught the jamb. My heart thudded back into my chest as I struggled to close it. I finally had to use the frame as leverage and lift up as I pulled.

I stood there, staring at the door and terrified in the dark. I put my hand against the painted wood. eventually, I got the courage to push on it. Bailey hadn't even touched the door, and it had opened.

It didn't move for me. My tense muscles—every fiber in my body—told me to run. I imagined fleeing the house in the middle of the night. I wouldn't even stop to put pants on. I didn't need shoes. I could leave. Alexandra could figure it out because it wasn't my problem.

Somehow, I managed to talk myself down and got back on the couch. To anyone watching, I probably appeared as cool as a cucumber, but inside, I couldn't stop screaming.

I pulled the blankets up and lay there, but the house listened. Waited. I managed to pry my tongue from the roof of my mouth.

"I asked you guys to settle down so I could get some sleep. Please leave the dog alone."

Chapter 4

March 21, 2003

"So, Alexandra, hey. This is a really dumb question. You didn't open the door to the porch, did you?" I couldn't decide if the door thing was more or less traumatic than the dream preceding it, but talking about the door was easier.

Based on the chewing sounds in my ear, I'd caught her on her lunch break. "No, that door is stuck shut, remember? Rebecca was really clear. I guess last time one of the kids opened it to get something, it took Ron, like, an hour and a sander to get the damned thing closed again. They access the porch from the outside, usually." She swallowed. "Why?"

I ignored my increased heart rate, playing with the phone cord. "No reason. I was just wondering."

"Was Bailey better last night?"

"Yeah. I told the ghosts to calm down after he got up the second time, and he settled right down." No air quotes in my voice this time.

She certainly sounded satisfied. "Good. Glad the night went better. Anything else?"

Nope. I had a history of sleepwalking—sometimes I had a hard time telling the difference between what I'd actually heard or what my brain had imagined. For all I knew, the scream was part of a very vivid dream. And the door could have opened on its own. Probably.

Alexandra read my silence like a book. "What happened with the door?" Even if she didn't know me better than anyone else in my life, she wasn't stupid.

Without making a sound, I took a deep breath, and then counted to three before I let it out. "At three, a horrible scream, like someone was being tortured, woke me up. The dog freaked out, and it opened by itself."

"Rebecca warned me about a new ghost that followed her home from one of her sessions. The other ghosts hurt her sometimes. That's what you probably heard."

I couldn't keep the sarcasm from dripping off my words at her casual tone. "Oh, is that all? Anything else I should know?"

"No, not really." More chewing. "Tonight is your last night. I'm meeting Rebecca in the morning, and she's paying me, so I'll give you some cash tomorrow, okay? We can meet for lunch. My treat."

"Yeah, great."

If I managed to make it without running screaming into the night. I changed the subject. "I may have met someone." My trip to the career center today had been useless, except for my run-in with a tall, dark, and handsome stranger. Just my type. "He's in the Army National Guard."

Silence stretched so long, I worried she'd hung up already.

"Are you ready for that?" she finally asked. "You've been through a lot in the last year. Maybe let the dust settle a bit?"

That invisible hand squeezed my throat again. I shook my head to shake it away as much as to disagree with Alexandra. "I can't live my life in the past. I want to move on."

"There's a difference between moving on from your past and ignoring it, hoping it doesn't catch up with you."

We'd had one of those really nice New England days that pop up now and again between when the snow is mostly gone and when spring starts in earnest. Temps got up into the seventies, so I'd spent a good chunk of my day cleaning up the tiny dirt patch at my apartment that might pass for a garden with enough imagination. In other words, I had found a way to stop myself from thinking about this moment, standing next to my car, staring at Rebecca's house.

A complete coward, I showed up early to get there well before dusk. If I arrived after dark, I think I'd be too scared to get out of my car. I may have also been hoping to run into Alexandra, so I wouldn't be alone. I opened the back of the car to grab my overnight bag and cursed under my breath. My book lay open on the floor of the car, but the bag itself had disappeared, along with anything to sleep in. At least no one would judge me for sleeping in just my t-shirt.

Bailey was happy to have the company, regardless of the reason. We played fetch and went for a walk. I felt obligated to give him a bath when he found a puddle to bury himself in. We checked on the animals together, but Rebecca's setup made it pretty easy for them to take care of themselves. I topped off their water and visited with them. It had been a while since I'd hung out with a horse, and I found myself really jonesing for a ride, then regretted not calling my trainer since I'd gotten home. She'd want me to come take a lesson, and I couldn't afford it, so I avoided her.

Bailey and I went inside when it got dark, and Winston came in with us. It was as if the house had been expecting me.

Anticipating, even. No matter what I called it, the hairs on the back of my neck rose as I locked the door behind me. Ignoring the tingling in my spine, I wrote a list of tasks to do in the morning instead of anthropomorphizing a building. Alexandra would be putting the house to rights ahead of the family's return home, but I wanted to make it easier for her if I could. I managed to settle down and read for a little while, but a chill settled over me I couldn't shake.

Bailey had to move for me to unfold the third blanket and pull it over myself, but he didn't seem like the type to hold a grudge. Even with three blankets and the dog on my feet, I shivered, so I doubled over the top blanket. Then the middle blanket.

Huddled underneath this pile, my teeth wouldn't stop chattering.

"This is ridiculous." I got to my feet and doubled over the last blanket. Shivering, I slid back underneath the pile and folded the end under to wrap my feet. I rubbed my legs together to generate some warmth. Was I coming down with something so suddenly? Just what I needed. Some plague with a fever.

Maybe he understood my mission, because Bailey stretched himself across my legs, adding a warm if squirmy and heavy top blanket. My top half shivered, but I finally fell asleep.

Chapter 5

March 22, 2003

Alexandra met me for lunch the next day and pushed an envelope across the table after the server had taken our order. "There's a little extra in there, since the ghosts gave you a hard time."

My hand hesitated over the envelope before I slid it off the table and into the back pocket of my jeans.

Alexandra scanned the café, her dark blue eyes missing nothing. Her mass of curly black hair had been partly twisted into a knot on top of her head, showing off the drop earrings she'd made. I had tried to replicate the style once, but my fine hair wouldn't do what hers did naturally, despite its thickness or how much product I used. All she had to do was throw on some eyeliner, and she looked like the most put together person ever.

I pulled my dirty PT sneakers farther under the table and tucked my hands between my thighs. "There was something last night, too."

She examined her water glass in the light before taking a drink. "Oh, yeah?"

"It was weird. When I went to bed, I was so cold. I had all the blankets doubled over and even had Bailey as a blanket, but I couldn't get warm. I thought for sure I was coming down with something."

She stared at me now, her mouth open slightly.

A shiver raced up my spine. "What?"

"And you're fine today?" Carefully, she set her glass down and twisted it on the table.

"Well, yeah, I wouldn't be here if I wasn't."

"Did anything else happen?" Her fingers framed the base of her glass. She focused on rotating the stupid thing with her thumb, avoiding me.

I frowned at her. "No, not really. I just went to sleep. I was fine when I woke up."

She glanced at me, then back to her glass. "It was the ghosts."

Slumping in my chair, I shook my head. "Is anything not the ghosts?"

Her eyes met mine. "They were standing around you—they knew you could hear them, so they were trying to communicate with you."

"Seriously?"

She shrugged. "It's well documented that the temperature will drop when ghosts are around."

Science had never been a strong subject for me, and I didn't know enough to tell Alexandra she was wrong. But if I conceded Rebecca's house was haunted, that meant ghosts had always been there.

The server arrived with our lunch, saving me from having to respond.

Chapter 6

March 20, 2010

The doorbell rang in rapid succession, so I hurried to neaten my stack of notes. "I'll be right there!" I called.

It was Alexandra, making sure I didn't chicken out. I didn't think she'd be able to hear me, but the bell didn't go off again. When I opened the door, she leaned against the frame, a sly smile on her face.

"About time." She evaluated my appearance as she stepped into my kitchen. I loved the black tall boots she wore over black skinny jeans. Not something I could ever hope to pull off. Her smirk turned into a frown. "What are you wearing?"

"What's wrong with it?" I plucked at my purple floral top I wore with my nice jeans and clean sneakers.

She sighed. "You look like you're going to the grocery store, not on a date."

"I have an investigation later."

She rolled her blue eyes at me. "Come home and change after dinner." She held up a hand. "I know, I know, you don't want to." She shook her head and strode toward the bathroom. I didn't immediately follow, so she beckoned me over. "Come on, I'll help you find something to wear. Can I help with your makeup, too? I have a cool idea."

Like a puppy, I trailed behind. I wanted to make a good impression, and Alexandra had amazing taste.

She paused at the bathroom door, but turned into the bedroom instead. "Let's find something better for you to wear first."

She rummaged through my closet, *hmm*ing and *tsk*ing at the choices. She pulled out a dark purple sleeveless top with some sparkle and a black jacket. She tossed both on my bed. "Start with that." She flipped through some hangers. "Do you not hang your pants in here? Where are your pants that aren't jeans? Oh, here they are. Wow, no options." A pair of black pants landed on the bed. "How tall did you say this guy is? Ooh!"

I wasn't sure how to feel about the level of excitement in the last syllable. "Five-ten, I think." She crouched on the floor to go through a pile of shoes while I changed into the outfit she'd picked for me. She came up with a pair of strappy silver heels like she held the crown of England in her hands. "Wear these."

My eyebrow went up and I shook my head. "I haven't worn those in forever."

She shoved them at me. "All the more reason to wear them. You'll probably be sitting most of the time anyway, but they'll make your legs seem miles long with those pants."

Not sure how she'd respond, I went on my own search in the closet and came up with a pair of plain black ankle boots with a short block heel. "How about these instead?"

She shrugged one shoulder. "Whatever you want. Those will be fine, too." Crossing her arms, she grinned at me. "Are you going to tell me about him?"

"His name is Josh. We've been chatting all week."

"You've talked to him on the phone, right?" One brow raised. "You have to make sure these online people aren't serial killers."

I snorted. "Is he going to tell me that? We used the site's messaging thing, and then Yahoo! after I got to know him a little better. I don't think he's a serial killer."

"That's good, anyway." She breezed out of the room and into the bathroom.

I followed, pulling at my shirt. With the mirror in front of me, I straightened the ruched three-quarter sleeves on the jacket.

"What else?"

"He says he loves horses and used to ride. Oh, he was a Marine, once upon a time," I said.

Alexandra frowned. "What does he do now?" She opened my makeup case and rummaged. "Girl, I have got to get you to Sephora for some new makeup." She pulled out a bottle of foundation and showed me the label. "I put this on you when you got married. It's old, throw it away." With a flick of her wrist, she tossed it into the garbage can. It hit the metal side with a *clang* and landed on the bottom.

"He works at the Shipyard now." My pulse raced and my smile widened. "I think we have a real connection, and when he asked to meet in person, of course, I said yes." I closed my eyes while Alexandra did my eyeshadow. "I think tonight is going to be a good night."

"I want you to be optimistic," she said, studying her work rather than at me, "but don't get your heart too set on anyone. Get to know them first."

"Is that big sister advice?"

"Big sister, best friend, whichever one you'll listen to." She did her best on the rest of my makeup and spent a few minutes giving some life to my hair, using products I never touched. She stood behind me in the mirror and smiled over my shoulder. "You looked good before, but now you're amazing. You're going to knock his socks off."

I had to admit she was right. I tugged at a spike of hair hanging over my forehead and smiled at my reflection. I loved what she'd done with my eyeliner, making my green eyes really pop. My eyes were my best feature, and I'd been accused of having a perfect nose before.

I caught her gaze in the mirror. All the amusement had left her face.

"Mel, no matter what, remember you're smart, funny, and gorgeous, and anyone who can't see that, it's their own fault. I want those words rattling around in your brain for the rest of your life." She perfected a piece of hair over my forehead before giving my shoulders a squeeze. She smiled again. "Now go have fun."

Calhoun's was my new favorite chain restaurant, if you could call two locations a chain. It had a family restaurant feel, but a little classier than average. Not quite cloth napkins, but also not cheesy décor all over the walls. Honest was a good way to describe it. It was what it was without putting on airs. Like me. I'd been here a few times before, but never to meet someone.

The hostess seated me. Within moments, a server poured me a glass of ice water. I ordered Sangria from the bar and kept my hands busy with my menu.

I had arrived early and, as I had anticipated, the crowd grew quickly. Every time the door opened, I hoped my date would appear. Emotions warred, but the anxiety he would stand me up fought the hardest. How long had it been since I'd been on a date?

A new group came in—dressed like a road construction crew. Not him. What time was it, anyway? I fought the urge to check my phone for the time and realized I'd left it at home.

Someone dropped something at the bar, taking my attention away from the door. I recognized the bartender as someone I'd gone to high school with, and I debated on whether to go say hi.

The bell on the door tinkled again, and a big guy walked in. Not quite fat, but stocky. He jerked his chin at the hostess and surveyed the restaurant. Brown hair, maybe brown eyes, but I couldn't tell from this distance. He wore a blue shirt and jeans, which is what he'd told me to watch out for. He wasn't unattractive, but I frowned a little at the beard. His profile pictures all showed him as clean-shaven. He at least kept it neatly trimmed.

I raised my hand to wave as he made a beeline for a guy sitting at the bar. I tucked my hand back down self-consciously. The door opened again, and the guy I'd been waiting for entered. Confident in my identification, I waved at him and kept a smile pasted to my face as he headed toward me. His profile pictures were definitely out of date. Not that I'd judge him for his weight, but he was at least fifty pounds heavier than his photos had showed. His hair was also much longer, falling over his face and ears.

"Hey." I stood and extended my hand with my practiced smile. "Nice to meet you finally."

Josh hesitated, examining me from my head to my toes. He frowned. "Yeah."

My smile faltered. "You find the place okay?"

He glanced around before sliding into the booth across from me. "It's not hard to find."

I sank into my seat, unsure of how to respond. "How was your day?"

He shrugged a shoulder and pulled his menu open. "It was a day. My ex is a bitch, and dealing with morons who are too stupid to breathe all day at work."

I sat back and tucked my hands beneath my thighs. "Where do you work in the Shipyard?"

He glanced up at me from his menu and frowned again. "Paint shop. And before you get any ideas, working at the Yard doesn't mean I'm made of money."

Holy cow. Did he think I was a gold digger because I asked about his job? My menu offered a necessary distraction, even though I'd practically memorized it. During our online chats, he had seemed so nice, but without inflection in text, maybe I'd been taking things wrong. Our calls had been rather short.

I glanced up at him. "Do you know what you're going to get?"

"I think so." He leaned out of the booth, then craned his neck up. "Do we even have a waitress?" His hand went up and, to my horror, he snapped his fingers at the server. "I want a drink," he called across the room.

Thinking I'd die of shame, I sank behind my menu as the server came over, a polite smile on her face. "What can I get for you, sir?"

"What do you have on tap?"

"Bud, Bud Lite—"

"Do you have Bud Lite Lime?"

"No, we don't."

"I'll take a Stella Artois in a chilled glass."

"I'm sorry, sir, we don't have that. The drink menu is on the back—"

"Give me a Heineken, then."

Her smile tightened. "Sir, the drink menu is on the back with our available beverages. The list is updated weekly."

He didn't even glance at the menu. "Do you have margaritas?"

"Yes, we do."

"Fine. I'll have a margarita. Double Patron Silver, salt on the rim, lime on the side." The moment she turned her back, he rolled his eyes. "I guarantee you, she gets it wrong."

My hand came up to cover my mouth. An unconscious gesture, probably trying to keep what I was thinking from spilling out. I would never be so rude to service staff. His behavior was abominable. But what could I say?

He looked around again. "Great, where did she go?"

"You just sent her to the bar to get your very specific drink order." My face twisted in confusion. "She'll probably be back in a few minutes."

"She should have taken my dinner order." He shook his head, then jerked his chin to get the hair off his forehead.

"Have you ever worked in food service?" I crossed my arms on the table. A bad day could be the reason for his brusqueness. Not a great one, but better than nothing.

He scoffed. "Only idiots work in food service."

Or not. "A lot of famous people have worked places like McDonalds. I worked at KFC for my first job."

He shrugged one shoulder, then stood his menu up at the end of the table.

I reached out and set it down flat.

He tugged it out of my hand. "No, you stand it up so they know you're ready to order."

"I know that." I grabbed the menu again, and pulled it to my side of the table, out of his reach. "She'll be back in a few minutes to take our order. We don't need to use signals."

"Well, before she comes back, we should talk about the check."

"I usually split the check on the first date." I opened my menu to find what I wanted. Having it in front of me would help me order.

"You have a usual? That's surprising."

My gaze flew to his, and my menu hit the table with a soft *thwap*. "What is that supposed to mean?"

The server arrived with Josh's drink. "Are you ready to order?"

He took the glass and examined it before setting it down. "I've been ready to order. Give me the ribeye steak, cooked medium. Not medium rare, not medium well. Medium." He shoved his menu at her. "Do you put real butter in your potatoes, or garbage butter-flavored oil crap?"

She had to be clenching her teeth behind her very professional smile. "I don't believe it's real butter."

"Fine. I want a baked potato—"

"I'm sorry, sir, we don't have baked potatoes."

Josh rolled his eyes. "What *do* you have?"

"Our side choices are on page two."

He waited, but when the server didn't list the options, he reached across the table to yank my menu out of my hands. He flipped it open and let out a dramatic sigh.

"What can I get for you?" the server asked, turning to me with her pencil poised over the order pad.

Please, do not let her think I'm anything like him. "Can I please—"

"I wasn't done." Josh snapped his fingers again, and I died inside. "Give me the mashed with the butter-flavored oil, and I'll have asparagus for the vegetable."

"We only have asparagus seasonally, sir. We have broccoli, carrots, or green beans."

"Which one of those is in season?" He rolled his eyes. "I bet they buy it in frozen." He flipped the hair off his forehead. "Give me the green beans. Do you at least have packets of real butter?"

"Yes, sir."

"Give me, like, four of those."

Embarrassed, I quietly brought my menu back across the table. "Can I please get the turkey BLT, but hold the tomato please?"

"Sure." The server jotted it down. "Fries okay?"

"Yes, please." I thanked her when she took my menu.

"Should you have gotten the salad?" Josh asked. He made me want to cover up.

"Excuse me?" My hands trembled underneath the table. Who even was this person? He hadn't been anything like this during our chats.

"The salad. Instead of a sandwich and fries."

"I'm not stupid, I understood what you meant."

"Didn't sound like it." He leaned on the edge of the table. "I think you should pick up the whole check because it would be more fair."

How the hell was that fair? I got a sandwich, and he ordered a twenty-five-dollar entrée. "Like I said, we can split the check."

"But seeing you misrepresented yourself, I think it's fair for you to pay the bill."

Not even knowing what to say, I stared at him.

"You didn't look this big in your photos. I wouldn't have come if I knew what size you were."

My blood boiled as my heart raced. "My profile photos are all recent within the last month. When were yours taken?"

"That's different. Women are shallow. If a guy isn't totally ripped or show how much money they have with a motorcycle or something in their pics, women don't pay attention." He sat back against the booth. "I'm a really nice guy, and women just blow me off and ignore me to date jerks instead."

There was so much to unpack in his statement that I couldn't pick any one thing to say.

"All I'm saying," he said, pursing his mouth, "is you misrepresented yourself, and I think I should be compensated for the false advertising."

"First off, I didn't advertise." The people at the table next to us were watching, so I lowered my voice. "My photos were real and untouched. Second, I shouldn't have to put my clothing sizes online to prove anything to anyone."

Our server came back with our plates. She slid my sandwich in front of me, and I thanked her. Josh's plate landed with a *thunk,* and the steak knife balanced on the edge slid into his beans. "The cooks wanted me to make sure your steak is how you wanted."

Josh glanced at me as he cut into the steak. "I probably should've told them I'm a Yelp reviewer, too. That gets me better service every time."

Sure, it does.

He nodded like an emperor at the Colosseum. Or maybe Henry VIII. "Tell the cooks they managed to do it right."

The server's tight smile reappeared. "Great. Can I get you anything else?"

"Yeah, why don't you have any A1 on the table?" He cut a chunk off his steak and stuffed it into his mouth.

"I will get that for you right away, sir."

"See what I mean?" He showed me the masticated cow in his mouth as he chewed. "As soon as she knew I was a Yelp reviewer, she was nicer to me."

"She's been nice this whole time." *Nicer than you deserved.* I picked up half of my sandwich, but could only manage to nibble the corner. This was, without a doubt, the worst date I'd ever been on. My appetite had fled.

The manager came to our table, holding the A1 sauce like a bottle of wine. "How is everything here?"

Josh jerked his thumb in the air in a sign of approval. So, more Nero than Tudor.

I'd lost count of how many times tonight I'd wanted to sink into a crack. "Very good, thank you."

Between the stress and Josh alternating between talking with his mouth full of food or chewing with it open, I picked at my dinner. He wolfed his down like it was a race, pausing occasionally to chug his margarita. He was scraping the last of his mashed potatoes off the plate when his phone rang.

He fished his phone out of his pocket and read the screen. "I have to take this. I'll be right back." He pushed himself out of the booth as he answered. "Hello? Yeah, I'm at some dive in Sanford."

I put my face in my hands. This was so horrible. The only decent thing he'd done all night was leave the table to take his phone call. I picked at my fries a little more, but only managed another bite or two of my sandwich.

"Everything okay?" the server asked, her hands full of plates.

"Yeah, just not that hungry."

"Do you need a box?" She added Josh's plate to her pile.

"Yes, please."

Several more minutes passed, and Josh still hadn't reappeared. I craned my neck to see out the front windows, but the sidewalk appeared empty. He was probably on the other corner where I couldn't see him. The server dropped off the box and a tray with the check clipped to it. "Whenever you're ready."

"Thank you." I packed my food to go, taking my time. The table next to me cleared, then the one across from us that had been seated after me. The hostess finished seating another party and I waved at her. "Excuse me. Did you see the gentleman I was with? Blue shirt, jeans?"

"He left about fifteen minutes ago."

My heart dropped. Wow.

The hostess waited for a response.

Heat creeped from my neck up my face. "Thank you."

I left a hefty tip for the server. Well worth a valuable lesson learned, and I scurried out with my leftovers.

As soon as I got home, I didn't even bother sitting down to log into the online dating profile where I'd met Josh. Ignoring the message notifications, I followed the steps to delete the account. It asked me if I was sure so many times, I gritted my teeth in frustration. Josh had been the icing on the cake. The last straw. There were more important things to do with my time.

"Some things just aren't worth it." My fingers tapped the mouse buttons without clicking, and I bit my lower lip. I didn't need a romantic partner to validate me or to build the life I wanted. As a matter of fact, now might be exactly the time to take the next step toward building it.

I slid into my computer chair, my eyes dropping to the clock in the corner. A few more minutes shouldn't matter. It took me a little bit of searching, but I found the phone number for the realtor who had sold Alexandra her house.

My gaze shifted to the clock again. "Crap." My search had taken longer than I'd thought.

After getting changed back into my jeans and sneakers, I was running late. And, of course, I got stuck on a back road behind someone going twenty under the speed limit. It's always the way.

I pulled up to the house. Cars covered the narrow driveway. I took the last available spot half on the grass and half in the driveway, hoping I wasn't blocking someone in. Our team leader, Jess, stood on the front stoop with a middle-aged couple, her thin arms crossed over her chest. She nodded a few times while a curly-haired woman made huge gestures with her arms as she spoke. A shorter man stood beside her, spinning a key ring on his thumb. Probably the homeowners.

Fidgeting more than anything else, I took my time checking my messenger bag to make sure I had my equipment. Digital voice recorder, K-II meter, digital camera, and I always had a spiral notepad and at least two pens with me. Two flashlights clinked together, one a stubby LED and a heavier one with red acetate taped over the lens. I also had a penlight on my keychain as backup.

With my digital voice recorder in hand, I flipped my bag closed and buckled it as the homeowners drove off. I changed out of my sneakers into my muck boots, pegging the legs of my jeans to fit inside.

"One of many valuable lessons learned during your military service, Mel," I muttered to myself. "Along with removing permanent marker from hard surfaces."

Knowing Jess wouldn't like it, I locked my car and pocketed the keys. If someone needed to get out, they could find me to move my car. I adjusted the shoulder strap and made my way to the front door. I stopped in the yard and shivered. The house sat very close to the road, only about fifteen feet from the edge. My research told me Capes were the most common house in the area for the 1850s time period, and this house certainly backed up that assertion. A central chimney poked through a rusting metal roof, and cracked and peeling white paint on the clapboard siding revealed a darker color underneath.

I shivered again and tucked my hands into the front pocket of my hoodie. Tonight's subject house occupied a corner lot, at the intersection between a main road and a narrower, paved right-of-way. Across the street, trees climbed up a steep hill. The lights of a house at the top winked through the woods. On the other side of the right-of-way, the neighbor's home seemed far away in the fading light, but the building was in much better shape. Cheerful historic reproduction lanterns cast light over pale green siding.

Turning back to the place we were investigating, I huddled into my hoodie to stop my shivering. This one had certainly been let go. It suddenly occurred to me that all the houses we investigated were run down, no newer than the 1960s. Another old one sat dark across the right-of-way. I frowned and couldn't remember the last investigation we'd done on a place that wasn't also coming apart.

With the touch of a button, my digital voice recorder started. I had MacGyvered a wrist strap onto it, which I slipped over my hand so both my hands would be free. As I touched the handle of the front door, my mother's snarky voice came from the back of my mind. *"Do you think you're royalty, using the front door?"*

I shook my head to clear those cobwebs.

Inside, wide pine floors had been painted pinkish-beige. Like the outside, the paint had cracked and peeled, revealing blue paint underneath. Probably lead-based. I fell in love with the old foyer with coffin-turn stairs leading up to a narrow hallway. Whatever railing had been on the stairs and lining the hall previously had been replaced with two-by-fours nailed together. I followed voices into a wide living room.

Faded floral wallpaper covered the walls from floor to ceiling. A bookshelf holding more dust than books tilted toward me, threatening to fall forward if anyone sneezed too hard.

"It's the floor," Jess said, focusing on her flashlight. "The whole thing is sloped toward the center of the house."

"Basement stairs added after the fact?" I asked.

"You know it." She jerked her thumb over her thin shoulder, her pale skin exposed by her gray tank top "Door to the basement is over there."

I nodded and walked around Jess, wondering how she could stand to have her long hair loose. I'd be afraid of sitting on it, or, worse, getting it full of cobwebs. I passed an enormous brick fireplace in the center of the room, which could have easily fit me inside, along with three other people. Beneath years—maybe decades—of soot, the original iron pot hanger rested against the wall.

My hand touched the latch of the basement door, and I froze. For no particular reason I could name, I didn't want to open it. I pulled my small LED flashlight out of my bag. The weight of it in my hand gave me the courage to open the door. I cringed at the loud creak. I flipped the switch on the inside wall. A light in a far corner of the basement came on, illuminating the stairs, and revealing they went almost straight down and had a ninety-degree turn at the bottom.

"Jesus," I said under my breath.

"What?"

Frank's hand appeared on the door, his deeply tanned skin standing out against white trim. By contrast, his pale watch tan practically glowed in the dim light.

"Didn't anybody ever tell you to wear sunscreen?" I grinned, so he'd know I was kidding. Mostly. "Young, tanned Frank is handsome, but when you get older, your skin is going to be like an old leather couch."

"Don't you know people pay more for leather furniture?" He pulled the door open wider so he could step around it. He peered into the dark opening, as I clicked on my flashlight to show him what I'd found.

"Jesus is right. Code lets them have stairs like that?" He withdrew a dark gray digital watch out of his pocket and strapped it on.

"Grandfathered." I stuck my arm into the stairwell to shine the light down. There were eight steps, each only about six inches wide. "If they ever need to pull a building permit, the CEO would make them fix it."

"You going down?" Frank grinned at me. "You know, all the best stuff is always in the basement."

"By all means." I gestured toward the stairs. "After you!"

"It's supposed to be age before beauty, but I'll make an exception." He ducked into the narrow stairwell. The low ceiling forced him to tilt his head to the side. He slipped halfway down and dropped an f-bomb.

"You okay?"

"Yeah, the railing is loose and so are the stair treads."

Great. The house wasn't only falling down, it was a death-trap.

Still on the landing, I tried to angle my flashlight so Frank could see. I hated steep stairs with a passion. Steep anything, really. I wouldn't go on ladders, either. But Frank was my boo-buddy (a name Jess hated) and where he went, I went.

I was halfway down when Frank let loose a string of expletives. I rushed the rest of the way. The rickety wooden stairs ended on a concrete pad.

"What is it now?"

"It's dirt." Frank took a leap to get next to me on the concrete. "Or it's supposed to be. It's actually mud."

Clicking my flashlight back on, I followed Frank's footprints where he'd walked over dry, hard-packed dirt, and it suddenly turned into slop.

"Oh, my God." I shook my head as my flashlight went over the foundation, made of giant stones stacked on top of each other.

Frank's flashlight clicked on, and the much brighter beam penetrated the dimness mine couldn't reach.

He whistled between his teeth. "Damn."

"Do you think they know their foundation is collapsing?" The stones in the middle of the wall bulged inward, and there were signs of lateral movement. I tried to orient myself. The whole house leaned into the back yard.

"They might, they might not." He shook his head and stepped back onto the dirt. "Fortunately, we're not here for that."

"I still feel bad." I raised my arm, my voice recorder dangling from its cord. A warning to Frank that anything he said would probably be twisted and used against him when Jess, Rachel, and Adam did the analysis.

Both of us turned our flashlights upwards, checking out the plumbing and the wiring. High EMF readings often came from cloth covered wiring, and unsecured plumbing could be responsible for strange knocks or bangs. Aside from some interesting DIY fixes to blend the old and new plumbing together, we didn't find anything loose or technically out of order downstairs.

"They're probably ready for us upstairs," Frank finally said. "Your boots are a mucky mess."

Frank was right. Thick, wet mud that reminded me of Texoma clay clung to the sides of my boots, and likely packed into the tread, too. "I'll leave them down here and work the rest of the house in my socks."

He scoffed. "They'll be full of holes by the end of the night. Some genius used horseshoe nails for the floorboards."

"Great." I pulled my boots off and crept up the stairs in my stockinged feet. I didn't have to say anything. Frank waited at the bottom of the stairs.

On my return to the living room, I ran into a young woman—a teen—and stopped short. "Hello."

She waved nervously, then smoothed her lanky brown hair behind her ear. "I'm Julie."

I waved, using the hand with the recorder on it, its steady red light letting everyone know it was on. "Nice to meet you."

"Are you Melissa?" She peered over my shoulder, her blue eyes wide. "And Frank?"

"That's us." Frank closed the basement door. "Julie?"

"That's me." She smiled. "Jess told me I'd be working with you guys tonight?"

"Sure," I said. "What do you have for equipment?"

She shifted her feet and averted her gaze. "I didn't know I was supposed to bring anything. This is my first time."

"Don't worry about it." I held up my voice recorder again. "This is a digital voice recorder you can get online. It doesn't have to be anything fancy, either. This one will record up to one hundred forty hours, so I leave it on the entire time we're at a location." I held up my small LED flashlight. "Flashlight, obviously because all the lights go out and you don't want to be stumbling around in the dark. Adam will tell you where the night vision stuff is. No flashlights on in those rooms, okay?"

Frank put his hand on mine to lower it. "This is supposed to be fun, stop being so serious." He smiled at Julie and stepped between us. "Learning on the job is better, anyway."

The lights in the kitchen flicked off and on.

I stared at Frank, eyebrows up.

"That's our cue," he said to Julie, still smiling. "We all meet before the investigation, and Jess outlines everything for us." He winked. "Kind of like a team huddle."

I followed Frank and Julie into the kitchen where Adam had the table covered in cords connected to three laptops. His HQ, he called it. I didn't pay much attention as Jess droned on about the house and what the owners had told her. I'd done this enough times that all the stories sounded the same: the owners hear noises they can't explain, creepy feelings, it must be ghosts. I rolled my eyes thinking about it. I'd already made a trip to the town hall and pulled the file on the house. My favorite part about investigations in these small towns were the town clerks who seemed to know everything about everyone and loved having an ear to bend. This house had been in the Thompson family since before the town had been incorporated. The last owner only used it occasionally for the first fifteen years, then it sat empty for the next twenty years, collecting dust and slowly falling in on itself. When she died, the heirs sold it as soon as they could to the current owners.

A sudden chill washed over me. I rubbed my arms and searched for a potential source of the draft. I shivered harder.

"The hell," I muttered under my breath.

"All set, Mel?" Jess asked.

Shit. "Yeah, I'm good."

Jess gave assignments, dividing the team into groups of two or three. The lights throughout the house were shut off. Frank, Julie, and I were sent upstairs. I wrinkled my nose at the musty odor, like towels left too long in the washing machine. The upper floor had been divided into four awkwardly shaped and partially furnished bedrooms. According to the town clerk, the last owners hadn't bothered to clean the place out, and apparently the new owners had just left it.

We sat in the dark, Frank and I occasionally asking the usual questions: why are you here, do you want to talk to us, do you want to be here? My K-II meter rested on the floor, the lights dark. A useless piece of equipment, anyway.

That reminded me. "Julie, if you're going to stick around, Jess does require everyone to have a K-II meter." I kept my voice as low as possible. I picked up my K-II and pushed myself to my feet. "We should go into the next room, Frank."

"Why do you want to move?" Julie whispered.

"That was Julie," I said for the recorder. "Julie, you shouldn't whisper. It gets distorted on the recording, and then when the analysis gets done, they might think it's an EVP."

"What's an EVP?"

She really was new. "Electronic voice phenomena. Basically, we can't hear something in real time, but when the tech team goes over the data, they might hear a ghost responding to one of our questions." Not that it had ever happened.

Enough moonlight came through the bedroom window across the hall that I didn't need my flashlight to navigate. The hallway, at least, was clear of junk. K-II meter in hand, I felt my way along the wall into the other bedroom. I stopped in the doorway, Julie and Frank close behind me.

"Is anyone in here?" I took two slow steps into the room, sweeping with my K-II meter. "We aren't here to harm you in any way."

"We just want to talk," Julie whispered.

I turned to face her. "That was Julie." Turning back into the room, a bed sat mostly obscured by shadow, the dim outline of a nightstand beside it.

"Do you hear that?" Frank asked.

No one moved.

"I heard a hum."

Several more seconds passed.

"I don't hear it." I paused. "Did you hear it again?"

"No."

I kept my K-II meter held out in front of me as I moved farther into the room, sweeping my arm for readings.

"We do that more to mark the recording so the techs can take a closer listen," Frank said.

Two of the lights on my K-II lit up and I jumped, almost dropping it.

"Say something else," I said.

"Is someone in here with us?" Frank asked the room.

"What is your name?" Julie whispered.

"Julie," I snapped. "Stop whispering. Talk in a low voice or don't talk."

"What the hell, Melissa," Frank asked. "You need to unwind. You need to get—have a drink."

Mindful of the digital voice recorder dangling from my wrist, I took a deep breath, then two. "I'm sorry, I'm a little wound up tonight. I'm sorry for being snappy," I said toward Julie's silhouette. "I'm not usually like this."

"Are you feeling something?" Julie asked, not whispering.

My free hand clenched and unclenched. The tension wasn't all because of Josh. Probably all the rushing around and then the race to get here. That always had me on edge. "Just a long day, I think." I swept the meter back toward the bed. Two lights illuminated and then went out.

"If there is someone here, we'd like to talk." I inched closer toward the wall. "The object in my hand has lights on it and you can make them light up."

Three lights came on, went to two, back to three. Dark.

"That was awesome." Frank moved closer to me. "Can you do that again?"

The meter remained dark.

"Julie, you ask something," I said. I wouldn't admit it, but I wanted to try to make up for being a jerk a minute ago.

"My name is Julie." She stepped closer to the window. "What's your name?"

I turned toward her, and as I did, the lights came back on. The first two stayed on, the third light flickering off and on. I waved my hand to encourage her to keep talking.

"Did you live in this house?" Julie asked.

"They might not know they're dead, just so you know," Frank said.

"Are you part of the Thomas family?"

"Thompson," I corrected. I took a step closer to the wall and the third light steadied.

"How will you get an EVP if you keep walking away?" Julie asked.

It took me a second to respond, I was so focused on the lights of the K-II meter. My stomach turned and threatened to climb into my throat. "It has a decent mic on it, and it's a small room." I glanced at Julie where she stood by the window. "I don't know that distance from the mic matters with the paranormal," I added. "Ask another question."

Frank cleared his throat. "That was Frank. How long have you been in this house?"

The fourth light on my K-II meter flickered. I turned toward Frank, and the meter went dark.

"How many—"

"Quiet, for a second." I swept back and the lights came back on. I did a wide sweep, slowly narrowing my range.

"It's the same place every time," Frank said, as if reading my mind.

Heart thumping, I pulled my small LED out of the pocket of my jeans and clicked it on, aiming it toward the wall. Shadows jumped across more faded wallpaper, a different pattern from downstairs. Sections had been torn away, revealing broken plaster and lathe beneath. The lamp and the nightstand were both old, but without being an antiques person, I had no idea which was older. A beige box with a cord running out of the back sat on the edge nearest to the bed. The blankets were rumpled, as if someone had gotten out of bed and tossed the covers back in a hurry.

"Didn't Jess say that the bedrooms up here were empty?" Without moving the K-II, I looked at Frank. He stared at the bed. "Frank?"

"Uh, yeah, the owners sleep downstairs, but they've had experiences in the rooms." He shook his head. "I think someone sleeps in here."

"Someone might have been." *It wouldn't be the first time we were lied to.*

I took a step closer, moving my flashlight along the wall. The K-II meter started going crazy, all the lights illuminating. I set my flashlight down on the bed, aimed toward the beige box on the nightstand. My free hand spanned the plastic case, and the K-II in the other continued going wild.

Julie said something, but I wasn't paying attention.

"What the hell?" It was an alarm clock, an old one. Like the one Bill Murray had in *Groundhog Day* where the numbers flipped down.

"It's a digital clock's granddaddy." Frank laughed. "I haven't seen a flip clock in at least twenty years."

I waved the K-II meter over it, and all five lights lit brightly. I swung the meter away and back. The clock was definitely the source of high EMF. "I don't think I've had my meter go this high before. This is crazy."

Frank checked his watch. "It's set to the right time."

"Well, someone is going to be mad at me then." Tracing the cord to the wall, I unplugged the clock. The lights on the meter slowly went out. "Definitely the clock."

"What does that mean?" Julie joined Frank and me in the corner.

"This meter measures Electro-Magnetic Fields, or EMF," Frank said. "It can detect paranormal activity. Ghosts can make it light up if they want."

I didn't believe that, but I couldn't say it. "It will also pick up on old or faulty wiring, or in this case, just a ton of extremely low-frequency electrical fields." I turned the K-II over in my hand, somehow disappointed in technology I didn't believe in anyway. "We sometimes get elevated readings around refrigerators when the compressor's running, too."

"Oh."

The light in the hallway came on, and Frank read his watch again. "It's barely been two and a half hours."

I wiggled the voice recorder at Frank again. "Jess is the boss. Time to pack it up."

Chapter 7

April 2, 2010

I walked away from the closing table with the keys to my first house. It wasn't much or anything special, but thanks to the burst of the housing market, it was mine. My excitement lasted up until the point I realized I had less than a week to move out of my apartment, and my Honda Accord wouldn't cut it.

Immediately after the closing, I went to my new house, compelled. I slowed as I turned into the driveway, giving myself time to take everything in. The dirt driveway went up from the road, and the house itself sat halfway up a large, wooded hill. The siding was my favorite. The builder had put a purple-gray vinyl on with white trim and a dark purple door. A bold choice, but it set this house apart from everything else that had been sitting on the market.

My Accord took the hill with a touch of the gas, and I parked on the gravel next to the house. There wasn't a single window on this side of the house, which I didn't like, but when I wanted to put a garage up, I would appreciate it.

I got out of the car, and drank in the surroundings, from the dead brown grass in the front yard and the layers of pine needles and leaves carpeting the ground beneath the trees. The silence washed over me like a refreshing shower after having lived on Main Street for so long. Despite the trees still being mostly bare, I could barely see my neighbor's house. In all other directions, scraggly pines and birch trees stretched their skeletal fingers toward the overcast sky.

Opening the front door, I somehow liked the house more than I had before, because now it was mine.

Home.

I smiled at the idea as I pulled up the butcher paper that had been protecting the new carpet from dirt and then took the plastic off the appliances. The kitchen was the perfect size and shape for me with butcher block countertops and white cabinetry. The kitchen ran into a dining area just big enough to fit the dining room set my grandparents had given me before they'd passed, the whole thing floored with maple. I didn't like the tightly woven commercial carpet in the living room—white, who used white carpet?—but I figured the sellers probably got partway through the build and had to cut costs, especially as prices continued to tank. A pair of half-walls between the hallway and dining area flanked the stairs into the basement. Clearly another half-finished idea, since there wasn't a door at either end of the stairs. Late afternoon light flooded in through the giant living room windows. I smiled again, imagining a garden with flowers blooming all summer long. Maybe some blueberry bushes.

I continued down the hallway, picking up the butcher paper and taking tape off of windows and fixtures. Fortunately, my first house had two full bathrooms, including one *en suite* to the main bedroom in the back corner of the house. The ranch-style home was on the small side, definitely smaller than the colonial I'd grown up in, but for just me, there was plenty of space.

My phone went off, echoing through the empty halls, and I jumped.

I flipped it open. "Hello?"

"Congratulations!" Alexandra and Sarah both shouted. It sounded like one of them had one of those noisemaker things. "Where are you?" Alexandra asked.

"I came to the house after the closing this morning. I'm trying to visualize things." Like pictures and photos on the empty white walls, and whether I should paint first.

"Oh." Alexandra whispered to someone, probably Sarah. "We have a surprise for you, so stay there."

"Well, I was heading out to go back to my apartment. I've kind of done what I wanted to do." Honestly, there wasn't much else for me to do here until I had some of my stuff. I needed to get some shelves on the walls, I decided, putting one hand on my hip.

"No, no, no. Stay there! We're on our way."

"Okay." I hung up, confused.

I went out to my car and rummaged around for something to do, managing to come up with a bottle of glass cleaner and a partial roll of paper towels. I set to washing grime off the windows. I had no idea what Alexandra had planned, but it made me nervous. She wasn't a loose cannon, per se, but her ideas fell short of the mark sometimes.

While I was all the way in the main bedroom, washing the windows facing the wooded hill behind the house, a vehicle crunched on the gravel driveway.

I strode to the front door, trying to peek out the windows on my way down the hallway. They must have parked next to the house. I stepped out onto the farmer's porch and walked to the end. My mouth went dry, and I think my heart stopped as I watched quite possibly the most attractive man I'd ever seen swing himself up into the open back of a U-Haul. My heart restarted in a mad flutter and heat crept up my face. He wore LL Bean like no man had any right to and had clearly stepped out of one of those only-in-the-movies firefighter calendars for the sole purpose of tormenting me. His dark blue plaid flannel shirt clung to him almost like a second skin, and my heart jumped as the muscles in his arms strained the fabric. My gaze dropped to his rear end and thighs as he bent over to pick something up off the floor of the truck. Heat flooded my face.

Sarah came around the back of the vehicle, bringing me back to reality. I'd been so caught up in watching this beautiful piece of man-candy I didn't even notice her car.

She smiled at me. "Surprise!"

"I can't believe you did this. I don't know what to say." Speechless for several reasons, I could only stand there and gawk. Tears welled and a lump formed in my throat. I had an excuse to bring my hands up to my flaming cheeks, and I hoped my high color would be attributed to their beautiful gesture.

"You can come down here and give us a hand. It wouldn't be fair to make Ryan do all the work!" Sarah said.

Alexandra dropped out of the driver's side and waved at me. "You know he loves it."

Ryan stepped to the edge of the truck's deck and leaned down to hand a box to Sarah. My tongue stuck to the roof of my mouth and I struggled to swallow.

One of Alexandra's brows came up and she grinned. "Mel, this is Ryan, he's a friend of Sarah's. Ryan, Mel."

Ryan walked over to the end of the porch and raised his hand up over the railing. "Nice to meet you."

I stuck my hand out to him. He had a nice handshake. Firm. He respected me as a person, but not hard, like he wanted to crush my hand. He had short brown hair—not quite short enough to be considered a buzz cut—and dark brown eyes searched my face from beneath even brows.

"Are you going to come down here and help?" Alexandra asked, hands on her hips.

I smiled, but tears choked me. Partly tears of relief, but also for the joy of having friends who cared.

Munching on a slice of cold pizza left over from lunch, I surveyed the room. The place could be way more of a disaster, but we'd come up with a good system to try to avoid a mountain in one room, mostly by making smaller mountains in all the rooms. I had forgotten how much stuff I had. After my ex—because I didn't like thinking of him as my husband if I could avoid it—died, I'd had a lot of his things put into storage, including a full living room set I'd sent down into the basement. Eventually, I would have to see if Goodwill or Salvation Army would come take any of it. Happy to find a few of my things I had forgotten about, my attention was drawn to Ryan hanging a picture on the long wall in the living room. Alexandra and Sarah had left a little while ago to pick their daughter up, leaving Ryan and me alone.

"You know, if you keep staring at my ass, I'm going to make you buy me dinner." He hadn't turned around, but I could hear the smile in his voice.

I ignored the flush heating my face and lifted my partially eaten pizza slice toward him like a toast. "I already bought you dinner, remember? And how do you know I'm staring at your ass?"

"Because if the roles were reversed, I'd be staring at yours. And who can resist this?" He winked at me over his shoulder and reached around to slap himself on the butt.

My blush deepened, but I won the fight to keep my tone casual. "Thanks so much again for the help."

"Again, no problem. Alex and Sarah told me they were planning this, and I'm happy to help." He stepped away from the wall and adjusted the picture to level it. "Is that good?"

I stepped closer to him. The heat of his body scorched me through my sleeve but I couldn't pull away. "It's great. You didn't have to, but I'm glad you did."

"You couldn't find your stool and it's painful to watch you try to hang it that high on your tiptoes." He looked down at me, the shadows on the planes of his face harsh in the bright overhead light. I already hated the soft white bulbs, and no one needed three hundred watts of it in one fixture. "How does it feel?"

I smiled. "Good. I forgot how much work moving was, and how much stuff I had. I'm kind of wiped."

He checked his watch. "Yeah, it's getting a little late." Grasping his hands behind his back, he stretched. His t-shirt pulled across his chest and lifted enough that I could see the top of his underwear peeking over his belt, along with flat, taut skin and a thin line of dark hair running into his waistband.

What is wrong with you? I turned toward a box on the couch, needing an excuse to avert my eyes. I probably resembled a Looney Toons character with my eyes bugging out of my head and my tongue lolling as I ogled him.

"I have to get the truck back. It was really nice to meet you."

"Nice to meet you, too." I forced my gaze to his to keep me from gawking at him more than I already had today. His chocolate brown eyes crinkled at the corners when he smiled. He smiled a lot.

Because he couldn't see me, I shamelessly watched him walk away. His blue jeans fit perfectly over his butt and legs, and my mouth went dry again as he trotted down the stairs. I jerked my head away as he turned onto the walkway, giving me a quick wave before he disappeared from view.

I stretched, and glanced at the clock in the kitchen. Definitely time to clean up and go to bed.

With the steaming water running over me, I leaned into the shower wall, exhausted. It had been such a long day, and I had more ahead of me. The water ran over my face, plastering my bangs to my forehead. I shut the water off and wiped my face.

Through the frosted plastic liner, the dark exterior curtain twitched and billowed out before falling back.

What was that?

After waiting a few seconds and the curtain remained still, I grabbed my towel to dry off. Probably a draft.

Snuggled in my bed a few minutes later, I wasn't quite ready to turn off the light. The excitement of being in my own house hadn't faded. I still hadn't decided what color I wanted to paint in here. White walls were okay in the rest of the house, but I wanted some color in my bedroom.

A concentrated effort had been made to keep the bedroom from being cluttered with boxes. A few hid behind the louvered bi-fold doors of the closet, stacked and waiting to be unpacked, but to an untrained observer, the bedroom looked lived in. Alexandra had a new hobby of paint-by-number, and she'd made me one with two horses, except she'd colored outside the lines to make one of them like my pinto mare. The first thing I'd done in here was hang it on the wall opposite the bed. Sarah knew me better than I'd realized because the three canvas prints hanging over my headboard were in the same configuration as they'd been in my apartment.

Exhausted physically, my mind wasn't quite ready to settle in for the night. In my head I made a list of all the things I wanted to accomplish tomorrow, first and foremost being getting down to the barn to ride. Tori got a little feisty with too much time off.

I also had upcoming assignments I needed to get done—damn, I also needed to get my internet switched over—and things to be done around the house.

BANG. Like someone had thrown a textbook against the wall. Inside my closet.

I sat bolt upright in bed, one arm clutching the comforter to my bare chest. What the hell was that? I sat there, tense, for several minutes. My harsh breathing drowned out anything else.

Inch by inch, I relaxed back into the mattress.

"It's a new house, it's going to settle. Settling makes noises, you know this." My voice didn't reassure me the way I'd hoped. How many times had our group gone out to investigate what turned out to be a settling house? Nothing to freak out about. Chalk it up to anxiety about being in a new place. By myself. In the middle of the woods. With less than stellar cell phone reception and no landline yet. My heart thudded in my chest, and I reached over to shut off the lamp. "It's fine, Mel, it's just the house," I said again and pulled the chain.

My mind finally started fading into sleep.

The brassy whine of trumpets sang faintly, punctuated by the deep timbre of a bass marking a quick tempo.

My eyes popped open, and I stopped breathing so I could hear. What was that?

I strained to make sense of the sound. Music. Like a big band era orchestra my grandmother would've listened to. Clearly, my half-asleep state had conspired with the excitement of the day, along with the physical exertion of unpacking, and I had imagined it. I took a deep breath and fell into a deep, dreamless sleep.

Chapter 8

April 3, 2010

There's something about taking the chaos away and organizing it all that gives me a sense of accomplishment. I didn't focus on the packing and the actual moving as much as the organizing part afterward, so maybe that's why I didn't hate moving as much as some people do. I hated helping other people move because I missed out on the best part.

I unwrapped another glass and put it into the cupboard, thinking of when my gram helped me unpack when I'd moved into my first apartment. I missed her every day and wondered how she'd feel about the family falling apart without her.

After unpacking the last glass, I smoothed out the newspaper, added it to the pile on the table, and broke down the box for recycling. I turned to go back to tackle the next box. The cupboard door swung open, but stopped the moment I set eyes on it, like it had been caught.

I stared, not believing my eyes. I hesitated for a breath before closing the door. My hand rested on the cool surface for a few seconds, and then I moved the door experimentally, trying to see why it may have opened on its own. I finally told myself the door wasn't hung quite evenly and made a note to adjust it.

Someone knocked on the door, and I leaned around the refrigerator. Ryan stood on the porch in jeans, a t-shirt, and a worn-out Red Sox cap, a cardboard box in his hands. I opened the door and let him in.

"Hey." He offered the box to me, and I took it.

"Hey, yourself." My heart fluttered. What was he doing here?

He smiled. "Alex asked me to bring this over on my way."

"I live in the middle of nowhere. Where were you going that this was on your way?"

I set the box on the couch and untucked the flaps. A box of random stuff Alexandra had collected from me over the years. Like way too many hair ties from my days of having long hair, lost at her house. Pretty useless stuff, unless Alexandra had used the box as an excuse to send Ryan over to see me. Ridiculous. I tucked the flaps together again.

"I also wanted to see how you were settling in. I hope you don't mind." He tucked his hands into his pockets and looked around. "You've been busy. Anything you can use some help with today? I'm pretty free for a Saturday."

I laughed. "You have a dishwasher in the back of your truck?"

"No, but I could."

My cheeks caught fire. I didn't know how to respond to my flip comment being taken in earnest. I needed a dishwasher—carpal tunnel and glassware are not a good combination—but I had accidentally asked him for something. I didn't ask for things, it wasn't me.

He took pity on me. "Look, how about this. I'm offering to help you with a dishwasher. Pick up, install, whatever, so call me if you need anything, okay?" He ran his hand underneath the band of his cap and gave me a small grimace. "Might be payment for something, anyway. Alexandra said I could ask you to help me out."

"What is that?"

"I have to go down to Boston with my dad for a few days. He's not doing great, so his PCP is sending him to a specialist. I don't suppose you could watch my dog while I'm gone?"

I winced at my pristine carpet and clean walls, but it would be nice to not be here alone, and I loved dogs.

I shrugged. "Sure, no problem."

The immense relief on his face made me glad I'd said yes.

"You saved my life. I'll introduce the two of you tomorrow. Can I give you a call later?

"Of course."

He smiled at me again and the warmth in the pit of my stomach started all over. "Great. I'll catch you later."

I waited in the parking lot at the Jetty, perched on the hood of my car with my arms wrapped around myself against the brisk wind off the water. Closing my eyes, I took a deep breath and imagined the wind blowing away my troubles and maybe bringing something good into my life.

Something hit my leg, and I jumped, nearly falling. A reddish-brown dog sniffed at my shoes.

Ryan stood at the other end of the taut leash, frowning. "Sorry, he gets a little excited."

I smiled like my heart wasn't thumping like a kettledrum. "Don't worry about it. Who is this?"

"This," Ryan said, pulling the leash a few inches shorter, "is Rexy. He's a teenager with selective hearing right now. Sorry about that."

"Don't worry about it." I lowered my hand so Rexy could sniff it. "Want to go for a walk?"

Rexy was one of those mutts that could have been any breed depending on who was observing and from what angle. Some people shied away because, oh, no!, a pit bull, others asked to pat him because they thought he was a lab. He definitely had some kind of hound in him, and the type refused to budge from the tip of my tongue.

In the end, Rexy had a short-ish brown coat with white paws and loved everyone. He bounded at the end of the leash, chasing the waves out and then racing back up the beach to avoid the lapping water. According to Ryan, Rexy had only so-so recall, a tendency to chase people hoping for love, and a long leash was easier than a misunderstanding.

Watching Ryan's infinite patience with Rexy's boundless energy and his interactions with the people wanting to pat the dog, I got to know Ryan in a whole different way. And the more I got to know him, the more I liked him, and the less self-conscious I became. He was very kind, and always ready with or for a joke. After all of my bad experiences and my ex haunting the back of my mind, it was nice to be able to relax. No pressure trying to be someone I wasn't—there was no way he would ever be interested in me, anyway—and the casual flirting back and forth was fun with nothing meant by it. I don't know if he didn't notice me side-eyeing him or ignored it, but I didn't think I'd get tired of looking at him any time soon.

We spent hours together on the beach until we were alone and the moon hung high in the sky.

"Don't you have to be somewhere tomorrow?" I glanced up at the rugged planes of his face in the moonlight.

His eyes had turned to gleaming pools, and with every crashing wave, I fought to not move closer to him. The wind gusted, and I didn't bother clearing the hair from my face. I shivered and told myself it was the wind rather than what I'd imagined in his eyes.

Our eye contact broke as he shrugged a little and reached down to pat a very tired Rexy. "I do have an early morning."

"I can take him back with me, if that works for you?"

"Yeah, that's good."

We parted ways, and Rexy slept on the backseat the whole way home. On one hand, I was exhausted, but somehow, energized at the same time. My mind kept going in circles over whether Ryan had really wanted to kiss me.

"Guys like that don't want women like you, Melisandre." I turned up the radio to drown out my the voice in my head.

Once home, I was far too awake to contemplate going to bed. Wrapped in an afghan, I sat on the couch with the dog, watching some ghost show or another. Rexy had one paw and his snout on my thigh, snoring loudly enough I had to turn up the volume on the TV to hear the narrator.

After being part of a paranormal group, I could identify most noises and occurrences in a house as having a rational explanation, so for the most part, I stayed away from paranormal reality shows. Other than *Ghost Hunters*, I always ended up yelling at the TV for the ridiculous conclusions people always seemed to draw.

Tonight, the only thing on was a marathon of *Ghost Survivors*, and my eye-rolling muscles were getting a workout. The first story had been miraculously solved with prayer to banish red-eyed demons. My favorite trope, aside from easily explainable things, was the infallible power of Jesus Christ to get rid of spirits. Apparently, ghosts were never Jewish or atheist. My second favorite: Ouija boards being dangerous tools and gateways for those same demons to access our world. I'd played shamelessly as a teen, and not a single dire warning had come true. I'd certainly never been possessed, even though my mother made me wonder occasionally if she had been.

I took a couple of cashews out of the jar at my side and popped them into my mouth, my eyes glued on the screen. The witness in the second half had just described an incident in her house.

"Oh, my God," I shouted. "Shelves fall down if you don't have the right wall anchors and, of course, the stuff on them is going to break." I shook my head and grabbed a handful of nuts. "Gravity plus drywall. Seriously."

The power flickered long enough to turn the lights off for a second or two before coming back on. I stared up at the light fixture, waiting to see if the power would go out completely. I squinted. I'd unscrewed three of the four bulbs, so why had all of them had been affected?

Rexy woke with a snort, startling me. He stared at the front door, twisting to look over his left shoulder. His hackles rose and he growled low in his throat. No part of his body moved other than his head, as he focused on something I couldn't see about six feet off the floor. His paw stayed on my leg as his eyes followed nothing across the room. He watched whatever it was into the kitchen, and then stared at the back door, the growl never fading.

The sound stopped abruptly.

Rexy wagged his tail a few times, put his head back on my leg with a sigh, and went back to sleep.

I couldn't breathe or move, not sure what had happened. The dog had been very consistent regarding the speed of whatever had crossed the room, and the height of whatever he'd been staring at hadn't changed.

I shivered and got up to turn on the back porch light. The dim yellow bulb worked hard to keep one small circle clear but didn't quite keep the shadows at bay. I'd been prey before, and some primitive corner of my brain warned me that I would be again. Someone watched me, hidden in the darkness among the trees.

Cursing myself for a paranoid fool, I taped up some of the wrinkled newspaper that had protected my fragile possessions over the glass in the door, and then more over the dining room window. I left the one over the sink—on the side of the house, not the back—uncovered. On my way home from class tomorrow, I would stop and find something better, but for now, I needed something to block the view in from outside.

Despite my precautions, every nerve remained on edge. I sat back on the couch with Rexy, who snored contentedly, oblivious of what he'd alerted me to.

Chapter 9

April 4, 2010

The next day, despite my fears, Rexy waited patiently for me to get home from the barn without trashing the place. Dusk had already darkened into night, and Rexy sat in front of the door as I opened it, wagging his tail with one of his toys in his mouth.

Everything seemed in order. "Good boy!"

With what I can only describe as a smile, Rexy stood up, his tail going ten miles an hour in his excitement. I reached down to scritch behind his ears and pat his sides.

I stood up, completely serious. "Rexy, where is your ball? Where's your ball?"

After dropping his toy at my feet, Rexy tore down the hallway to the bedroom, across the hall from mine, where I'd tossed his other toys. I expected him to come right back. When there were no paws thumping down the hallway by the time I put my backpack away, I followed him.

"Rexy?"

I stopped dead in my tracks in the doorway to the bedroom across from mine. Rexy sat facing the blank wall, barely giving me a glance over his shoulder. His dingy, yellow tennis ball rested between his feet, and his tail wagged a mile a minute. With a whine, he picked the ball up, scooched closer to the wall, and dropped the toy.

It's what he did when he wanted someone to throw it.

To a blank wall.

I swallowed around the lump in my throat. "Rexy?"

He looked at me over his shoulder again, tongue lolling, then turned back to bark at the wall.

A plush hedgehog lay next to my foot. I picked it up and squished it so it would squeak.

Rexy practically fell over himself coming to me. He sat at my feet the same way he'd done to the wall a moment ago. I held the toy near my shoulder and squeaked it again.

"What's that?" I asked, trying to ignore the tightness in my chest.

Squeak.

Tail still wagging, he scooched his butt closer to me. His front paws came up from the floor and he barked.

"Good boy!" Instead of dropping the toy into his waiting mouth, I threw it so it landed next to his ball.

Tongue lolling, Rexy bounded the few steps to the wall. He sniffed the hedgehog, and then picked up his ball and dropped it at my feet.

"Where's your toy?" I asked.

Rexy picked up his ball and trotted out of the room.

I walked slowly to the wall he'd been sitting in front of. As if afraid of being burned, I hesitated to reach out and touch it. My fingers flexed the moment before they touched the paint. My fingertips dragged over a normal wall.

"What a weirdo." I shook my head as I bent down to pick up the stuffed hedgehog.

I collected the rest of Rexy's toys. Halfway through the doorway, I caught one from the corner of my eye I'd missed. As I picked it up, fingernails dragged across the wall behind me. The hairs on my arms raised and I clutched the pile of dog toys to my chest. My lungs refused to draw in air and my heart thundered as I backed down the hallway. I couldn't stand the idea of having my back to the open door and waited until I reached the middle of the living room to turn around. I dropped the toys to the floor and sat on the couch with my head in my hands.

What in the hell had just happened?

Trying to put it behind me and forcing myself to breathe, I brought Rexy out to relieve himself. Back in the house, I sat on the couch and patted the cushion next to me. Rexy hesitated but, one foot at a time, he climbed onto the couch. I rubbed the side of his neck until he sank onto the cushions with his head on my lap. My patting and stroking of his ears didn't stop. He licked his lips and gave a contented sigh, and I leaned into him, equally relaxed.

I kept one hand on the back of his head, picked up the remote, and turned on the TV, wanting to decompress a bit before I started dinner. Memories of a door swinging open in the middle of the night nagged at my mind, and I shoved them away. I watched a few minutes of History Channel, trying to figure out what the program was about.

Rexy picked his head up off my lap in the same moment I heard something. Footsteps? Someone walking across the wooden planks of the farmer's porch. I muted the television and we both turned our attention toward the front door.

With the lights on inside and the exterior lights off, my living room reflected in the glass.

Footsteps on the far end, beyond where I could see. Heavy work boots, from the sound of it.

I held my breath, waiting for someone to appear in the light spilling out from the living room, waiting for Rexy to jump up and see who was at the door.

The clock on the wall above the television ticked and tocked, but no one appeared, and the footsteps didn't come again. After what had happened yesterday, I didn't want anyone sneaking around unseen, so I got up and turned on the porch light.

Definitely no one there.

Leaving the porch light on, I sat back down. I watched the silent images moving on the TV screen for a few minutes, but I couldn't bring myself to turn the sound back on.

What if the footsteps came back?

I went back to the door, straining to see into the darkness.

"Let's go out, Rexy," I said, grabbing his long leash off the end of the couch. If someone was in the yard, the dog would pick up on it.

He circled around the yard and did his business, but I didn't rush him back inside. The fine hairs on my arms and neck tingled and the sensation of being watched weighed on me like a wet blanket. I slowly moved around the yard, letting Rexy sniff at everything he could reach from the end of his leash. Even in the back yard, where I was most uneasy, he gave no indication anything was wrong.

He started digging at something, and I stopped him. I gave one last scan before giving up and going back into the house.

Without waiting to be asked, Rexy hopped onto the couch. He rested his head on the arm, facing the door, and licked his chops. With a half sigh, half groan, he closed his eyes.

I sat next to him and patted his back. Soon, he snored.

Flipping through channels, I wasn't interested in sitting through anything. Unable to relax, I shut the television off and headed into the kitchen to make dinner.

Chapter 10

April 5, 2010

Ryan picked Rexy up the next afternoon. It was on the tip of my tongue to ask if the dog made a habit of trying to play fetch with blank walls or growling at nothing. I decided I didn't know Ryan well enough to bring it up, and I probably misunderstood what had happened, anyway.

I waited for Ryan to leave the driveway before going down the front steps, car keys in my hand. The weird big band music had happened again last night for just a few seconds before I fell asleep. The only thing I could think of was my neighbor had a record playing (what else could it be?) and I'd devised an experiment to test my theory.

My car's dashboard lit up when I turned the key to Accessory mode. I flipped through the stations until I found a classical station. How loud should it be? I turned the knob until it reached nearly intolerable levels and then rolled down the windows.

The distance as the crow flies between my house and my neighbor measured less than half of what it took for me to walk down my own driveway and up theirs. A Toyota hatchback sat in the driveway, and the front yard had a series of retaining walls and stairs made out of railroad timbers. The shrubs were just leafing out, but had freshly laid mulch spread around their trunks. At the top of the stairs, the railroad tie steps alternated with gravel landings, and flowerbeds flanked both sides. Much nicer than my strip of gravel leading from the driveway to the front steps.

A nicer front door too. The oval lite had a diamond-pattern sandwiched between the layers of glass. I compared it to my own full-lite door as I rapped my knuckles on the cold fiberglass.

The door opened and a stooped lady with gray hair peeked over thick-rimmed glasses. "Can I help you?"

My ears strained to hear my car radio. "I'm Melissa—Mel. I just moved in next door," I said, pointing over my shoulder with my thumb. "I thought I'd say hello."

She straightened a bit, then adjusted her glasses. "I'm Dorothy, but everyone calls me Dotty." She stepped onto the porch, closed the door behind her, and then stared at me until I wanted to squirm under her scrutiny. "You know the same person built both of our houses?"

Not what I expected. I took a step back as she leaned closer. "I think my realtor may have mentioned it."

Dotty made an expansive gesture with one arm. "He might as well have put the loam on with a saltshaker, there's so little of it. I had to have more trucked in." She adjusted her glasses again and crossed her thin arms over her chest. "Are you going to do anything with your yard? Landscaping?"

The line of questioning had me off balance. "Um, I guess? I haven't really thought about it yet."

Reaching behind her for the doorknob, she nodded. "You have a good night, Mel. I have bread in the oven."

She slipped back through the door and closed it firmly. A lock clicked on the other side.

That was a weird interaction. Still on the top step, I strained to hear my car radio. Nothing.

On the walk home, I concentrated on keeping my footsteps as light as I could and continued to listen. Already halfway up my own driveway with my car in sight, the music still hadn't reached me. Then suddenly and with perfect clarity, a violin and piano sang a lively duet. Which was even weirder.

I sat in the car after turning it off. Clearly Dotty wasn't the source of the sound. Between our houses the ground rose into a steep hill, a steeper drop, plus her house had to be on a hill at least twenty feet higher than mine. Maybe I'd been there during a commercial break, and the voices didn't carry as well as the music would have. That made sense to me.

But that night, I lay awake in bed, staring into the darkness as my mind raced, wondering about the noise. After nearly an hour of tossing and turning, I got up and dug through mountains of boxes and found a fan for white noise. I refused to acknowledge to myself it was because of the music.

More tossing and turning later, I decided maybe I needed a drink of water. I swung my legs over the edge of the bed. The moment my feet hit the floor, *crash*.

I fumbled with the lamp on the bedside table. I pulled the chain a few times, but the light didn't come on.

I pulled a flashlight out of the drawer and clicked it on. Swinging the beam around the room, I searched for the source of the crash. The light stopped at the bathroom door and went back. The painting Alexandra had done lay face-down on my dresser.

With the flashlight resting on the dresser top, I carefully lifted the painting by the edges of the frame. The glass had cracked almost the entire way across with a few spiderwebs radiating out. In the wall, the nail still faced the ceiling, firmly embedded in the drywall. I checked the back of the picture. If it had been hung correctly, the nail would've seated into the back of the frame. To come off of the wall, it would need to be lifted up and out.

I replaced the picture on the wall, broken glass and all. I tried a few different ways, but every time I tried to balance the picture in a way where it could fall off the wall, gravity pulled the frame down over the nail. There was no way to not hang it correctly. I couldn't figure out how it fell. I left it face down on my dresser.

It was an easily navigable journey to the kitchen, so I left the flashlight behind and didn't bother to turn any lights on. I felt my way down the hallway, my left hand trailing along the wall. My fingers went over the trim and door to the craft room, then they bumped into the doorjamb on the other side. My fingers went over the trim. A small hall closet stood right next to that door with the trim for both butting up against each other. I stopped as my fingers traced the door.

Why was it open?

I pushed, and the door clicked closed. Open doors were a thing for me, so I'd definitely closed it. When had I opened it at all? I shook my head and walked into the kitchen. The blue lights for the microwave and stove clock were more than enough light for me to grab a glass and fill it from the tap.

On edge, I stood in the corner and faced the back door. Being in a new house would unnerve anyone, I reminded myself. There were new sounds and smells to get used to. The environment was so much quieter, too. And darker. Had living on Main Street for so long ruined me for the country living I'd always wanted?

"It doesn't mean anything, Mel." But the windows continued watching, so I brought my water with me down the hall.

After the perceived brightness in the kitchen, my eyes weren't quite ready for the darkness of the hallway. With baby steps, I went forward, my hand tracing the top of the half-wall over the basement stairs. My right hand holding the glass crashed into something and water splashed everywhere.

"What the fuck?" My free hand fumbled over the wall for a moment before I found the light switch.

I squinted against the sudden brightness of the overhead light.

The closet door stood all the way open, most likely pushed when I walked into it.

"I know I closed this."

Setting my almost-empty cup down, I closed the closet door again and listened for the *click*. Without turning the knob, I pulled on the door. It held fast. I pushed the knob this way and that to test it, but no matter what I did, the latch held firm in the strike plate.

The hairs on the back of my neck lifted and my muscles tensed, ready to fight or flee. I shut the light off and waited in the dark, trying not to breathe in case it covered any sounds. The fan in my bedroom hummed and the motor in the refrigerator whirred.

Nothing else.

I released the breath I'd been holding and shook my head as I picked up my water. "It's a new house. You have to get used to it." I reached out for the closet door, which was still closed, as it should be. "You just didn't close it all the way the first time, that's all."

With what was left of my water in my hand, I went back to bed.

Chapter 11

April 11, 2010

A week later, feeling brave, I gave Ryan a call. I couldn't tell what I wanted more, for him to pick up or let it go to voicemail. At least if it went to voicemail, he could blow me off and be done with it. I'd prefer that to him—

"Hello?"

I almost fell out of my chair. "Ryan, it's Melissa."

"Hey!" He sounded genuinely happy to hear from me. "What's going on?"

"I've been busy with classes, mostly." I didn't know how to finish. "I was wondering what you were up to today."

"Not much." There was that happy tone in his voice again. "What's up?"

"Well..." I hesitated, knowing how weird my next words were going to sound. "I'm actually doing some research for a thing and was wondering if you'd want to come with me." I paused again, just for a heartbeat. "To a cemetery."

Silence stretched across the line for several seconds. "Sure. Do you want me to meet you there or...?"

"It's out in Newfield, so I can pick you up?"

We made arrangements, and I hung up the phone.

When I picked Ryan up, I expected something—a look, a comment. My jeans had seen better days, and I had settled on a pair of worn-out sneakers. On the other hand, his jeans made my mind go places it shouldn't. He smiled when he got into the car, and we exchanged pleasantries about the weather. For the first time in days, the sun had come out, and discussing that took up the beginning of the drive.

"So, where are we heading?" he asked, slapping his hands against his jean-clad thighs.

"It's called the Trafton Cemetery, or maybe the Trafton-Straw Cemetery. At least, that's where I'd like to be heading."

"But you aren't sure?"

"Unfortunately not. I won't know for sure until we get there. There are so many little family plots in these older rural communities it can be hard to know where something is without knowing where it is. So, I know Trafton is the one I want, and I know I'm heading in the right direction, but I won't know if the cemetery we're going to is the right one until I can check out the headstones."

"And what are we researching?"

I hesitated. "I'm working on a local ghost story."

"Cool. What's it about?"

"Well, the legend is Gideon Straw and his family lived in Newfield, and his daughter, Hannah, died on a blustery night in 1826. Sometimes she died in childbirth and other times it's unknown causes. But with the ground being frozen, they buried her under the kitchen floor and put a gravestone in the floor. Supposedly, Hannah was unhappy with this and haunted the house."

"That's pretty interesting. What's at the cemetery?"

"Hannah, if I've done my research right."

"And what's the research for?"

I glanced over. He had one leg stretched out in front of him, and the other tucked up against the seat, with his knee leaning against the door. One arm draped over his raised knee, the other rested on the center console. He'd rolled his sleeves up, and my mouth dried at the sight of the sculpted muscles of his forearms.

Clearing my throat, I focused on the road. "At the risk of being unpopular, I actually do a lot of this kind of research to debunk local ghost legends. I read this particular story, and it didn't make sense. Almost everyone built their house on a foundation with a basement. There aren't floorboards to bury someone under. I checked into it, and the genealogy doesn't match up, either. The story doesn't really stand up to scrutiny very well." I glanced down at my printed directions. I couldn't remember the name of the road I was supposed to be taking. "Kind of annoys me when people make things up and it goes wild, and no one bothers with things like facts." I glanced at him again, admiring his profile. "It was repeated in a regional newspaper a few years ago and it irked me."

"You do all this because it bothers you?"

"Pretty much." I shook my head. "I think, at some point, someone started questioning the genealogy, and it went around it was actually a woman named Margaret, and they called her Hannah instead, or maybe it was Cyrene Straw. But Cyrene is in the same cemetery and wasn't born until 1845, and lived until 1924."

He nodded. "Does the story not matching mean the haunting isn't real?"

"First, just because the story is completely wrong doesn't mean there's no ghost." I sat back in my seat with one hand in my lap and the other on the top of the wheel. "It could still be haunted and have the wrong background. Kind of like everyone saying they're related to Pocahontas because it's a recognizable name. There's some weird East Coast thing about claiming native ancestry I've never understood." I glanced at him and bit the inside of my lip to stop my rambling, but it didn't work. "My grammy was from West Virginia, and when we talked about our family history, she'd scoff. 'Everyone says they're related to an Indian Princess! Our ancestor found some fat —'" I didn't want to repeat the word Gram had used "'—woman sitting in a cornfield.'"

We both chuckled a bit, and I shook my head again. "Anyway, generally speaking, I don't think hauntings or ghosts are real, but there's not much anyone can do to prove or disprove it. I prefer to err on the side of there being a rational explanation rather than the place is haunted." I let out a deep breath. I'd been wrapped up in the research for weeks, and having a willing ear had me a little excited. "You really want to hear all this? I can kind of go on and on about it."

He nodded. "I don't believe in ghosts, either, but I like history. Especially local history."

"Well," I said, my mind turning over to find the best place to start, "Gideon Straw built a colonial style home on what's now Elm Street, in the Historic District in Newfield. I checked it out on Google, did a drive by, and the house is actually there.

"Then I started checking out the genealogy. Ira and Hannah Chadbourne had a daughter, also named Hannah. Hannah, the younger, married Daniel Straw, who was the son of Gideon Straw. That makes Hannah his daughter-in-law. Are you keeping up?"

He chuckled. "I think I can manage."

"Sorry, I didn't mean to imply anything. Genealogy can be complicated." I peeked at him from the corner of my eye. He stared through the windshield with a neutral expression. At least he wasn't asleep. "In this case, there was no Hannah Straw who died in 1826. Hannah's mother, Hannah Chadbourne, died in 1826 and was buried in Limerick, but the younger Hannah didn't marry into the Straw family and become Hannah Straw until 1839. Thirteen years after her mother passed away. Her mother never set foot in the house that's supposedly haunted.

"When Hannah's father died, she had her mother moved to the same cemetery to be reburied with him, and she had a new matching headstone made. She was living in the Gideon Straw house at the time, and the old headstone made its way to the house. I talked to Ruth Ayers, who wrote a book called *The First Families of Newfield*, and I have to tell you, she was exasperated when I told her the reason for my call. She's heard the legend, and runs into the same problem I do most of the time: the lore is more interesting, so no one is willing to let facts get in the way.

"Ruth said the old headstone was being used as a kettle cover at one point. It was just a thing hanging around the house. It's still there today, as far as she knows. It was there in 1995 when she published her book. She told me what I already knew: Hannah Straw lived to a ripe old age until 1899, and she's buried in the Trafton-Straw Cemetery. I think she called it 'Tafton', minus the 'r', but I don't know if that's how she talks or not.

"I unraveled the entire story using Google and a couple of genealogy websites, so it would be hard to argue the 'haunting' supposedly resulting from this specifically tragic story is true."

I let out a deep breath and glanced over at Ryan. He watched the trees whizzing by the car, but seemed to be listening. "Are you sure I'm not boring you?"

"Not at all." He grinned at me.

I glanced at my printed directions and tried to keep my eyes on the road at the same time. "The problem is there's no cemetery across from the house like Ayers said. I found a historic map that showed some of the family plots and who was living where." I glanced at him. "Did you know old town maps had people's names on them? So cool. Anyway, I'm basically guessing that maybe this is the right one. It's also entirely possible it's a private plot and wasn't labeled on the map."

"Is it big?" he asked.

I shrugged, setting my directions down. I took a right. "There were over a dozen people buried there, but that doesn't mean it's big. It's more or less a needle in a haystack. And if I can't get to it from the road, I can't go check it out without the owner's permission since I'm not related to the people buried there."

"What do you get if you find this place and you're right?"

The smile on my face couldn't be helped. "I already know I'm right, but I want as much evidence of it as I can get."

I slowed down and pulled onto the shoulder to let the car behind us pass. The cemetery was supposed to be in this area, somewhere on the right. I pulled back onto the road, driving slowly as I scanned both sides. A monument came into view.

I pulled onto the shoulder and put my hazards on. "We're here. Maybe."

Ryan brushed his palms on his jeans and unfolded himself from my car. Making sure I wouldn't get creamed by oncoming traffic, I got out and went around the front of the car where he waited. His gaze searched the stone monuments, over and through the white picket fence around the cemetery.

He fell into step beside me. "So, debunking, huh?"

"Yeah. I've always loved doing research, and this is at least interesting, being local history and all." We walked together and I pointed at the rusted hinges sticking out from the granite posts as we walked through. "The gate is long gone, probably wrought iron collected during World War II."

We headed toward the large monument in the center of the cemetery. The ground, soaked with melted snow, squelched under our feet.

"I don't know when the Hannah Straw legend started, but I'm pretty sure it will outlive me."

His brows drew together, and he gestured to the ground. "Why are these all sunken?"

"The coffins collapse after a while." We got to the monument, and my shoulders slumped. "I don't think this is the right place, but let's look around."

We reached the other end of the cemetery, checking each headstone. Not a Straw or Chadbourne to be found. We were in the wrong place.

"Bummer, I was so sure I found it."

"Does finding it really matter if all the public information is there?"

I shrugged and we headed back to the car. "Kind of. More for me to say I did it and maybe snap a picture than for any other reason. It feels unfinished if I haven't gotten all the way to the end."

"What else do you do for fun, other than debunking ghost stories?"

"Well, I'm a full-time student right now. And I have my horse." My face heated a little. "I'm also part of a paranormal investigation team, so I guess I really spend a lot of time debunking ghost stories." I bit my lower lip. "And I'm not sure how you feel about it, but I started doing all the Hannah Straw research a few months ago, and now I'm going to use it for one of my classes." I covered my mouth with my hand, suddenly embarrassed. "I spent this whole time rambling on about ghost stories and didn't let you get a word in edgewise. I'm sorry."

He shrugged and grinned. "It's nice to talk to someone who's excited about what they do. I don't believe in ghosts, but the investigation thing sounds interesting."

I stopped in my tracks. "Really?"

"Yeah. We should hang out again, and you can tell me more if you want."

I smiled. "I'd like that."

Chapter 12

April 30, 2010

One afternoon, as I fell through the doorway, my arms loaded with my first full load of groceries in my new house, the phone started ringing.

I answered out of breath. "Hello?"

"It's Jess."

"Hey." I squished the phone between my ear and my shoulder, and set my grocery bags on the table. "What's up?"

"We did the nursing home investigation in Portland last week, remember?"

"Sure."

"While we were there, we were talking about you, and how you haven't been going on investigations lately."

"You know I'm busy, going to class during the day, and then I have a mountain of assignments to finish." I didn't mention I didn't feel like dealing with the group. Besides, it was a volunteer gig.

"Everyone has a day job, Melissa," she said. "And they all come on investigations. The nursing home was a very big deal, you knew that. We'd been planning it for months."

Closing my eyes, I pinched the bridge of my nose. "There are fourteen other people on the team. I didn't think it would be an issue if I didn't go on every investigation. I didn't think anyone would miss me."

The silence over the line had me wondering if we'd been disconnected. "The Portland thing was three floors, and we could have used the help."

"Well, I'm sorry I couldn't make it." I shrugged and threw my hand in the air. "I'll do better next time. When's the next investigation? I'll make sure I'm there."

She sighed. "I'm actually calling to tell you there won't be a next time. The other thing we discussed was your negative attitude about ghosts. You're being kind of a bummer."

My jaw dropped. "What negative attitude?"

"You know, after what you said happened when you were at Rebecca James's, we expected you to be more open-minded."

"So, the problem is that I don't think everything is haunted?" My neck already ached from holding the phone on my shoulder with my face. I started unpacking the grocery bags. "What would you like me to do? Fake EVPs? I told you, I don't do that. It's wrong."

"Well, you don't have to poo-poo over the evidence the other people find."

The soup can in my hand landed on the table with a *thunk*. "Jess, seriously, one of the things I debunked was Julie and Frank talking about getting a Mountain Dew out of his car. Do you want me to not say anything when someone thinks they found an EVP, but it's actually the team whispering? I told her so many times not to whisper because it would mess with the recordings."

Jess didn't speak, and I imagined her expression, red-faced and seething, as I put carrots in the crisper drawer. "We don't want someone so negative on the team, and lately, you haven't been coming at all, so we think it's best if we part ways."

"Okay, no problem." I didn't wait to say goodbye, just hung up the phone. No need to prolong the inevitable with the inane.

Then I sighed, disappointed. Jess's group was the only one local to me I could be part of, and even though I'd never found any evidence—and more often than not, found the perfectly reasonable explanation for someone's paranormal experience—I still had fun most of the time. I considered calling her back, but decided against it. If nothing else, I'd learned Jess never changed her mind.

I finished putting the groceries away and sat at my computer desk. Leaning back in my chair, I drummed my fingers on the desktop. My experience at Rebecca's was why I'd joined a paranormal group in the first place. When the group had shut down, I'd joined Jess, and I'd been with them for a while. I could try to find a new group, but the clock told me I didn't have enough time before meeting Alexandra and Sarah for dinner.

After running through the shower, I grabbed my towel and wrapped it around myself. As I stepped out of the tub and adjusted the knot on my towel, something kicked on in my brain, and my gaze crawled to the mirror.

Steam coated the four-by-eight sheet of glass, and I could only assume my washing it earlier in the week had created the bizarre pattern. Just above the faucet, nearest to the door, a face, reminiscent of Munch's Scream with x's where the eyes should be, stared back at me.

My logical brain fought with my sympathetic nervous system over whether to analyze or run.

I don't know how long I stood there, frozen except for my pounding heart, before I wiped the image away.

"It was just steam, and that thing where you see faces in things. That's all it was." My voice sounded about as confident as I felt.

I ran the water in the sink to get my hand wet and wiped a section of the mirror clear. My eyes didn't fit my pale face, and my hair stuck up at odd angles from scrubbing it with the towel.

"Get it together."

Alexandra waved at me from a table in the corner when I walked into the restaurant. I'd never been here before, but Sarah had a reputation for finding obscure places with amazing food. There were only two menus on the table.

"Where's Sarah?" I asked, sliding into the booth. A glass of red liquid with fruit floating in it waited for me.

"Got you Sangria." She slid a colorful menu toward me. "There was an emergency at work, so she got called in after we got here. I've been abandoned without a car, so I may end up going home with you."

"Wouldn't be the first time."

She grinned and wiggled her eyebrows at me. "I gave up trying to pick you up in high school."

My heart thudded. If Alexandra had ever given me any indication—I forced old feelings aside. I'd missed my chance. "We're better as friends. And could you imagine my parents' reaction if we'd dated?"

Her dark blue eyes arrested me over her menu. "Your parents were such unbelievable homophobes, they could've walked in on us having sex, and they would've made up their own reality to avoid it." She rolled her eyes and went back to reading. "Then they would have erased it from their collective memory."

"I'm not going to argue with that because I can't." I sipped my drink—Calhoun's made the best, but I liked this a lot—and browsed my menu. "Bummer about Sarah, she always has good stories."

Alexandra shrugged one shoulder. "It's nice for just the two of us to get together and catch up sometimes. How's the new house?" She'd always been good at reading me, maybe because we both had narcissistic mothers who were toxic in their own special ways. She must've read something in my hesitation. "What's wrong with the house?"

I fidgeted with the corner of my menu and wouldn't meet her eyes. "There's been some weird stuff happening. I'm having a hard time adjusting to the quiet and the dark outside of town, I think."

Completely serious, she set her menu on the table and folded her hands on top of it. "What's happening?"

I told her about the bang, and the weird big band music. I told her about the picture falling, and the dog. I couldn't bring myself to tell her about the mirror, it felt too silly.

She listened intently, and then nodded, her gold hoop earrings swinging. "I'll have to check it out some time."

"That's it?"

"That's it. Oh, and I'm having another glass of wine."

My low tolerance for alcohol—and not realizing this particular establishment had fifty percent larger glasses than I was used to—had me too buzzed after three glasses for me to be able to drive safely. Always cool and collected, she offered to take me home. We laughed and sang along with the radio, and no one thought about ghosts.

When we got to my house, I rummaged through the closet in my craft room to find a blanket and a pillow so Alexandra could crash on the couch. Already two in the morning, we both wanted to pass out. Sarah's quick emergency had turned into an overnight at work, and I could bring Alexandra home on my way to class in the morning.

I walked down the hall, more than a little unsteady on my feet. The moment felt right, and I launched into a song from an old Disney movie. At the opening to the living room, I started giggling and doubled over from laughing.

"Here you go, Alex."

She looked up from her phone where she sat on the couch, and glared daggers at me. "You get a pass because you aren't in your right mind."

I pressed a finger to my lips. "Shh. Don't tell him I told you, but Ryan calls you Alex. He says Alexandra is too much of a mouthful."

She rolled her eyes and shook her head, simultaneously securing her mane of hair at the nape of her neck with an elastic. "I won't say anything. Not until he calls me Alex to my face." She stood enough to take the bedding from me and sat back on the couch, setting it beside her. "You like him, don't you?"

I scoffed. "It doesn't matter." I imagined Ryan at six-feet, two-inches towering over Alexandra—only a hair shorter than me—while she explained to him precisely why she would never, ever be Alex, and I started giggling again, drawing another glare from her. "I think I'm going to go to bed before I get myself in trouble."

She rolled her eyes and turned back to her phone. "Why don't you do that?"

My goofy smile stayed glued to my face as I stumbled down the hallway to bed. I couldn't get the mental picture of Alexandra taking Ryan down from my mind. Not bothering with pajamas, I stripped out of my clothes and slid between the sheets naked, and turned the bedside lamp off.

Alexandra had already shut the living room light off, and the darkness took over.

I don't know how long I lay there—how many moments or breaths had passed—when suddenly, Alexandra's form appeared in the doorway, silhouetted by the faint green glow of the smoke detector in the hall. Before I could even register her presence, she dove onto the end of my bed, somehow getting under the covers in one smooth move.

"What the hell, Alexandra?" I sat up, holding a corner of the blanket to my chest with my arm. "Are you okay?"

Her voice came from under the blanket, muffled like she spoke into the mattress. "There's a man on your porch."

My buzz evaporated. Instant sobriety. "What?"

"There's a man on your porch. He's wearing, like, a green plaid flannel." The blankets moved, and her fingers appeared around the edge as she pulled them away from her face. "He was staring at me."

My heart raced. I slid out of bed and grabbed my robe.

A pale hand snaked out from under the covers and grabbed me. Only my heart in my throat stopped me from screaming.

Her eyes gleamed in the dim light, surrounded by shadows. "Don't go."

"I have to go."

Detached from myself, like I was watching a movie instead of in my own body, I crept down the carpeted hallway, not sure what I would find. A pale bluish glow bathed the room. The waning moon hung low in an overcast sky and cast weak light through the tall windows. At the end of the hallway, I paused. The closet door was barely open, and I pushed it closed. My neck might break from the tension in the muscles as I peered around the corner to the front door.

The hairs on the back of my neck rose and my skin prickled. Something had to be there, which kept me on edge.

A hand closed on my shoulder, and I about jumped out of my skin. "Judas Priest, Alexandra, are you trying to give me a heart attack?"

Clinging to my arm, she peered around me, staring at the empty space in front of the door. "He was right there. I saw him"

I wavered on my feet and leaned against the wall for balance. "We can go outside and check it out if you want. How are you with a rifle?"

She stepped back, her brows drawn together. "Are you crazy?"

I gestured to the front door. "If I have a prowler, I'm not going out unarmed." My words slurred. "And I'm not bringing your wife to a fun gight." I blinked and wiped my face. "Not bringing a *knife* to a *gun fight*. But I might not be the best person to be handling a weapon right now."

Rolling her eyes and shaking her head at the same time, she put her hand on my shoulder. "I don't think it was a prowler. Let's get you back to bed."

I widened my eyes in make-believe shock and clapped my hands to my cheeks, warm with drunkenness. "Was it a *ghost*?"

Alexandra didn't laugh and steered me back to my bedroom.

Chapter 13

May 1, 2010

Once I sobered up, I didn't remember much about the previous night. A fuzzy memory of Alexandra seeing something stood out. Pale and withdrawn, she didn't speak during the whole ride back to her house, and I wasn't sure I wanted to be the one to bring it up. If she wanted to talk about it, she would.

She didn't call me for the rest of the weekend. I texted her Monday, and didn't receive a response, no matter how many times I checked my phone. Classes on Tuesday provided a great distraction until they were over for the day. Finals loomed as the semester wound down. I only had one class at this point that I questioned how well I'd do. I expected the other three would be a breeze. I could take one final online, but the other three were in-person this Thursday.

When I got home, in my driveway, Ryan sat on the chrome back bumper of his truck, legs crossed at the ankles. The visor of his ball cap hid his face as he stared down at his phone.

My heart jumped into my throat to flutter there like a butterfly, and I tried to tamp it down. Him remaining completely oblivious to my presence helped, but my face heated anyway as I parked next to him. More than ghosts, he'd been on my mind all day.

"You like him, don't you?" Alexandra had asked.

He put his phone away, but didn't move.

I grabbed my school bag off the passenger seat and swung it over my shoulder. "Hey. You're early."

"I am." He pushed off his truck, standing in one smooth motion. "How was your day?"

"Not bad. Thanks for coming out, I really appreciate it."

"No problem." He grinned. "You helped me, I help you. It all works. Why don't you tell me what's going on?"

As I climbed the steps, I tried to come up with the best way to say what I wanted to without sounding like a crazy person. He followed me into the living room and closed the door behind him as I dropped my backpack on the couch.

"I've been hearing some weird noises at night, and I don't know what it is," I said.

"Okay, where are you when you hear the noise?"

"In bed, usually."

He flashed a wicked grin. "Are you trying to lure me somewhere? It never happens like in the movies."

It took me a few seconds to realize what he was talking about. My cheeks caught fire when I finally got his meaning.

"Sorry, I had to." He placed his hand on my arm, and his smile was anything but apologetic. "Your bedroom is the back of the house, right?"

He walked past me, but instead of going down the hall, he headed down the basement stairs.

"Where are you going?" I asked, following.

"There's a lot of stuff in basements making weird noises, especially in a new house. Let's go see what monsters might be lurking under your bed."

The end of the stairs opened into bare space. In the corner to the left, under my bedroom, the closed and locked bulkhead door. In the corner stood my well pump, then a water softening system, then the boxy blue contraption with copper pipes coming off of it—the boiler.

Ryan rapped on the bulkhead door. "This is a nice door. They don't usually put these in spec houses."

I frowned. "What's a spec house?"

"Instead of the owner of the subdivision working with a builder to put up custom homes to buyers, they build a house and then try to sell it."

"Oh." I crossed my arms. "I knew he built the house to sell, but didn't know what it's called."

He shrugged it off. "Spec houses aren't as common as custom-built, but you get more buyers with a turnkey house." He frowned at one of the pipes running up to the ceiling. "This isn't code." He stood on his toes, sliding his hand between the copper and the floor above as the fabric of his shirt pulled across his wide chest. "You're supposed to have more space between your hot pipes and flammable surfaces." He pulled a pocket knife out of his back pocket and used it to tap the pipes, then the big silver duct coming out of the back of the boiler. He read the yellow tag dangling at his eye level. "I'm going to give you the name of a heating guy I like. You're close enough to needing service on this that he can come do that, bleed the air out of your pipes, and get this up to code." He patted the pockets of his pants. "Do you have something to write with?"

"Upstairs." I frowned again.

How did the boiler need to be serviced already? In my head, I ran over my recent expenses. I'd depleted a lot of my savings with a down payment I had technically not needed and closing costs. The extra cost of gas added up to more than I'd anticipated, too. And how would I clear the snow out of my driveway this winter? The weight of being in too deep settled onto my shoulders.

"Just a second." Using his knife to tap each one, he counted the floor joists. "Eighteen on center…" He took a step away from the exterior wall, stood in front of the boiler, and touched the floor joists. "Your bed is probably right here?"

If I didn't stop frowning, my face was going to stay stuck that way, but I couldn't help it. "I think so?"

He reached around and tapped the silver duct again. "This is your power vent. I'll check outside and see if anything is stuck. That can make all kinds of different noises." He slipped the knife back in his pocket. "Get me something to write with, and I'll give you the guy's number."

Ryan followed me up the stairs, but the shivers I got from being watched warmed me this time. My face heated, too. Without lifting my eyes from the floor, I dug a pen out of my school bag. He scribbled a name and number on the back of one of his business cards. Our fingers touched when he handed it back to me, and the heat intensified. Knowing how awful the creeping red clashed with my pale skin made it worse.

"You okay?" he asked.

Great. Now he thinks I'm having some kind of meltdown. "Yeah," I said with a weak grin. "Just a little warm."

He smiled, and the warmth sank into the pit of my stomach without leaving my face. I had to get over this before he decided I was a complete moron.

"It's late spring, so he should be able to see you pretty quick." He tucked his hands into the front pockets of his jeans. "Are you doing anything tonight?"

"Me?" *Yeah, dumbass, who else is he talking to?* My fingers played with the edges of the business card. I'd done too much driving today. "I'm pretty much in for the night, I think. I was going to make dinner if you'd like to join me?"

He smiled again. "I'd like that."

Having Ryan with me in the confines of my house was much different than out on the beach. My nerves tingled as he moved around me. I knew exactly where he was even when I couldn't see him.

"Do you want some help?" he asked, standing near my elbow.

I took a deep breath to steady myself. Beneath the clean aroma of his body wash was a very distinctive male scent that reminded me of a campfire and fresh cut wood.

"How are you at chopping onions?" Without raising my gaze to his, I shoved the cutting board and knife over to him.

Without hesitation, he picked up the knife and started a fine dice I could only envy. When I cut onions, the pieces always ended up too big.

"I'm making you nervous," he said quietly. I used the same tone on my mare when she spooked about the wind blowing, or whatever invisible things upset horses. "If you want to take back your invitation, that's fine."

Taking another deep breath, I braced myself against the counter. When I tried to catch Ryan's gaze, he focused on the cutting board. My shoulders sagged as some of the tension left. "It's been a while since I shared a kitchen is probably the best way to explain it, I think."

"Well," he said, using the edge of the knife to scrape the chopped onion into a neat pile, "if there's anything I can do to help, let me know. Where do you want these?"

The onions were dumped into butter sizzling in the bottom of a pot on my smooth-top range. I stirred with a wooden spoon and watched them change color. I moved two thick carrots from the counter onto the cutting board and pushed the knife toward Ryan.

He started peeling and sniffed appreciatively. "I love that smell."

"What smell is that?" I dumped in a handful of minced garlic. A few seconds later, my mouth started watering.

"The onions mostly, but the butter, too. Half rounds?" He held the knife poised over one of the peeled carrots.

"That's perfect." Grinning, I tipped the pot to separate the butter from the onions and garlic. "If you like real butter, you're going to like my food. The secret ingredient to pretty much everything is butter. Real butter, not fake."

Leaning so close his body heat warmed me, he sniffed the steam coming from the pot. "Be careful. If you feed me, I'm going to keep coming back. I might be hard to get rid of."

I dumped flour into the butter and whisked it smooth. "The way to a man's heart is through his stomach." I glanced at him. "Or so the saying goes."

"My mother has always been a really bad cook, so I'm easy to please." He chuckled. The knife moved over the carrots quickly, chopping them into even semi-circles. "She burns pasta. Everything else is either under or overcooked."

"That sounds bad." I poured my homemade bone broth into the pot, whisking it into the roux. "My mother held herself out as a brilliant chef, and heaven help anyone who didn't lavish her with compliments over whatever Betty Crocker recipe she added salt to and called her own. I still get mad over her cranberry bread."

"Sounds like an interesting thing to get mad about." He slid the chopped carrots into the pot as I stirred.

"I didn't have the best family life growing up. I, uh, distanced myself from them. Joined the Air Force to get away from them, actually. My mother made the most delicious cranberry bread at Thanksgiving." I remembered being stuck on base over the holidays, begging her over the phone to send me some of her holiday goodies. My pleas had fallen on deaf ears. She couldn't be bothered. I shook the memory away. "Anyway, my sister felt bad for me and there was a whole cloak and dagger thing for her to give me the recipe. She made me promise to never say anything, because my parents would've been furious if they'd found out she shared my mother's secret recipe." I put the cover on the pot and turned the heat down. "I bought a bag of cranberries to make it. The recipe was—verbatim—on the back of the cranberry bag." Shrugging, I turned to the sink to wash my hands. "Since then, it seems like I find one of her recipes she 'invented' every time I open my cookbook."

"You have a sister." He leaned against the countertop.

"Technically." How was that his takeaway? I dried my hands and smoothed the towel over the oven handle. "We haven't talked in a long time. An older brother, too. It's been even longer since I spoke to him. Excuse me."

He leaned out of the way so I could push the cabinet door behind him closed. I still hadn't adjusted the hinge, and it fell open for no reason whenever I was in the kitchen.

"And your parents?" He crossed his arms.

"Dead." I grabbed potatoes and put them on the cutting board. "They died not long after I got out of the military." Answering the question on his face, I added, "Car accident, about seven years ago." With the edge of my knife, I scraped imperfections off the surface of the potatoes. "Do you have siblings?"

He pushed himself away from the counter and dropped into one of the wooden dining chairs. He sat sideways with one arm draped casually over the back and the other arm on the table. When had he taken off his shoes? "Just me. My parents divorced when I was in high school. No step-siblings, either."

After setting the timer, I poured two glasses of lemonade and brought them with me to the table. "You get along with your parents?" I handed him a glass and took the seat closest to him.

"My dad and I are cut from the same cloth." He took a deep drink. "That's good, I like it." He cleared his throat. "My mom and I, well, we have some spiritual differences."

The cold glass chilled my lower lip as I sipped. Keeping my eyes on him was easier now than it had been not long ago. He didn't elaborate, so I had to ask. "Like, you put pineapple on pizza and she doesn't?"

He laughed and fidgeted with his glass. "Nothing that serious." The pause stretched, and his jaw worked. "She believes in things that makes her vulnerable to people who want to take advantage of a nice lady. Auras and chakras and ghosts and fortune telling. You name it, she probably believes it's the answer to life." The tips of his fingers bounced against the tabletop, his dark brown eyes fixed to the motion. "A year or so ago, my mother got a tarot card reading. She said the woman was 'terrifyingly accurate' with the cards. When the woman told her I had a curse attached to me, my mother fell for that, too. Gave the crook hundreds of dollars for magic candles and a handful of rocks."

"That really sucks." I cringed, and not just because his mother had been conned out of some money.

My tarot deck rested in the nightstand next to my bed. I couldn't read my own cards to save my life, but I'd read for other people on more than one occasion. I also had a small wooden box of tumbled stones on my dresser I believed had special energy. At this very moment, I had a chunk of rose quartz in my pocket.

"No." He exhaled noisily. "The part that sucked was the 'curse' took way more over the next six months. I happened to be there when the tow truck showed up to repossess her car."

"Ouch." I touched my thumb to my lower lip and gave a smile bordering on a grimace. "Dare I ask why she thought you were cursed?"

"The timing, mostly. Things had fallen apart with my wife and it had gotten really ugly by then."

The word "wife" hit me like a bucket of ice water. I pulled away and dropped my hands into my lap. "I didn't know you were married."

"I'm not anymore." He wiped his face with his hand.

I was good with changing the subject. I wasn't ready to go down the rabbit hole of unpleasant spouses. "Do you mind if I ask how much your mom lost?"

He leaned back in his chair again. "The initial card reading cost about fifty bucks, but that was a 'discount price'. The initial curse diagnosis ran about three hundred. Then, of course, she had to come back every couple of weeks for a new reading to see if the curse was gone, so another hundred every time." He didn't quite count on his fingers, but they twitched as he mentally tallied up the costs. "Naturally, the curse was very powerful and resistant to the 'usual' remedies. Every few weeks, it would cost her anywhere from two fifty or more to buy spells and prayers or whatever other nonsense the scam artist made up to get money out of my mother." He shrugged one shoulder and frowned. "All in all, I think probably four grand."

"That is so horrible." I leaned forward and rested my elbows on my thighs. My dangling hands almost touched his knee. "I feel so bad for your mom being taken advantage of like that. Was she able to get anything back?"

He ran his hand over his brow. "No. Naturally, it was all cash."

"So, what happened?" I sat back again. "I'm sorry, I'm being really nosy."

"No, it's fine." He sighed. "The bank took her car. I had to pull every string I had to keep her from getting evicted from her apartment. I missed so much time off my job sites having to cart her around that I finally rented her a car. Of course, at the same time, I was getting hit with attorney's fees and dealing with that whole mess. Thank God her bank was local, and we were able to refinance the car, and she got it back. The whole thing drained my finances so bad that I'm still trying to recover from it. My father really came through for me when I needed it."

"What did your father do?" I went back to the stove. Weight built in my chest—envy, maybe—at all the family togetherness and helping each other out.

"I guess, technically, he sold me his house. As soon as the divorce judgement got finalized, he put my name on the deed so I could borrow against the house while we untangled everything."

The timer beeping saved me from having to respond. Physics made more sense to me than cohesive families, and my entire knowledge of physics came from elementary school science. Not knowing what to say, I started cutting the potatoes into chunks.

"What are we making?" he asked.

"Baked potato soup. My own recipe you won't find anywhere else." Food I could talk about all day long. With a grin, I lifted the cover. The ingredients were melding together and my mouth watered when I got a whiff. "We had the best chow hall on base, and they had a baked potato chowder. When I got home, I made it a mission to come up with something of my own." The potatoes went into the pot with a bit of thyme. I stirred and waited for it to come back to a boil.

"And what's your new mission?" he asked from a step behind me.

I shivered from his nearness, glad to have a steaming pot to blame for the heat rushing to my face. "I'm going to learn how to grill next." With the spoon, I gestured toward the back door. Wrinkled newspaper still covered the window because I couldn't justify spending money on something better. On the other side of the door, on the tiny porch, stood a small gas grill I hadn't been brave enough to turn on yet.

"What's with the newspaper?" He lifted the tape and raised the corner of the paper.

Five or six feet from the edge of the porch, a scar in the land marked where heavy equipment had dug into the earth to level the area around the house and dig the foundation. Above the exposed sand and rocks, the land rose steeply upward. It peaked and then dropped nearly one hundred feet. I hated the back of the lot. What was I going to do with it?

He wiggled the corner of the newspaper to get my attention back. The opposite corner came free.

"Sorry, thinking about landscaping."

"What's with the newspaper?" he repeated. "You put it over the window, too?"

"I don't like having uncovered windows is all. Side effect of living in town for years."

He frowned toward the living room. The giant windows were big enough for a fully-dressed firefighter to climb through were bare of any type of dressing or covering at all.

"I like the light in the living room." It sounded like a question and defensive. I replaced the cover on the pot and wiped my hands on my jeans. "We have about twenty minutes until dinner."

He smoothed the tape back in place. "I still have to go outside and check your vent. Why don't you come out with me and then you can show me around?"

"Sounds good to me." I turned the heat down on the stove again. With the pot of soup bubbling away, we headed outside.

Chapter 14

May 11, 2010

In bed that night, I put myself diagonally across the queen-sized bed. I'd fallen into the habit of only sleeping on one side, but I had the whole thing to myself. Time to let go of old ways. After rolling over, I faced the windows overlooking the backyard. The closed blinds behind the drawn curtains blocked almost all the meager star and moonlight filtering through the trees.

A small white light hit the ceiling and disappeared.

I stared, not sure if I had imagined it.

It returned. Really just a flash on the ceiling, less than a second.

Then there were two dancing together, and I sat up to stare at the lights bouncing around on the ceiling like lightning bugs stuck in a jar. They must have been coming around the blinds, and then through the gap between the wall and the curtain rod.

A third light joined the dance along the ceiling. I clutched the sheet against my breasts, partly to convince myself I was actually awake and seeing this. I hadn't turned my fan on, so I could hear if Ryan dislodging the stuck flappy thing on the vent pipe would make the music-like sound stop. Now, the blood rushing in my ears deafened me. I held my breath, straining to hear footsteps or anything else.

As quickly as they'd come, the lights disappeared.

Dragging the sheet with me so I could keep it wrapped around myself, I pushed the curtain aside. The blinds were down and fully closed, as I'd expected. I ran my finger along the gap between the window frame and the blinds. It wasn't much, but enough to let some light through. But where had the lights come from? I left the curtains pulled back and sat on the edge of the bed for a while, waiting to see if the lights would return.

After a few minutes, I lay back down. I stared at the ceiling, counting my heartbeats and half wanting the lights to reappear, but half terrified they would.

My cell phone vibrated across the nightstand and dragged me out of a sound sleep. I squinted at the caller ID before flipping it open. "Hello?"

"Hey, it's Sarah." No tone or inflection in her voice to give me a clue what it could be about.

"Good morning." I lay back against the pillows, one hand on my forehead. Sarah never called me. It was almost always Alexandra.

"I am so sorry to do this to you, but could you take Olivia for us for a couple of days? I can bring her pack and play and everything over. Our regular sitter is down with the flu and we're really in a bind." Her hand went over the phone, and she said something I couldn't hear.

Clearing my throat, I wiped the sleep from my eyes. "Yeah, I can do that." My drowsy mind tried to remember my finals schedule and what time I had to be up the next morning.

"Do you have any not-baby friendly stuff out? She is into absolutely everything right now."

"Nope." I'd have to lock a door, but giving Sarah too much information never ended well. "Worst thing she can get into are some DVDs, nothing breakable."

"Thank you so much, Mel. I owe you big time! I'll pack her up and come drop her off. Alexandra is sitting with my dad, and I really want to get back to the hospital. Thank you so much!"

"Oh, Sarah, I'm sorry, don't thank me yet."

"What's wrong?"

I ran my hand through my hair. "Ryan's dog has been here. Is that going to mess with your allergies?"

"As long as you vacuum and she doesn't come into direct contact with the dog, it should be fine. Is the dog there now?"

I told her no and swung my legs out of bed. I apparently had some cleaning to do.

She thanked me again.

"No problem."

The room across from mine seemed like a good spot for Olivia. Mostly empty anyway, it was close enough to hear her during the night, but not so close that I'd wake up every time she rolled over. She'd been sleeping through the night since four months old, but Alexandra often said Olivia rose early.

After vacuuming and rushing around the house to make sure there was nothing dangerous out, sweat dripped from the ends of my short hair and my damp t-shirt clung to my chest. I only took a quick rinse in the shower, so I wouldn't be wet and naked when Sarah showed up. I peeked around the curtain at the mirror, which I had thoroughly scrubbed. No faces this time. After toweling off, I threw on some jeans and a long sleeve shirt. I was pulling my socks on when the doorbell sounded.

"Coming," I yelled, half trotting down the hallway to get to the door.

Sarah stood on the porch with Olivia on her hip, two bags slung over her other shoulder, and a box-like thing at her feet.

"Thank you again so much," she said as I opened the door. She slipped past me and neatly deposited a duffel bag and a diaper bag on my couch without moving the baby off her hip.

Olivia studied at me with wide blue eyes, her fingers in her mouth.

"Hey, peanut." I waved at her, giving her a bright smile. She had grown since the last time I'd seen her.

Olivia turned her face into her mother's shoulder and hid.

"She's a little cranky this morning because I woke her up early." Sarah reached outside and grabbed the other thing off the porch. "This is her pack and play. It's kind of self-explanatory to set up once you have it out of the case. I am going to grab her car seat for you, so you aren't stranded here."

Sarah jiggled the baby on her hip and pulled off Olivia's crocheted hat, exposing sparse blonde hair. "You're going to stay here with Auntie Mel." She gave the baby a noisy kiss on the cheek.

"Mow, mow."

"Yes, Auntie Mel. Can you say Auntie Mel?"

"Mow!" Fingers went back in the mouth.

Sarah kissed the pink cheek again and set Olivia on the couch to unzip her coat. The baby gawked with wide eyes, now interested in everything surrounding her. The next several minutes consisted of Sarah rattling off instructions like I would remember any of it.

I jumped in when Sarah paused for breath. "No sugar, no sacrificing the baby to appease angry gods. Got it."

The eye roll I got in response was epic by any standard and I grinned.

"You have our cell numbers. Alexandra has better reception at the hospital than I do, so try her first." She took Olivia's hand and kissed the chubby fingers, but Olivia was working on climbing off the couch. "I'll put the car seat in the back of your car. Once I leave, I have to be gone or she'll get upset." Sarah hesitated, watching Olivia toddle her way to my entertainment center and the colorful DVD cases. She let go of a long breath. "I'm sorry, this is the first time she's been away from us overnight. And with everything going on with my dad in hospice..."

"She'll be fine." What could I do but try to diffuse the situation with some inappropriate humor? I touched her elbow. "Seriously, no sacrifices."

She rolled her eyes, but relaxed. "Alexandra keeps telling me I'll get used to the sense of humor, but after five years, I haven't yet." She shook her head. "One last thing, if she gets up at the crack of dawn, leave her be. She'll entertain herself and fall back asleep. Call me if you need anything." She blew a kiss at the baby. "Bye-bye, my precious!" she crooned, and breezed out the door.

Olivia seemed pretty cool with Sarah leaving, but I unpacked some toys a distraction, anyway.

"Looks like it's just you and me, kid." I shook one of the toys, a stuffed star, and bright lights turned on and it sang "Twinkle Twinkle Little Star," catching Olivia's attention.

I sat on the couch, holding the singing star in front of me like a shield.

She came at me, arms extended for the toy. "'tar! 'tar!"

It warmed me to see this little kid, so innocent and whole, and I understood Alexandra's fierce protectiveness of her mini monster. She and Sarah were negotiating having a second one, but only if they could use the same donor as they had found for Olivia. I was all about it, this tiny human being one of my favorite people. This was our first time alone without her mothers.

Olivia grabbed the star and gave the toy her full attention. It stopped singing, so she handed it to me to fix, her blue eyes irresistible.

I gave the toy a good shake, and the lights came back on. "Do you want to come help Auntie Mel set up your room? Come help me!"

I slung the diaper bag over one shoulder and grabbed the pack and play. Moving sideways to keep an eye on Olivia, I took my time walking down the hallway. She was pretty good on her feet by now, but I didn't want her getting distracted and lost in the wrong room. I jerked to a stop, but I couldn't turn around, so I backed up. The strap of the diaper bag had caught on the doorknob for the closet door.

"At least this time I know why it's open." I slipped the strap off of the knob. With my hip, I bumped the door closed.

In the room at the end of the hall, Olivia clutched her toy in one hand and squatted on the floor to pick something up I couldn't see.

Glad Sarah didn't see that. Alexandra and I were of the "let her eat dirt" mindset, but then again, you could probably eat off Sarah's floors, they were so clean.

I realized I didn't have a place—or food—to feed my friend here. I'd have to find something.

Olivia helped me set up her bed, then ran up and down the hallway for toys to throw into it. I sat on the floor and helped, but then she wanted to climb in to throw everything out again.

There were worse ways to spend my days.

Olivia had a very easygoing nature—unlike the very intense Alexandra—and at just under two years old, provided good enough company. I put her down for a nap as instructed (Sarah, clearly anxious over Olivia's first overnight away, had left a written list of everything she'd rattled off in the pocket of the diaper bag) and flipped through my statistics notes, half-heartedly reviewing for tomorrow's final.

The star toy went off. My friend was awake!

I tucked my notebook back into my bag and set it back in the hall closet—doorknobs still thwarted the little Miss—and headed down the hallway to pick her up. That infernal star toy was still going off, longer than it usually did. I pushed the bedroom door open, expecting Olivia to be standing in her pack and play, the brightly flashing toy clutched in her chubby fist.

She slept soundly, face down with her butt in the air, her mouth open, and drool spilling onto the sheet. The star toy glowed in the middle of the room, playing its song. I picked it up and flipped the switch to "off." The battery must have been dying. I wasn't sure if she'd still want to play with it without the lights and sounds, but I set it back on the floor where she must have thrown it.

Rather than go back to studying I didn't need to do, I decided to clean a little bit more. My earlier cleaning spree had me motivated. I could wait to vacuum until Olivia woke up.

As I finished the dishes, her voice traveled down the hall, so I dried my hands and went to her.

Standing on her toes, bouncing up and down with her hands braced on the rail of the pack and play, Olivia pointed excitedly toward the center of the room.

She smiled at me when I came in the room. "Isaac!"

I picked her up, my back toward whatever she pointed at.

Insistent and still pointing, she strained to see over my shoulder. "Isaac! Isaac!"

Turning, there was nothing but the star toy, sitting silent on the floor. She must've named it. Far be it from me to question her choices.

I squatted with Olivia against my front and grabbed the toy. I tried to hand it to her. "Here's Isaac."

She pushed it away to jab her little finger at something behind me. "Isaac!"

"Okay, my dear." I kept the star in my free hand. I'd see if I could find some new batteries for it.

In my arms, Olivia struggled, still pointing and calling, "Isaac!" She let loose an ear-splitting shriek when I closed the door behind me, then dissolved into tears. "Isaac."

Unnerved, I carried her down the hall and into the living room.

Olivia moved on quickly when faced with the pile of toys on the floor while I swapped out batteries in her star. She was so absorbed in a stuffed bunny I didn't want to give the noisy lights and music toy back quite yet. Her chubby fingers examined the hard glass eyes of the rabbit with such intensity, she didn't move when the phone rang.

It was Sarah, probably calling to check in.

I picked up the receiver. "Newfield Zoo, you've reached the Monkey House. How can I help you?"

"Oh, ha-ha. Aren't you hilarious?"

I could practically hear Sarah's eyes rolling.

"I do what I can."

"How is she?"

"She's fine, playing with her toys." I crossed my free arm over my stomach, tucking my hand under my elbow. "I replaced the batteries in her star, they were getting low."

A heavy pause. "That's weird, those were brand new batteries. I replaced them this morning."

"Oh." I bit the inside of my lower lip. The tester had said they were dead before I tossed them. "Hey, really quick. Who is Isaac?"

"Isaac?" The confusion in her voice came through loud and clear.

"Yeah, Isaac." I had literally nothing else to clarify that statement and hoped she'd know what I meant.

"That's my six-year-old nephew, why?"

Olivia had moved on from her bunny. She handed me two of her giant blocks, and I pushed them together for her and handed them back. "Olivia was talking about him after her nap. I thought she had named her star toy Isaac."

"Oh." Sarah paused. "She doesn't quite understand the name thing yet. She thinks all six-year-old size boys are 'Isaac,' and all eight-year-old size girls are 'Emma.' It's a thing with her right now because her cousins are the only kids she knows."

My heart thudded, and I had to peel my tongue off the roof of my mouth. What the hell had Olivia been pointing to? "How's your dad?"

"He's still hanging in there." She sighed, and my heart broke for her. "The doctors warned us he might for a few days before...well, before, so now it's a waiting game."

The last week had been hell for Sarah as her dad went from being in remission to metastasized cancer, cutting his life span down to less than a week. Shitty doctors are shitty.

"Olivia can stay here as long as you need her to, so don't feel like you have to rush back."

"It means a lot to us, Mel." Tears filled Sarah's voice, and I winced. "We both feel bad leaving her there, but I really need to be here with him, and Alexandra insists on being here for me. I'll call back tonight around six-thirty to sing Olivia her goodnight song, okay?"

Glad I could do something to help them out, I fought back my own tears and cleared my throat. "Sure, but call the house phone, because cell reception can be kind of sketchy."

"No problem."

I hung up, my eyes on Olivia, who was currently banging her star on the floor trying to make it go off. What the hell had she seen earlier?

Chapter 15

May 12, 2010

Ryan arrived around six, carrying a pizza with one hand, some cut flowers in a plastic sleeve resting on top of the box. A six-pack of Sam Adams swung from his other hand.

I answered the door with Olivia on my hip, pink-cheeked and glassy eyed. Side effect of all the screaming she'd done when I didn't have whatever she wanted to eat. It was definitely not peas or hot dogs or macaroni and cheese. She couldn't have been too mad at me, though, because she rested her hot little face on my shoulder as I opened the door.

"Well, this is a development." Ryan stepped inside. He grinned at Olivia. "Who is this?"

I jiggled the baby a little on my hip. "Olivia. She's Alexandra's, and by the default rules of made-up families, she's my niece. Sarah's dad decided to pull the plug yesterday, and Sarah wants to be there." I bounced my hip again, trying to get a smile out of a very cranky toddler.

I missed my actual sister, and I'd never met her three kids The years had passed so quickly I'd lost track.

Smiling down at Olivia, I forced some cheerfulness into my voice. "We're hanging out for a day or so."

"Very nice. I thought she looked familiar, but babies all look the same to me." He touched her nose, and Olivia reached out with both arms for him to hold her.

"Here, let me take those." I took the pizza and flowers in one hand and handed Olivia off.

He had one arm under her butt, holding her close to his chest while she patted both his cheeks and smiled.

I sniffed at the flowers, my mind racing. Why did he bring me flowers? They were stargazer lilies—my favorite—but the aroma of pepperoni competed with their fragrance.

"Those are from Sarah," he said, answering my unasked question. He pulled his head to the side to avoid the baby hands aimed for his mouth. "She said thank you, and good luck on your finals." He made a face at Olivia and she smiled. "How old is she again?"

"She'll be two in a few months."

"Terrible twos?" He turned his face away from her exploring hands, and she giggled.

My smile came naturally, watching the two of them. "Not at all. She's very well-behaved at the moment, even though she didn't appreciate my cooking."

He laughed and jerked his head back before she could jam her fingers up his nose. "Friendly, isn't she?"

I set the pizza on the table and pulled a chair over so I could grab a vase from the top of the cabinets. The loose door hung open, so I pressed it closed.

"She can be a little shy with new people. Hell—I mean, heck—she's shy with me some days depending on her mood."

"I'm surprised she took to me so fast." He stuck his tongue out at her and glanced at me. "Because, you know."

I stepped down, cradling the glass vase against my chest. "Because what?"

"Well, she has two moms, so I figured men would be extra scary or something."

Shrugging, I set about trimming the stems and arranging the flowers while Ryan entertained Olivia. "Sarah's dad has been very involved until recently. That's why her house is so spotless. His immune system was shot because of chemo. She also has a brother, and her sister is married, but they're out in Vermont. Alexandra's dad is around as often as he can be. Everyone wishes it was more, but her mother is a piece of work."

He made a noise that sounded like interest.

Pursing my lips, I tried to decide how much to say. I'd known her long enough I didn't think she'd be offended if I shared. Especially with Ryan.

"When Alexandra came out—and she came out because she was dating someone she really liked, before Sarah—her mother did not respond well. Made it all about her and how it would affect her. Put up a big stink with Alexandra about how the family wasn't going to approve. It caused a pretty big rift in the family." I grabbed plates and set them out, along with the Yahtzee! game I'd unpacked earlier. "It took Alexandra about a year before she had the courage to approach one of her aunts on social media about the whole thing. Her mother had lied about everything. She was trying to hide it because *she* was embarrassed. No one else batted an eye."

"That sounds pretty rough." He sat down with Olivia on his knee, and turned her so she faced the table. She reached for the dice with chubby hands.

I swept the choking hazards out of her reach, so she grabbed the score pad instead.

"Rough came after. Alexandra was really upset and confronted her mother, and things got ugly. That whole situation is why you never, *ever* call her Alex to her face." I served him a slice of pizza and smiled at his attempt to balance the baby and keep her from snatching the slice before it got to his mouth. "Her mother called her Alex as a way to humiliate her, like she was less of a woman for being gay."

I gave Olivia a piece of sausage, which she popped into her mouth. She kicked her legs and bounced, finally happy with something I fed her.

Ryan stared at me. "She's lucky to have you."

I glanced at him. "We're lucky to have each other. We've been sisters for a long time." I grabbed a pizza wheel and cut a bite-sized piece off my slice. Olivia smashed it in her fist before pushing it into her mouth. I smiled. "Guess the kid likes pizza."

"What kid doesn't?"

"Between lunch and dinner, I was starting to worry she wasn't going to eat the whole time she was here. I think pizza is allowed." I reached for her. "I'll take her so you can eat. She spent a lot of time screaming, and I don't think I'm quite ready to eat yet. Still feeling a little frazzled." I cut more bites for Olivia.

Silence stretched between us, and he cleared his throat. "I'm not sure how to follow that up."

I smiled at him. "I'm sorry, all that was pretty intense, wasn't it?" I bounced Olivia, and she smiled. I grabbed her sippy cup of water and offered her a drink, which she took. "I should have warned you ahead of time, things can be pretty intense with me, or with Alexandra. I'm always afraid of scaring people off." I made a face at the baby, and she grinned. Water dribbled down her chin. "She and I don't think anything of it at this point, but my life has been a string of abusive relationships, starting with my family, and that's my life." My voice rose an octave, and I made a silly face at Olivia. "Drama's part of the package, isn't it? Yes, it is!"

"You should know me well enough by now that I'm not going to get scared and run."

My head made a non-committal motion along with my shoulders. I'd barely scratched the surface. He'd probably run screaming if I told him about my ex.

Olivia took a piece of pizza on her own, and I watched her eat because I found I couldn't look at Ryan. "You never know what people will be able to take or not take. I have a lot of baggage." I shrugged, hoping I appeared far more nonchalant than I felt. "Like, a lot."

He grabbed another slice of pizza, avoiding my gaze. Like I'd run if he made eye contact. He was right. I might.

The silence shook me, and words tumbled out of my mouth. "Families are complicated, some more than others. People get judgmental when it comes to families." I balanced Olivia with a hand on her belly as she leaned across the table.

He opened his beer. "What do you mean?"

I kissed Olivia's sweet-smelling but sparse hair. "People see it as the child's responsibility to maintain the relationship with the parents. Especially when the child is a daughter. I was an instant black sheep when I stood up to my parents. My own siblings haven't spoken to me in years. What little family I had left when I cut my parents off had disowned me when I didn't go to their funeral."

"That's pretty harsh."

I shrugged one shoulder. "My mantra is 'it is what it is'. I should have it tattooed on my forehead, I think it so much. I have Alexandra and Sarah, and Olivia. Alexandra's dad was kind of a stand-in for me, at least until things fell apart with her mother."

"You don't talk to her mother, either?"

The inevitable judgement rolled across the table. This always happened. People with healthy families just couldn't grasp that not every family brimmed with sunshine, love, and support. Not even found families.

"After the way she treated Alexandra, how could I? Alexandra's girlfriend broke up with her over it, and it broke Alexandra for years. How could I maintain a relationship with her mother? That would have been an absolute betrayal."

Olivia pushed at me with sauce covered hands, wanting down. I set her on her feet, but snatched her wrists to wipe her hands with a napkin before setting her loose. I had less luck with the pizza sauce on my shirt.

"We're very protective of each other. There's an unspoken code. Her mother tried to play us off each other for a while, and a lot of it happened when Sarah was having a hard time getting pregnant with Olivia. We were a united front, and both of us stopped talking to her, and stopped engaging."

Olivia disappeared around the corner, and I hopped up to follow her.

Ryan's hand caught my arm, stopping me. "I *am* judging you. You're not the woman I thought you were. Honestly, you're more."

Rather than relief, tension filled me. "Really?"

He smiled at me, a dimple appearing on his left cheek. "Really. Now go catch the kid."

I made my way down the hallway. The damned closet door was cracked open again, and I bumped it closed with my hip.

Olivia had made her way to the toilet and was trying to climb it, so I gave her the praise Sarah had mandated on her list. I helped Olivia balance on the edge of the seat, and had to be excited and clap when she peed. She clapped, too, a huge smile on her face.

Ryan's voice came from the hallway, just outside the open door. "Sounds like fun in there."

"She's very inconsistent right now, but if she asks to use the toilet, I have to help."

I braced my knee against the vanity and leaned Olivia over the sink to wash her hands. I cringed on the inside, but we sang "Twinkle Twinkle Little Star" while we washed. Olivia joined me with her baby voice, really just saying "little 'tar" over and over until we were done.

I caught Ryan's gaze in the mirror, and I blushed scarlet. "I'm sorry."

"No, it's cute."

"Sarah was pretty insistent I follow a few routines from home."

I went across the hall to change Olivia into her jammies, and had just settled on the floor with Miss Squirmy between my knees when the phone rang.

"Crap, I bet that's Sarah. Can you grab that for me?"

He disappeared down the hall. He told her everything was fine and ratted me out about the pizza. He said "I don't know" a couple times as he came up the hall, probably in response to Sarah's questions.

I had Olivia zipped up by the time he got back. She examined the pendant attached to my neck by a thin silver chain, picking it up with tiny fingers and tucking her chin to her chest. I studied her face, fascinated by her complete absorption in the activity.

Ryan handed me the phone, and I tucked it between my ear and shoulder to keep my hands free for containment of the tiny human.

"Hello, Mama."

"How is she?" The exhaustion in Sarah's voice sucked all the energy right out of me. I hoped she at least got some of it for herself.

"She's fine." I pried my pendant out of Olivia's hands before she could garrote me with the chain. "She didn't like what I made for dinner, but liked the pizza Ryan brought over. She had water with dinner, not milk, and she actually asked to potty."

"What a good girl! Can I talk to her?"

"Do I hand her the phone?"

"Put me on speaker."

I did. The moment Olivia heard her mother's voice she pulled the phone from my hand.

"Mama!"

I felt like an intruder listening to Sarah talk to her daughter, so I kept quiet. Sarah sang Olivia their special bedtime song, with Olivia joining in about halfway through in her chirpy baby voice.

"Good night, my precious! Mommy and Mama love you!" Sarah blew a kiss through the phone. "You can take me off speaker."

I released Olivia. She walked to Ryan, who picked her up. I didn't want to ask, but I had to. "How's your dad?"

She sighed. "Still hanging in there but the doctor said he won't wake up again. It's going to be a long night. Alexandra went home to take a shower and grab the mail, then she's coming back." Sarah cleared her throat, and she spoke again without the hint of tears. "Bedtime is seven on the nose. She might fuss a little bit, but let her, she's used to it."

My brain took a second to realize that "she" referred to Olivia, not Alexandra. "Okay. Define fuss?"

"Whining and maybe a little crying. She should settle down in about fifteen minutes, and if she doesn't, you can call me. She might wake up in the night and do the same thing—give her a little time to self-soothe."

One corner of my mouth tipped into half a frown. "Well, if she's crying, shouldn't I go check on her?"

"Use your judgment, but try not to run in and pick her up. Usually, she gets herself back to sleep."

"Got it."

"And, Mel? I packed some cereal for her to have for breakfast. No cold pizza."

I couldn't tell whether I should laugh or be offended. "Okay."

She sighed. "It's not you, it's her mother who likes cold pizza for breakfast."

Mother always referred to Alexandra, and I smiled. "Anything else?"

"Thank you, again. So much."

"We're having fun. She'll probably be sick of me by tomorrow, but we're doing good here."

"Give her a kiss for me, and one for Alexandra."

"I will, and thanks for the flowers."

Ryan stood in the doorway, leaning against the frame as I disconnected, watching me and Olivia.

I smiled at him. "I'm sorry, I have to get her to bed soon. Then my time will hopefully be my own, assuming she goes down."

He shrugged and pushed off the wall, tucking his hands into his pockets. "Take your time. Do you want to watch a movie? Or we can play a game? Pick your poison."

Olivia chose that moment to launch herself at my face, and I caught her, but almost fell backward.

"How wholesome of you. Why don't you surprise me?" I blew a raspberry at Olivia, and she giggled. "While you're here, do you mind checking out a door for me?"

"No problem."

Olivia went down quickly. Ryan had stretched out on my couch—shoes off again—and had his hands folded behind his head, eyes closed.

"Are you awake?"

He sat up and blinked a few times. "Yeah. Long date. I mean, day." He stood and stretched his arms behind him. "You said something about a door?"

My knuckles rapped on the closet door at the end of the hall. "This door keeps popping open, and I can't figure out why."

"It latches?"

I nodded.

For the next few minutes, Ryan opened and closed the door, pulling it this way and that. He asked me a few questions, which I answered. Finally, he frowned at the door.

"Well, it's probably one of a few things." He held up his finger. "The door isn't plumb." He held up a second finger. "The frame isn't square." Third finger. "There's an issue with the latch plate. There's something called reverse pressure. Even though the door is latched, just enough pressure is happening it's slipping off the strike plate. How big of an issue is this for you?"

Shrugging, I leaned against the half wall behind me. "It's annoying when I walk into it in the middle of the night. Or I don't notice it's open and catch something on the knob."

He opened the door. "You just keep your backpack in here?"

"And a couple of coats."

His turn to shrug. "It's not like you have kids in the house all the time and have guns in there or anything. If it's only annoying, you have to decide if you want to rip the door apart trying to fix it. Something breaks and can't be patched together, you're out a couple hundred bucks."

The cash register in my head rang. "No, it's mostly annoying." I smiled. "At least now I know I'm not going crazy, and the house isn't falling down or something."

We passed a pleasant evening playing Yahtzee!, and munching on some cookies he had brought in from his truck. "My mom made them," he said, as if testing me.

"They're really good." I didn't think I was ready to talk about mothers. Especially mothers who baked cookies.

He took his turn, then I rolled the dice and marked my score. "There, I think I won."

He sighed. "I think you did, too. You cheated."

"Clearly."

"Winner picks up."

Chuckling, I stood and put the pieces back into the box. I slid the box off the table and headed for the living room. My mother's nasty voice intruded, which I fought hard to tamp down. Very few things upset me quite like thinking of her. On way too many levels. Because then I started thinking about my sister, and my niece and nephews I had never met, and—

Distracted, I walked straight into Ryan. I looked up at him, and within the space of a heartbeat my cheeks burned.

He held my arms to steady me. "You okay?"

"Yeah, sorry. Not paying attention." I drew in a deep breath, and I got a good whiff of him, like fresh cut lumber and something underneath like leather but not quite His heat seared the front of my body.

He stared into my eyes, and his lips parted ever so slightly. Dark brows drew together, and his gaze softened, dropping to my mouth. My breathing quickened and when the flush creeped up my neck, I didn't care. I couldn't stop staring at his mouth. His hands on my arms moved toward my shoulders. The tip of my tongue peeked out to touch my upper lip. He leaned closer and his breath caressed my face. I shivered and my eyelids lowered. If he didn't kiss me, I might die.

Suddenly, a banshee wailed from down the hall.

"What the hell?" I tore from Ryan's grip and launched myself toward Olivia's room. I shoved the door open so hard, it bounced against the doorstop and closed behind me as I picked Olivia up from her makeshift crib.

In the nightlight's dim glow, her little face had scrunched up and turned bright red, and the sounds coming from the little body seemed impossible. Stiff as a board in my arms, fat tears rolled down her cheeks. I patted her back and shushed her, shifting my weight from side to side to rock her.

The door opened, and Ryan appeared.

"Everything okay?" His voice barely made it through the wailing in my ear.

"I think so. Sarah said she might fuss a bit, but this is not fussing." I rubbed Olivia's back in a circle, patting every now and again, trying to settle her.

"Definitely not what I would classify as fussing, for sure." He ventured into the room and touched one wet cheek with his finger.

Olivia wanted none of it and turned her face into my neck.

Ryan winced at the wailing. "I'm sorry, but I have to go. Are you all set?"

"As all set as I'll be. I'll talk to you later." I bounced Olivia. Her cries frayed my nerves. "Can you hit the living room light and lock up on your way out please?"

He doffed an imaginary hat.

Olivia had finally started to breathe in between screams. By the time the red glow of his departing taillights filtered through the closed blinds, the high-pitched wailing had faded to a more normal crying.

I'm not sure how long I stood there, rocking and bouncing Olivia, but eventually she stopped crying. I brought her into the bathroom with me and used a tissue to wipe the snot and tears off her face.

"There you go, tiny peanut."

She smiled at me, her mouth a black void in the dim light. I shuddered and felt like a terrible person for the reaction, even though it was involuntary.

"Yeah, let's not do that."

I changed her diaper on the floor and set her back in her make-shift bed. She seemed content to clutch her blanket, and her eyelids closed. She rolled over, tucked herself in a ball over her blanket, and released a sigh.

I headed toward the kitchen for some water. I froze halfway down the hall.

Heavy footsteps on the porch. Someone in work boots.

Had Ryan come back? I hadn't seen the lights come back up the driveway, but I wouldn't have from the kitchen.

My heart leaped into my throat, and I didn't breathe, straining to hear. I couldn't be sure, but it sounded like someone was walking the length of the porch toward the end of the house. Away from the front door, toward the parking area.

And it didn't make sense for it to be Ryan. He would have at least knocked on the door, if not come right in.

Still holding my breath, I crept down the hallway and peeked around the corner. The footsteps had stopped.

Whoever it was, all they did was stand there on the end of the porch. If I turned on the living room light, they would be able to see me through the full-lite door, but I might not be able to see them. The plastic glow-in-the-dark star I'd glued to the switch plate so I could find it with the lights off glowed faintly on the other side of the room.

What if they'd been waiting for Ryan to leave?

After a quick gasp of air, I ran across the room on my tiptoes, flattening myself against the exterior wall. I forced myself to breathe tiny gasps so I wouldn't pass out, but the footsteps continued their steady pacing. I reached over and flicked on the porch light.

The steps stopped.

I craned my neck to peer out the front door. Most of the porch was visible, but not the corner nearest the house at the end. Next to the window of the room where Olivia slept.

"Fuck this," I said under my breath.

Still on my toes, I ran across the living room, avoiding the light spilling in from the porch as much as I could. I snatched the portable phone and ran down the hallway to Olivia's room. I peered through the doorway, searching for a shadow on the blinds.

Nothing.

Hiding at the end of my hallway, I dialed.

"9-1-1, what's your emergency?"

I gave the dispatcher my address and my name. "I'm home by myself with a baby, and there's someone outside. Some guy is walking around on my porch. This has been going on for a few nights. Someone keeps walking around my property in the middle of the night, and I think they were outside my window with a flashlight last night."

"Do you know who it is, ma'am?"

"No. I only moved in recently." I clenched and unclenched my free hand as if that would stop the shaking.

"We'll send a deputy out, ma'am."

She took my number, and we hung up. I checked on Olivia, who still slept soundly in her pack and play. No shadows came through the blinds, and I didn't hear anymore footsteps. I could my rifle out, but decided against being armed when the cops arrived.

Phone clutched in my hand, I paced up and down the hallway, peeking in on Olivia every time I reached her door. I wanted to move her into my room and lock the door, but I also didn't want her to start screaming again.

Was that a shadow on the blinds?

I stood, frozen, and stared at the window for the space several deep breaths. Waiting.

There was no one there. No shadows, no footsteps.

I resumed my pacing. When was the deputy going to get here?

It seemed like forever before a pair of headlights slowed at my driveway. In reverse, the car pulled up the drive and stopped halfway up the hill just before it curved into the parking area. The porch lights reflected off the dark light bar on top of the car.

I sighed in relief and went to the front door.

The hatless deputy stepped out of his car and spoke into the radio on his shoulder. He was a few years older than me, and in the yellow porch light, his short hair could've been black or dark brown. I waited until he ascended the porch to open the door.

"Evenin'," he said. "Do you want to tell me what's been going on?"

I told him what I'd told dispatch about the footsteps I'd been hearing late at night. I didn't know the lights on my ceiling were from a flashlight, but what else would they be? I told him about that, too.

He pursed his thin lips and his gaze scoured the yard before he turned back to me, his thumbs hooked in his duty belt. "You live out here alone?"

I nodded. "Yes, sir."

Absently, he scratched behind his ear. "I didn't see anyone when I came up, so if someone was here, they're gone. You have any cameras?"

Shaking my head, I crossed my arms. "I don't. No security system, either."

"You have a dog? Or any firearms in the home?"

"No dog." My brain scrambled. Had I broken some law or rule, and I was going to get in trouble if I said yes? "I do have a rifle."

The deputy nodded again. "Best alarm you can have is a dog, swear to God. As far as the other…" He tucked his thumbs back into his belt. "Well, make sure if someone breaks in, you shoot them in the front, not in the back."

"Excuse me?" A frown tugged at the corners of my mouth, and I struggled to keep the shock off my face. Did he seriously just tell me to shoot someone? What was happening right now?

"And if you shoot them outside, make sure you drag them back into the house. It's different if you shoot them in the house instead of outside."

Stunned, I watched him as he trotted down the porch steps and walked the length of the path to the side of the house. He didn't step off the gravel, and then he got into his car and left.

I shut off the porch light, and wrapped my arms around myself.

I checked on Olivia, who still slept soundly, her blanket tucked underneath her body.

Freaked out by the footsteps, I left the fan in the window off. I needed the silence, just in case something happened. I lay awake for quite a while, staring at the ceiling in the dark.

Finally, I relaxed. In the seconds before I drifted off to sleep, a big brass band played a song I didn't know.

Chapter 16

May 13, 2010

After a few hours of tossing and turning, my alarm went off. Bleary-eyed, I got ready for class. I waited until the last possible moment to wake Olivia, but when I opened the door, she stood in her pack and play with a smile, shaking the rail.

"Good morning, peanut," I said. "How did you get all of your clothes off?"

Hands braced against the rail, she bounced on her toes with a giggle.

"Mostly off, anyway." Picking her up, her onesie pajamas trailed behind, still wrapped around one foot.

Olivia didn't have any problems with the way I fumbled with her diaper. Instead, she amused herself by squirming in every possible direction, laughing the entire time. I zipped her jammies back up just as the doorbell rang.

"Who is that?" I set her on her feet. "Let's go see!"

Sarah stood at the front door. My heart hurt by the exhaustion on her face. She lit up when Olivia helped me open the door.

"Hi, my precious." She scooped Olivia into her arms and gave her a noisy kiss on the cheek.

"Your dad?" I didn't want to ask, but it felt insensitive not to.

"He let go around four this morning." Sarah buried her face in Olivia's thin hair. Closing her eyes, she breathed in deeply.

"Why don't you get her situated in the car and I'll finish packing her up?"

No more words were spoken as I helped Sarah pack the car. Olivia bounced happily in her car seat, singing to herself.

I put my hand over Sarah's on the car door before she could climb in. "I never know what to say in these situations, but I want you to know I'm here for you guys." A lump formed in my throat. I didn't know her father, but my heart hurt for her. "You guys are family. If you need anything, let me know, okay?"

Sarah nodded and slipped into the car.

With my arms crossed, I watched her do a three-point turn and head down the driveway.

I sighed and wiped my face with my hand. My day hadn't even begun yet and I already wanted to go to bed.

Sitting in traffic on my way home, I dialed Alexandra.

"How are you holding up?" I asked.

"We're okay." Her voice was flat. Tired. "I think some of the shock wore off. I don't know if he did it on purpose or not, but her father spent the last three days planning his own memorial service. I think it may have done more to prepare Sarah than anything else."

"I'm really sorry to hear that. So you know, I'm on my way home from Portland right now. If you need me to pick anything up for you or watch Olivia or anything, let me know. I have my last final to take in—" I glanced at my car's clock "—three hours, but otherwise I'm available."

"Sarah and Olivia went over to her brother's."

My hackles rose, thinking Alexandra had been uninvited for some reason.

"They wanted to spend some time alone, and I had to hang out here to sign for a package," she said, answering my unasked question. "Life goes on, I guess, but I'm so exhausted right now, I don't think I could handle all the emotions everywhere."

"What are you doing?"

She paused. "Are you up for coffee or something? I'm so overwhelmed with all of everything, and there's not a thing I can do about it. I'd like to sit and talk with someone about literally anything else."

"Of course."

We worked out the logistics of when and where to meet. As I flipped my phone shut, I got a text notification from Ryan.

Hope your finals went well.

I'd give him a call later, I decided, not knowing if he knew about the current situation.

My finals had gone well, and it was a relief to have a week or so of no classes before summer session started up. The movement of the car on the long stretch of country highway relaxed me, and I regretted offering to meet Alexandra. All I wanted now was a nap.

"Wake up, babycakes." I straightened myself behind the wheel. "You still have one more final to get through."

We met at the little breakfast and lunch place that, once upon a time, we'd met at for lunch once a month to make sure we caught up with each other when things were crazy. Alexandra sat in our usual booth, her hands wrapped around a warm mug like it anchored her to reality. Several empty sugar packets littered the table.

"Hey," I said. I hesitated before sitting down.

"Don't you dare," she said with raised brows. "The hug rule is still in full force and effect, so just don't." She stuck the spoon into her mug and stirred.

"You never drink tea." I slid into the booth. An ice water with lemon awaited me, condensation clinging to the outside of the glass.

"Sarah is trying to give up coffee, so I have to, too, because solidarity. Torture. Whatever you want to call it." She took a sip from her steaming mug and grimaced before dumping another packet of sugar into it. "How were finals?"

"They were fine. The classes were pretty easy, and I took enough notes that I felt like I did okay. I'm concerned about this online one. I suck at statistics, and the professor is a brilliant math guy, but a shitty teacher."

Alexandra rolled her eyes. "I always hated that. It's like they're so absorbed in whatever subject that they assume everyone else is, too."

"I really am sorry, Alexandra." I squeezed the lemon into my water and dropped the rind onto the ice. I poked it below the ice layer with my straw and then stirred it.

"I appreciate it, but really, I need to talk about something else right now." She raised her hand to flag down the server. She asked for a slice of pie, whatever they had. "How are you settling into the house?"

"Pretty good." I stirred my water some more, imagining music as the ice tinkled against the glass. "Finding a bunch of problems with the house, though. I have a cabinet door that won't stay closed, my hallway closet keeps opening on its own, and my boiler makes some really weird noises at night." I paused, wondering if I should continue. Might as well. "And don't freak out, but I had to have the cops out last night."

Alexandra went perfectly still, her eyes fixed on me. "Is everything okay?"

Sitting back in the booth, I pressed my hands into the vinyl-covered cushion. "I'm not sure. I think someone is prowling around my house at night."

"Like a stalker?"

I shrugged one shoulder. "The house was empty for a while, maybe someone lived there before it sold. I keep hearing footsteps at night, and weird noises I can't explain. Last night, Ryan stayed until around eleven or so—"

Alexandra cut me off with a sly grin. "Ryan was at your house late?"

The tone of her voice had my cheeks hot. "Yeah, he came over for dinner. And that wasn't the point of the story."

"We'll get back to it. Ryan left at eleven..." she prompted.

"And not fifteen minutes later, I heard footsteps on the porch. I was scared, mostly because Olivia was in the house with me, so I called the cops." I lifted my glass to drink and then set it back on the table. "I think the other night someone was prowling around the backyard with a flashlight. It's starting to really freak me out."

"Well, if they didn't have a flashlight, they'd break their neck on that hill." She sat back, looking at me like a cat at an unsuspecting mouse. "What did the sheriff say? Did he find anything?"

"Finding implies searching, and no, he didn't find anything." I sipped my water instead of playing with it. "He didn't use these exact words, but he basically told me to set up cameras, get a dog, and shoot them."

"That's reassuring," she said dryly. Her blue eyes held mine as she sipped her tea. "Have you considered the other possibility?"

Uncomfortable now, I shifted in my seat. "What other possibility is that?"

"That maybe you aren't chasing a prowler, not a tangible one, anyway." She let the words hang over the table, her fingertips tracing the rim of her mug. "I think your house is haunted."

My eyes rolled as I fell against the back of the booth. "What is it with you, and everything is haunted? Is your house haunted, too?"

Dead serious, Alexandra shook her head. "No. I made sure before we bought the place." She held up a finger. "Think about it. Weird noises you can't explain, doors opening without explanation, footsteps. Dammit, Mel, I *saw* a ghost on your porch."

"There are explanations," I said. "Ryan said the flappy thing on my exhaust pipe was stuck, which could have been part of the noise. And the door wasn't put in right, he said. The cabinet is probably a loose hinge, and I keep forgetting to look at it. As far as you seeing something..." I frowned. "We'd both been drinking. Maybe it was the prowler."

One slender brow raised. "Really? So, you think I made it up?"

Her tone made me cringe. "Not that you made it up, I'm sure you thought you saw something."

"Mel, not everyone is a lightweight with booze. I did not imagine anything." She thanked the server for the blueberry pie and dug in. "I'm telling you, the moment I walk in the door, my hair stands on end and I have the heebie-jeebies until I leave the property. You have ghosts." She pointed at me with her fork. "You keep doing what you're doing, but eventually, you aren't going to be able to ignore it. You're haunted." She shoved her plate at me. "This is really awesome. You have to try it."

Chapter 17

Ryan's dad had another health scare, but Ryan called to see how my finals had gone. I don't know what I said that set him off during the conversation, but he insisted I finally get the dishwasher I may or may not have been bellyaching about since I'd bought the house. Normally, I'd cut my nose off to spite my face, but the sin of letting Ryan help me beat handwashing dishes.

Then, of course, Ryan insisted on installing said dishwasher, and I have to say, having him lying on his back on my kitchen floor half under my sink was pretty great.

When I was home alone, the weirdness continued. The footsteps freaked me out the most, only ever happening after dark, and in sets of four. One night, it had happened repeatedly until I went outside in my robe. Like an idiot, I stood in the middle of my driveway for almost forty minutes. The footsteps settled down a little bit, only waking me up occasionally instead of several times a night, every night. I was back to turning my little fan on to drown out the weird noises from my power vent. Alexandra's words had gotten to me, and the idea that maybe I was haunted never left the back of my mind.

I arrived home from riding Tori and pressed the code into the deadbolt I'd installed. As I pushed the door open, the back door closed in front of me. I knew, with absolute certainty, the door had been locked when I left, but the new curtains on the door were still fluttering.

I wrinkled my nose. The odor of cigarette smoke permeated the room.

I stood there, stunned for the space of a few breaths. Without knowing what may have possessed me, I turned and ran back out the front door. Leaping off the porch, I almost took a digger at the bottom of the steps. I ran toward the parking area and around the back of the house.

There was no one there. If someone had been in my house when I arrived home, they couldn't have left and be out of sight already. I pressed my hands to my cheeks and forced myself to breathe. Maybe the door had been left open just enough that the change in air pressure when I'd opened the front door made the back door close. The explanation worked if I could ignore the fact that I checked both doors to make sure they were closed and locked before I left. I had installed the electronic lock to give Alexandra and Sarah access to the house, but hadn't assigned them a code yet. No one could have gotten into my house—with my permission—other than me.

I went back into the house cautiously, not sure what I might find. The cigarette odor had disappeared, but the fact it had been in my house at all bothered me. I hated that smell. Someone had told me once that smells were the one sensory perception capable of bypassing the conscious mind to take a nose-dive into the subconscious. My mother had smoked, and the stink of it brought memories back I wanted to forget. On one hand,

I worried someone had managed to get into my house while I wasn't home. But after my last experience with the deputy, I didn't want to call again. Especially since I hadn't put cameras up yet.

After thoroughly checking the first floor for unwanted visitors, I changed out of my breeches and into a pair of yoga pants. I'd offered to feed Ryan again. Tonight, I was going to make meatloaf and mushroom gravy. Getting started would help me feel normal. I grabbed my ingredients and pulled my potatoes out of the cabinet. Drat. My big pot had been stashed in the basement.

I skipped down the stairs and flipped the light on at the bottom, which opened into the center of the basement. Around the wall to the right, I had set up a second living room I never used—the TV wasn't even plugged in—and to the left, all my unpacked boxes. Things I didn't have room for or wasn't quite ready to sort through stood in neat towers stacked chest high. On the opposite end of the basement, behind the stairs, were my washer and dryer.

I turned left and stopped so fast, I lost my balance and had to grab the wall to stop myself from falling.

Every box, every bag, had been opened.

I checked the nearest box. Books.

The next one had some mismatched curtains in it, still neatly folded.

I struggled to wrap my head around this. They'd all been folded shut, but not taped. I could understand if one could come open if it'd been packed too full, but this?

Nothing had been disturbed aside from the boxes being opened. Forgetting the reason I had come down in the first place, I ran upstairs and picked up the phone.

Alexandra picked up in the middle of the third ring, sounding out of breath. "Hello?"

"Hey. I need a reality check." Our code for needing the other to talk straight.

"Sure, what's up?"

Letting out the breath I'd been holding, I told her about the open boxes in the basement, hearing the back door close, and the cigarette odor when I walked in.

She shifted the phone. "Was it locked?"

Not the response I expected. I tucked my arm across my stomach as my brows furrowed. "Was what locked?"

Now Alexandra sighed. "The back door. Did you notice whether it was still locked?"

Like an idiot, I hadn't checked, so I did now. "The knob is locked but the deadbolt is open. I know I checked the deadbolt before I left. I know it was locked."

The weight of her pause came through the phone line. "It's possible someone broke into your house. You're calling me freaking out about it, so I think you want to call the Sheriff's Department, and want validation from me."

I twisted the ring on my right pinkie. "You really think someone was in here?"

She sighed again. "If they were, they didn't make much of a mess, but yes, it's possible." I imagined her shrugging, the slightly exasperated expression she'd have on her face. "Get off the phone, call the the cops, and while you're waiting for the deputy, why don't you look around and see if anything is missing, okay?"

"Okay. Thanks." I hung up and stared at the phone for a minute before I dialed dispatch. I explained about the door closing, and the open boxes.

She said a deputy would be out shortly.

I didn't have an awful lot for jewelry, mostly sterling silver stuff that cost less than fifty bucks a piece, usually much less. Due to some recent break-ins in the lakes area, I kept my wooden jewelry box in the bottom of my closet instead of my dresser where robbers would expect to find it. Kneeling on the carpet, I went through my jewelry box, checking for empty spots. Aside from the ring on my right hand, everything was present and accounted for.

As I closed the bottom drawer, I hesitated, then reopened it as far as it would go. In the very back corner, the slot where my engagement ring and wedding band had sat for the last four years was empty. I wracked my brain. Had I moved them, and I was only remembering they were there before? When was the last time I'd seen those two items? Set with sapphires and diamonds, my wedding set was the only jewelry I owned with any value. A chill went through me. Someone had been in my house, going through my things when I wasn't home. I'd been violated. Again.

Rather than spend my time pacing, I decided to head back into the kitchen to work on dinner. I got everything ready, but I didn't want to go back into the basement until after the deputy had gone.

Someone knocked on the door as I chopped potatoes. I jumped about a foot in the air, cutting myself with my chef's knife for good measure.

"Dammit." I grabbed a paper towel and wrapped it around my finger to staunch the bleeding.

A different deputy from last time, thinner, younger, and balding, scanning the yard from his vantage point on the porch. His white patrol vehicle sat halfway up the drive, facing toward the street. He turned to me as I opened the door, and I dragged my gaze from his pistol to his face. He had an air of generalized boredom like I had wasted his time, which didn't help my anxiety. Without asking to come in, he stood on the porch while I explained about the door, and about the boxes, and told him about the missing wedding rings.

"Best thing you can do is check out the pawn shops and see if they have them. Act like you're there to buy. If they think you're looking for stolen property, they won't help you." He handed me a business card. "If you find your rings in one of the shops, give me a call."

Dumbly, I read the card. "Okay, thanks for your time." I had déjà vu when he strode down the gravel walkway to give a half-assed search around the house before walking back to his car.

I sighed and closed the door, and then leaned against it. I don't know what I'd been expecting, but I guess I'd been hoping for more than a brush-off. My mind went to Alexandra, who had clearly said what she thought I'd wanted to hear. I shouldn't have called.

With a shake of my head at my naivety, I went downstairs for my stock pot. All I wanted was some validation I wasn't crazy, was that too much to ask? Or maybe I was losing my mind.

Hugging the pot to my stomach with one arm, I focused on my feet on my way up the stairs. When I got to the top, I glanced up. My gaze made it halfway up jean-clad legs and caught a glimpse of a dark blue shirt before my brain registered a person blocking my way.

I screamed—really screamed—and dropped the pot as I stumbled forward. It landed with a *thunk* on the carpeting, and the lid rolled in a circle around his feet. A hand on my arm kept me from falling backward down the basement stairs. I gasped for air, but it refused to come, and I clutched the arm that held me. Tears streamed down my cheeks by the time I recognized Ryan's face.

He put his other hand on me and bent to stare into my eyes. "Holy hell, Melissa, are you okay?"

The air rushed into my lungs with a croak, then went in and out faster and faster, sounding more like a panting wheeze than actual air.

Ryan guided me over to the couch and sat me down. "Are you okay?"

My hands trembled. "I'm sorry."

"What for? I called when I walked in. I thought you heard me. I didn't mean to scare you, sweetheart." His hands went over the side of my face, my hair.

I grabbed them and squeezed, focusing on the texture of his skin underneath mine, the roughness of his palms against my fingertips.

My heart raced, and I fought to regulate my breathing. Iron bands had wrapped around my ribs, and I couldn't get any air.

I apologized a few more times as I tried to compose myself. "I wasn't expecting you to be standing there. All I saw—" I clenched my jaw and covered my eyes, trying to will the image of an airman in a skin-tight t-shirt out of my head.

I imagined Tori and I were cantering across a field. Wildflowers bloomed around us, waving in the wind. The sun warmed my face, and nothing could hurt me. I uncovered my eyes, my hands clenching and unclenching.

Ryan went into the kitchen. I took a shaky breath as he reappeared with a glass of water.

He sat next to me on the couch. "Tell me what you need."

I took a few sips and set the cup on the coffee table. I still had the bloody, wadded up paper towel in my hand.

Without saying anything, I went into the small bathroom and turned the light on to tend to my wound. My hands still shook, but my pulse had slowed from a galloping racehorse to a more reasonable pace. My nerves thrummed. The internal battle over that pesky fight-or-flight response had begun. Stupid sympathetic nervous system. I washed my hands and gave myself a bandage.

Healthy or not, the emotion immediately following my trigger was anger. At that douchebag airman for assaulting me. And at my sergeant for telling me I shouldn't have punched someone. At least the squadron leadership seemed to take it seriously after two more of my fellow female Airmen came forward. I had a whole lot of anger I couldn't let go of, but I preferred it to being afraid.

More composed, I walked back to the living room where Ryan played on his phone. He twitched, and slipped it into his pocket, like he didn't want me to see him on it.

"Everything okay?" I asked.

"Is everything okay with you?"

"Yeah, it's been an interesting day." I explained about the door, and the boxes, and cutting myself, and the deputy not making me feel any better.

His brows went together, and he stood up to give me a hug. "I'm sorry. That is definitely creepy."

Being folded in his arms felt right, even though the position of my neck didn't. I pushed away, but kept my hands on his chest for a few more seconds. His heartbeat kicked against my palms.

"Maybe I should get a dog. It's what the first deputy suggested. I was going to wait until I figured out where I'd be working, but maybe I don't need to wait."

He nodded. "No, you're right. Wait until you're settled and know what you're going to have for hours." He paused, opened his mouth as if to speak, then closed it.

"What?" I asked.

He pointed his thumb over his shoulder, toward the stairs. "I don't think I've ever seen someone with a startle response like that."

"That's one way to describe it."

The smell of roasting meatloaf permeated the air, reminding me I had a meal to finish preparing.

He followed me into the kitchen, and I resumed my chopping. Somehow, staring at the cutting board was easier than looking at him. I had nothing to be ashamed of or embarrassed about, or so my therapist had been telling me for almost a decade, but it was still hard. Like admitting weakness.

I put the potatoes into the pot, turned on the burner, and then laid the knife flat on the cutting board. "You had no way of knowing this, but I have PTSD. I have pretty good control over my triggers, but occasionally, I don't." I shrugged. "Sorry I didn't tell you before."

He paused. "Is there anything I can do to help?"

Shaking my head, I set about putting potato scraps into my compost canister. "Not really. Just be aware of it, I guess."

A long silence stretched. "Before you went into the bathroom, you said you saw something? You don't have to tell me."

Leaning against the counter, I put all my weight on one foot and crossed my ankles. Staring at my socks was easier, too. "I was assaulted when I was in the military, and your shirt is the same color the guy had on." I looked Ryan in the eye. "My mind playing tricks on me."

He nodded. "Did they at least catch the guy?"

The laugh that came from my mouth sounded more like a cough and didn't contain an ounce of actual mirth. "Catch him? Me and ten other women told the MPs who he was. There was no catching."

"I guess I meant to ask if he at least got arrested."

The weird laugh bubbled out of my throat again. My therapist said it was a stress reaction. "In response to the complaints, the airman got moved to an all-male dorm. He graduated and moved to his next duty station. He continued his life like nothing happened. My knee got screwed up and that's why they dis-charged me, but I found out that all of us who filed complaints were discharged early under some pretext or another. Two years later, I had two guys in suits at my door from OSI, and they're investigating. I relive the whole thing all over again, give them the contact information for one or two of the other women I was still in touch with. Then, some JAG from a base in Georgia calls me, and I had to relieve it all over again for him. Do you know what happened?"

Ryan shook his head.

"Fuck all. Fuck all happened. The JAG defending that piece of shit trashed every witness but me and two other women, saying they were 'unreliable'. And then, the whole thing got dropped without a word to anyone, or at least, not to me. Two years later, I get another phone call. It's another JAG, this time from Colorado or something. He's at his next duty station and he's raped someone, so they want to dig up the old assaults. So, I relived the whole thing all over again. Again. Do you know what happened?"

"I'd like to say he got put away, but by how angry you're getting right now..." He held up his hands.

My mind went immediately to the airman who had walked in during my assault and did nothing. I forced myself to breathe and unclench my jaw.

"Seeing how angry you're getting, I don't think that's what you're going to say."

"You're right. They dropped the whole thing. Again." I took a deep breath and let it out, trying to quiet my anger. I wasn't angry at Ryan, I told myself. Another deep breath, and release. "They called me about six months ago, wanting to dredge it all up again. The two other 'reliable' witnesses they had refused to get involved. So did I." I shrugged. "I feel terrible about it, but the first two times, I thought to myself, Mel, if you don't say anything now, he's going to go on and do this to someone else. So, I set my own feelings aside and talked about it, and he did it again, anyway."

I shrugged and turned toward the stove. The potatoes were boiling. I covered the pot and turned the heat down. I wiped the counters down and focused on my dishcloth.

"The sad fact of the matter is, what happened to me, a tiny, insignificant little cog in the wheel that is the machine of the United States military, didn't matter. There's nothing I can do to help anyone else." I rinsed my dishcloth and hung it over the faucet before facing Ryan. "It took me a long time, and a lot of hours on a couch to come to terms with that. There's nothing I can do."

The defeat weighed on me. I turned back to cooking, so I didn't have to face him. A weight lodged in my throat like I might to cry, but there weren't any tears left. My mind raced, partly a side effect of my being triggered. I couldn't concentrate, so I worked in silence, too aware of Ryan's presence behind me.

He texted furiously, a scowl on his face.

"Are you sure everything is okay?" I grabbed my water and took another sip, my throat too constricted for much more.

He shook his head, glaring at his phone. "Yeah, it's fine."

"Not to be a nag, but you don't look fine. You look pissed." I started on my gravy, and kept glancing over my shoulder at him.

Still on his phone, he clearly didn't want to talk about whatever it was, so I left it alone.

Ryan's phone sat face down on the table by the time I finished washing my hands, and his expression hadn't gotten any friendlier. I worried about setting him off if I said anything else about it. He'd never been mad at me, but for the first time since I'd known him, I had nothing to say.

The house phone rang, saving me. Alexandra's number popped up on the caller ID.

"Hey, are we all set for tomorrow?"

My brows furrowed. "Tomorrow? What's tomorrow?"

"Sarah and Olivia are at her sister's in Vermont and my house is being fumigated. You said I could come crash on your couch?" She waited a moment. "Is any of this ringing a bell?"

My mind struggled, but I still had no idea what she was talking about. "Yeah, sure, no problem."

Her frowning voice came over the line. "I talked to you about this a month ago."

"I'm sure you did, but there was a lot going on and I forgot." I moved the phone away from my mouth so she wouldn't hear me sigh. "But it doesn't matter, come on over. Bring food."

"Better, I'm bringing wine." Her voice had become cheerful. "We can pop in some Mel Brooks and make it a girls' night in."

Smiling, my earlier tension drained. "That actually sounds really fun."

"Cool beans. Catch you tomorrow!"

I hung up, still smiling.

"What was that?"

Something in Ryan's tone got my hackles up.

"Alexandra." Snippier than I intended. Meaning, I meant to be snippy, just not that much.

His face relaxed. "I'm sorry. I have a situation going on and it's putting a lot of pressure on me."

My eyebrows raised and I shrugged. "Do you want to talk about it?"

"Not right now." He shook his head, still focused at the phone in his hand.

"Can I do anything to help?"

He ran his tongue over his teeth and grimaced. "There is, actually, but I don't want to impose."

"Okay, so ask, and I reserve the right to say no." I smiled, crossing my arms.

"Could Rexy come hang out with you tomorrow? Maybe for the weekend? I think I need to go deal with this. My dad will be fine on his own, but he can't get Rexy out for walks or anything."

I waved him away. "That's not imposing. Of course, Rexy can come over." I laughed. "I might need to put a sign over the door about not collecting any more strays. I'll be full."

He smiled, but I could tell his heart wasn't in it. Even though dinner came out perfect, I found myself too anxious to eat much, partly from my episode earlier but also being worry about Ryan's behavior. Not long after dinner, he took off.

It was too early for bed, but too late for anything other than to watch TV. Without homework or studying, I'd been cast adrift.

Alexandra's voice intruded. *"It's possible someone broke into your house,"* she'd said. And she hadn't meant it, I could tell by her voice. *"You have ghosts,"* she'd said over lunch with a cat in the cream expression.

I rummaged through my closet until I pulled out my messenger bag. The digital voice recorder and K-II meter sat in the bottom with my flashlights, chastising me for abandoning them. I pulled both out, one in each hand. Before, I had considered the K-II more for show than function, but could it help me tonight?

All of my dangerous toys were isolated in the bedroom, closest to the living room. On the floor of the closet, behind the bifold doors was a box full of cords and gadgets, but my digital camera wasn't in there. I pulled out my webcam, having to untangle the cord as I did. It wasn't much, but better than nothing.

For the next half-hour, I set up the cam and finagled the USB cable through the bedroom window, trying to decide which angle would be best. I finally settled on the stairs. It was unlikely an intruder would vault over the railing. Or so I'd hoped.

My investigation setup complete, I paused in front of the bank of switches by the front door. Compared to some of the investigations I'd been on, this was pretty pitiful. But better than nothing, I reasoned.

Before turning off the lights, I recited the date, time, and location, and left the recorder going. With a flip of a switch, I was plunged into darkness. In the time it took for my eyes to adjust to the darkness, I realized that, without any camera equipment, it wasn't even necessary for the lights to be out. I frowned. Was there a reason for the lights to be out, or did we do it to ourselves for ambiance?

"Every investigation you've done has been in the dark," I said, using my not-whispering low tone for the recording. "If it ain't broke, don't fix it."

The trouble was, I'd left my flashlight in the bedroom. Between the light coming from through the front door and the pale blue glow of the clocks in the kitchen, I figured I could make the journey without killing myself. My fingertips trailed across the wall until I got to the hallway. I switched hands to let my left hand guide me along the half-wall to my bedroom.

I crashed into the hallway door face first. Surprised, I stumbled forward and bashed my head against the door again as it recoiled from its bounce against the trim.

I swore as I brought my hand to my sore nose. Fortunately, my hard head would be more likely to break the flimsy hollow-core door than the other way around. I fumbled for the knob and closed it, resisting the urge to take revenge with a hefty slam.

"Pain in the ass. A barrel bolt is only a couple bucks," I said to the door. "That'll fix you right up. Asshole."

Satisfied, I continued down the hallway for my flashlight.

Chapter 18

May 21, 2010

Alexandra sat on my couch, her feet tucked underneath her with a glass of wine in one hand and her phone against her ear. "I know. Yes. Okay. Yes. Yes. Okay. Give Olivia kisses for me. Love you, too." She sighed and set the phone on the coffee table. "I love my family, but it's exhausting having to be on all the time."

Rexy stopped snoring, sat up, and stared at us. Apparently deciding we weren't interesting, he lay back down with a groan.

I took a sip from my own glass. Alexandra had brought a new brand of red over, and I enjoyed it very much. "For what it's worth, you and Sarah are basically my relationship goal."

She rolled her eyes. "That's why you've been single so long." Leaning forward, she topped off her glass from the box on the coffee table. "So, you've been hanging out with Ryan." A statement, not a question.

I sipped, and considered telling her my investigation had turned up nothing to throw her off the scent, but that would make it worse. Then she'd know something was up. If she had any idea how attracted I was to him, she'd never let it go.

"He's nice. I'm trying to help him out as much as he helps me." I gestured to Rexy with my glass. "But he acted really weird last time he was here."

"Weird how?" Her gaze locked on mine over her glass. "He's always been pretty chill."

"Checking his phone every second, upset over something—like, really upset—and refusing to talk about it." I topped off my own glass.

"Stuff happens," she said, checking her phone. "He had an ugly divorce. It's still pretty fresh. It's tense. Not everyone can part amicably. I was lucky in that sense."

"If you can part amicably, do you really need a divorce?" Maybe I needed to stop drinking. After I finished this glass.

"Sometimes stuff doesn't work out. George and I were married for a hot minute out of high school. A man so deep in the closet that he didn't realize we'd married each other for the same reason: to play straight for our families. Speaking of which." She reached around the arm of the couch for her pocketbook. She fished around for a minute before pulling out an envelope with my name on the front. "For you."

"What is it?"

She nodded at me to open it, smirking, so I did. I couldn't stop my smile as I pulled out the ivory card.

"A wedding invitation? This is great!"

She held up a hand. "Well, we're engaged. I don't want to run off to Vermont like a thief in the night to get married, and the date is TBD for now. I think Maine might legalize at some point in the near future, so we're sending engagement announcements-slash-invitations to the people we want to have there." She smiled like the cat that got the cream.

Breaking one of the cardinal rules of our friendship, I gave her a hug. She let me, patting me on the back, and I could hear the smile in her voice. "It's going to be small, maybe twenty people. No attendants or anything fancy, and we're having a notary perform the ceremony."

"You're still going to get dressed up though, right?" I sat back on my side, pulling my feet onto the cushion. "Oh, please let me help you find a dress!"

She scoffed. "Of course. Sarah's big into this whole wedding thing and she's really anxious for us to be able to set a date." Her smile changed. "Of course, we'll have to wait until after the new baby."

"*What*?!" I jumped up, some of my wine sloshing out of my glass and onto the carpet, but I didn't care.

Alexandra and I clinked our glasses together, her cheeks flushing pink. "We got our positive a couple weeks ago. It's very hush-hush, but obviously you're on the inside."

I shook my head and couldn't stop smiling, only partly because of the wine. "This is so much! I am so happy for you both."

She smiled the soft, gentle smile that only appeared with her fiancée and daughter. "I'm happy for me, too." The softness disappeared, replaced with determination stronger than steel. "My mother is not being invited, either. To any of it. Just so you know."

Raising my hands in mock surrender, I shook my head. "I am on your side on this one. You won't be getting a hard time from me at all!"

"Good." She relaxed and smiled at me. "I knew I could count on you."

After cleaning up from dinner, we opened a second box of wine and watched *Men in Tights*. Laughing felt so good, we popped in a second disc afterward for a double feature. Eleven finally rolled around and we had to admit defeat.

I groaned, leaning my head back on the couch. "I find the older I get, the earlier I want to go to bed."

"Staying up all night is definitely not as much fun when you don't want to. Like your infant won't stop screaming because she's teething." Alexandra rolled her eyes and brought her glass into the kitchen. "Oh, nice, you got a dishwasher."

Close behind her, I opened the door and pulled out the top rack. "I did, indeed. Works great, love it." We loaded the machine together. I glanced at the window over the table one too many times, because Alexandra noticed.

Without actually rolling her eyes, she rolled her eyes at me. "What's the matter?"

Shaking my head, I held both my hands up in front of me. "Nothing, it's fine."

"Are you sure?"

"Yeah."

While Alexandra brushed her teeth in the bathroom, I pulled some blankets and pillows from the closet and tossed them on the couch. I took Rexy out for one last potty break before bed and stood on the porch swatting at bugs while he sniffed endlessly for the perfect place to pee. I searched the night, into the shadows beyond the porch light, and shivered.

Finally finished with his business, Rexy bounded up the stairs and followed me into the house. We passed Alexandra at the end of the hall, and we said goodnight.

Settling into my own bed, I realized I hadn't heard from Ryan at all today. I checked my phone again. No missed calls, no texts.

Sleep found me easily tonight, courtesy of the wine and the laughter.

In the foggy place between sleeping and waking, someone whispered my name.

"Mel, I think someone is here."

My eyes shot open. Alexandra's silhouette hovered next to me. Rexy lay at the foot of the bed and hadn't lifted his head off the mattress to warn me someone was there who shouldn't be. I grabbed my robe off the corner of the headboard and put it on over my jammies. Armor.

"What happened?" I slipped out the bedroom door, heading toward the living room.

Alexandra grabbed my upper arm, and I took a deep breath to keep from screaming. Her hand clutched at me, so I slowed my pace.

"I was on the couch, texting Sarah. I set my phone down and heard footsteps on the porch." She pulled my arm, forcing me to turn and face her. "It was him. The man in the flannel. He had a dog with him. And the dog came to me and sat down and then..." She swallowed hard. "The dog barked once, and then disappeared."

My heart thudded in my chest, and I couldn't get enough air. "Rexy." The croak came out so low, I don't think even Alexandra heard me. "Rexy." Better.

The dog jumped off the bed and sauntered down the hall like he had all the time in the world. Rexy's ears perked and he trotted into the living room. He circled a spot in the center of the room, sniffing the carpet.

Alexandra's fingers turned to claws in my arm. I pried them away, confident I'd have bruises from her grip.

"That's where the dog disappeared."

My wine-soaked mind struggled to understand the words coming out of her mouth. Was someone here, on the porch, or did she think she saw a ghost dog?

Alexandra flipped the light on and strode to the couch. She stuffed a few items into her pocketbook before slinging the strap over her shoulder. Then she collected all the pillows and blankets into a heap in her arms, and came back to me.

Not sure what was happening, I reached out to take them.

"Hell no," she said, twisting away from me. "I'm sleeping in your room tonight. I'm not staying out here by myself. We can either share the bed or you can take the couch."

Stepping aside, I backed into the closet door and stumbled as it closed the last couple of inches and latched shut.

"Come on, Rexy." I patted the outside of my thigh.

He stayed right on my heels on my way back to the bedroom.

Alexandra had made herself a cocoon on the side of the bed next to the windows.

Sliding between the sheets, I wasn't sure what to say. "Do you mind if the dog sleeps on the bed?"

The bed moved as she scooched over. "He can sleep in the middle."

Rexy didn't need much encouragement to climb onto the bed. He settled between our legs with a grunt and a sigh. The dog fell asleep far easier than I did, my earlier relaxation having evaporated. Alexandra breathed deeply beside me. I tried for a while to sleep, but finally admitted defeat.

The light of my computer monitor had me squinting. I did a search for paranormal investigation teams in the area. Jess's group came up first, and my cursor hovered over it. No, I needed someone who didn't know me.

The next one down had an address in Springvale. They were still using an old Angelfire site with way too much neon green on a black background. I went through a few of their pages, which assured me that, in spite of their cruddy site, they might be a decent enough team. Using the contact form, I sent a message to the group. Nothing to do now but wait. Satisfied

I'd finally done something about my problem, I headed back to bed.

Halfway down the hallway, the odor of cigarette smoke hit me again. I grimaced and continued down the hall. After only taking a few steps, it disappeared completely. My grimace turned into a frown. That didn't make any sense.

Then I heard it.

Footsteps.

Not on the porch this time. Outside on the gravel.

"Rexy," I hissed. "Rexy."

He jumped off the bed and followed me. Alexandra didn't move. Good. I closed the door behind me.

On my way down the hall, I stopped in my office and grabbed my thirty-aught-six out of the closet and loaded it. My shoulder banged into the open closet door, and I bit back a swear. I was going to take the damned thing off the hinges until I could put some kind of lock on it. I'd had enough of that nonsense, too.

There might be an accident if I tried to hold him and the rifle at the same time, so I didn't bother with Rexy's leash. The doorknob chilled my palm as I pulled the front door open, letting the dog out ahead of me. I didn't know if I'd actually shoot someone for lurking outside my house in the middle of the night, but the cold wood of the stock grounded me as I stalked outside.

Rexy leaped off the porch and sniffed around the walkway. As soon as my bare foot touched the porch, his head snapped up, his attention drawn to the gravel parking area on the dark side of the house.

Barking every time his feet hit the ground, he galloped around the corner and disappeared. I ran behind him, my rifle gripped tight in both hands, the muzzle pointed toward the ground.

Rexy had raced up the hill behind the house into the woods. Standing alone in the middle of my driveway, I shook my head. There was no way to know whether he'd come back on his own or if I needed to grab a flashlight and go after him.

It took a moment for me to realize that where I stood the porch lights didn't reach. For months, I had feared this darkness, and now I stood in the middle of it. Strange shadows moved around me, and I squinted. There was no fog tonight, and I couldn't figure out why or how the air appeared hazy between me and the porch.

My breath caught as Rexy bounded down the hill toward me, tongue lolling. Sighing with relief, I let the rifle dangle from my left hand to free up my right to pat the outside of my thigh. "Come here, boy!"

Rexy flew to my side, skidding past me.

"Good boy!"

We left the darkness together, and I resisted the urge to check over my shoulder as I stepped into the house.

Sneaking back into bed felt weird, but I didn't want to wake Alexandra. Rexy settled back between us. I reached down to stroke his silky ears and my eyelids grew heavy.

"Did you find anything?" Alexandra's voice sounded scared. Vulnerable.

I swallowed. "No."

"I didn't think so." Her hand reached around and patted my arm. "It's okay."

Lying in the dark, I hoped she was right.

Chapter 19

May 22, 2010

Alexandra snuck out of the house before I got out of bed. I loafed in front of the television for a few hours until I figured Tori had had enough time in front of her round bale to not be too cranky with me. Then I got changed to ride. As I headed for the front door, the phone rang. I didn't recognize the number.

"Hello?"

"Hey, this is Joel from Paranormal, Inc. I got your email from our website."

"Oh, hi." I leaned against the wall. "How are you?"

"I'm good. So did you see on our website that we're a new group?"

My brain scrambled. "I must have missed it."

"Well, I wanted to make sure you knew in advance. We've just formed from a few different groups in the area. A lot of people see that on the site, so we haven't been getting a lot of requests. I might have a mutiny on my hands if I don't get us some searches soon."

I waited. What could I say?

"I was wondering if we could come out tonight?" he asked.

Aside from my reluctance to entertain the idea my house was haunted, there really wasn't a good reason for me to put this off. Wanting to maintain my ignorance should have been a good enough reason. "I guess that would be fine." Rexy's tail thumped against the floor, attracting my attention. "I do have a dog, though."

"That's fine."

I glanced at the clock above the television. "Do you know what time?"

"It's getting dark around eight, so would seven-thirty work for you?"

"Sure, no problem."

Tori was a good girl for me, but my mind pressured me to get home to tidy up the house before the team came by. I hurried to put things to rights while chastising myself for being silly. The group wouldn't care what state my house was in, but it had been drilled into me at a young age that having people in your house meant you cleaned. So, I turned on CMT and danced my house clean. Rexy stayed on the couch, wagging his tail when I walked by. Fortunately, the vacuum didn't seem to bother him.

A stranger with a goatee knocked on my front door just as the sun dropped behind the mountains, draping my yard in purple light. I opened it a crack. "Hello?"

"Hey, I'm Joel."

I leaned around him. Three other cars lined my driveway. More than half a dozen people milled about, pulling equipment from trunks and backseats. Some of it I recognized, some I didn't.

I stepped back, and Joel came in, holding a laptop case.

"Do you have a table or a desk we can set up as a command center?"

"Sure, in the kitchen." I led him into my small dining area and gestured to the table. "So, what do you need from me?"

"Well," he unzipped the laptop case and pulled out a very expensive-looking machine, "once the rest of the team gets in here, I'll introduce you to everyone, and I'd like you to talk to us about the house, the things you've been experiencing. For now, how old is the house and how long have you lived here?"

"I bought the house April, and it was brand new. "

His expression said he didn't believe me. "What was here before?"

"Nothing but vacant land. Unless you count the trees."

I could tell I'd lost him by the way he glanced away to set up his laptop. No one wanted to investigate a new house when an older one would be so much more interesting. My statistical analysis on the age of houses Jess's team worked on came to mind, reminding me I'd never actually done it.

"So, no buildings or residences of any kind?" Eyes glued to his screen, he clicked to open a few programs I didn't recognize. "Any deaths on the property? Native American burial grounds?"

I won the battle to not roll my eyes, shaking my head instead. "Not that I know of, no."

"Hmm." He plugged his laptop into the wall. While his programs booted up, he pulled out a couple of digital cameras.

I decided to walk away. I didn't want anyone from this group to know I used to be part of someone else's team. I needed to let them work and find what they'd find. I reminded myself I was the client now.

In total, the team had nine members, including Joel. I forgot everyone's name pretty much the moment I learned them. We walked around the house as I explained the weird big band music, and the footsteps in the woods, on the driveway, and on the porch. We discussed the service on the heating system, the stuck vent flap. I told him about the opening closet door and cabinet I still hadn't gotten around to fixing.

No one seemed able to wrap their heads around the concept of a brand-new house being haunted. They might have been in the same camp as me: the activity wasn't a great indication of a haunting. A couple members of the team checked their watches or phones while I explained things. I was losing them the way I'd already lost Joel.

When I explained what Alexandra had seen in the corner, the tall man in the flannel, I got some of their attention back. Joel navigated an experiment while I stood by and watched. The team was very excited to realize the apparition Alexandra had seen had been in the house, standing in the corner, not on the porch. Re-energized, they dispersed throughout the house in teams of twos and threes with their cameras, flashlights, and voice recorders. Just before lights-out, I sat at the table with Joel, who typed and clicked away, setting up the camera system for a live feed. Cameras covered my house, except my craft room, which had remained oddly weirdness free. Maybe I should let Olivia sleep in there.

Joel, very dedicated to keeping an eye on the team and seeking any kind of anomalies, didn't take his eyes off the computer screen. He did chat with me about a few different things, like my water quality and whether I took any kind of psychiatric medication. In all, the team let the equipment run for about three hours before calling it when no one had any experiences.

On his way out the door, Joel explained the process of going through the evidence. I listened, nodding in all the right places, and let him practice his spiel on me so he'd be better at it for the next people who called him for help. Joel left last, and I respected him as team leader for it.

I closed and bolted the door behind him. As soon as the last pair of taillights left my driveway, I shut off the porch light. Leaning against the door, I wasn't sure how I felt, except relief I had finally shared this burden with someone. One way or the other, I would have some kind of answer.

The call from Joel came the next afternoon, much sooner than expected.

"We didn't find anything."

Suddenly, I realized how much I had wanted validation for my experiences, even hoping my own investigation had been wrong. Is this what I had done to clients when Jess broke the news to them?

No. Even Jess would explain how things had happened, how she reached her conclusion. Joel shut me down completely.

I said all I could say. "Okay, thank you."

Hanging up the phone, I was both relieved and disappointed. On one hand, maybe Alexandra would finally be satisfied and stop telling me my house was haunted every time something bumped in the night. On the other, my rational explanations weren't holding much water these days.

Chapter 20

May 25, 2010

In spite of Alexandra's concerns about a potential haunting, Olivia was coming to stay the night with me again. Alexandra had to take an overnight shift and Sarah got called in. Sarah tried to be subtle as she glanced around my living room. She handed Olivia to me, and I set the baby on her feet.

"What's the matter?"

"Alexandra said you have ghosts."

My cheeks warmed. "I don't, actually. I just had a team out, and they said no. No ghosts." There. I had taken the coward's way out by telling Sarah, who would definitely tell Alexandra.

She nodded and dropped the diaper bag on the couch. "I'm very curious about the whole thing." She smiled at me. "Alexandra has always been a believer, tells me she can see and feel spirits. I haven't closed my mind to the possibility of an afterlife, but I also haven't had any evidence to that effect."

I needed to change the subject. "How are you feeling?"

Her hand went to her lower abdomen. "Good, actually. I was worried because I was so sick with Olivia, but things seem to be going a lot smoother with this one so far." She grinned and knocked on the wooden trim of the closet door. "We'll see how it goes, I'm still early in."

She did that wave at her daughter where the fingers folded into the palm. "Bye-bye, Olivia!"

Ignoring her mother, Olivia went for the bag on the couch and dumped it. Toys spilled onto the floor.

"Completely disinterested." Sarah shook her head, her lips pursed with one corner of her mouth tucked in. "No rejection is so harsh as your child not caring whether you're around or not."

"But when you come to pick her up tomorrow, she's going to greet you like she hasn't seen you in a year. You know that."

Her expression brightened and her pale blue eyes sparkled. "I know. I always feel like a celebrity when she comes running to me. Have a good night, and call me if you need anything." She blew a kiss at Olivia and went out the door.

I picked up a stuffed donkey and made it walk toward Olivia. "We'll have fun though, right?"

Olivia and I had a successful dinner and spent some time playing on the floor with her toys. I found myself fascinated with her interest and determination to understand everything around her. She would sit with absolute focus, trying to figure out how this toy or that worked. Eventually, she'd hand it to me so I could make it do its thing, and then take it back to make it work herself.

We skipped a bath. Instead, I washed her face and hands before snapping her into her jammies. She followed me into what I now considered her room and reached over the side of the pack and play for her star.

"'tar!'"

"You want your star?"

"'tar!"

"What do we say?"

"'tar plea!"

Smiling, I handed her the star, making sure it was on. Instead of making the lights and sounds go off and playing with it, she set it down in the center of the room and turned to me with a smile. I'm pretty sure all the color drained out of my face.

"Why did you do that?"

Olivia beamed and pointed to the corner. "Isaac."

I gaze followed her finger, wishing I could see what she did even as I hoped I wouldn't. "Okay. Isaac can't play with your star because it's time for you to go to bed, okay?" I picked her up and settled her down. I made a mental note again to talk to Alexandra about getting a crib or something here for her. "Good night, Olivia."

She waved at me, sitting upright in the center of the pack and play. "Nigh."

I closed the door behind me and crept down the hallway without turning on the light.

At the end of the hall, I reached out with my hands. After one too many collisions between my face and the closet door, I'd finally learned. Sure enough, the door hung fully open, blocking the hallway. My school bag rested on the floor of the closet, leaning against the back wall. After a moment of rummaging, I pulled out a pen cap. With the closet door closed, I jammed the thin end into the door to wedge it closed.

For the next hour or so, I watched TV, flipping through the channels when commercials came on. When I was finally tired enough to go to sleep, I turned it off, and then stood to stretch.

The clock ticked, then a *click* came from the hallway. The clock ticked again, then *pat*, quieter than the clock.

The clock kept counting the seconds as they ticked by, as if nothing had happened. I released a deep breath and shook my head. Even if I'd heard something, nothing that soft could hurt me. But when I got to the wide doorway to the kitchen, I shivered, and the fine hairs on the back of my neck stood up. An ominous presence waited in the shadows of the kitchen, but I steeled my spine. I was alone in the house, and nothing here could hurt me. Without turning on the light, perhaps foolishly, I used the blue lights of the oven and microwave to get a glass of water to bring with me to the bedroom.

As I took my first step into the hallway, *thud* came from the closet and I jumped. The door burst open in front of me, and my school bag tumbled out. My pens, all separated from their caps, spilled from the front pocket onto the floor in front of me. My heart sped up and I stopped breathing.

I bent down to pick it up a cap that had come to rest inches from my bare foot. Squinting in the dim light, the plastic was pitted like someone had chewed it. No one else used these pens, and I didn't have a habit of snacking on them during class.

My heart pounded as I stuffed everything back into the bag, but the zipper didn't respond to my trembling hands. I gave up and tossed the still-open bag into the back corner of the closet and slammed the door shut.

And I didn't wedge a pen cap in the door.

Olivia's screaming woke me from a restless sleep. I tore my bedroom door open as I struggled to tie my robe. I halted in the doorway, my arm extended and hand reaching for the hall light switch.

Between me and the switch stood a dark mass. My height, maybe shorter, a blacker than black shadow like the darkness the porch lights struggled to keep at bay. It rippled in front of me.

The world slowed. As my heart raced and my muscles froze, Olivia's screams pierced my ears.

I had to get to her, and that need overrode my hesitation. I charged through the shadow. A jolt went through my entire body like the wet day I'd touched a metal gate without knowing the electric fence was on. Just like then, my fingers went numb and my chest ached.

My lips tingled as I picked Olivia up, her face red and wet from crying. I patted her back to soothe her. The shadow had disappeared, but the hairs on the back of my neck remained standing.

Her stupid star still sat in the middle of the room, the lights blinking as it played "Twinkle Twinkle Little Star." My heart galloped in my chest, and I choked on a gasp.

Still trying to get Olivia to stop crying, I turned on the bedroom light.

For the first time, the deep shadows from outside had followed me in. The light stopped abruptly, unable to hold back the darkness in the house. My whole body screamed for me to leave. I couldn't breathe. Olivia screaming in my ear wasn't helping the situation.

Both of us eventually calmed down, and I settled her back down with her blanket. I picked the star toy up and shut it off. I stared at it for at least a minute before prying the cover off and pulling the batteries out. Enough was enough. I threw the toy on the floor, not caring where it went.

My fear turned to anger, and I yanked the covers over myself so hard, the end came untucked. Not able to sleep if the sheets tangled around my feet, I got up and remade the bed.

Sliding back between the sheets, I shivered. As my eyes drifted closed, Olivia cried again. Not the same scream as before, but I jumped out of bed. Nothing stopped me from turning on the hall light. As I entered the room, the star toy rocked on the floor as if it had been set down a second ago.

I turned on the light to banish the shadows before picking up Olivia. She wailed, her forehead pressed on my shoulder. Her cries slowly subsided into occasional whining, so I lay her back down in her bed. She fussed for a few minutes, turning this way and that, but settled with a sigh, and went still as she drifted back to sleep.

Before I even made it back to the bed, she cried again. I turned on the light in my bedroom. Then I turned on the light in the hall, and the overhead light in Olivia's room, which startled her enough that she stopped crying. She squinted in the light as I picked her up and held her on my hip. Grabbing the pack and play with my other hand, I dragged it toward the hall. The stupid thing bumped into the wall, then the doorframe.

I banged into the wall a few more times before I realized the bulky pack and play wouldn't fit through the opening. Growling, I hit the release buttons on the sides to fold the stupid thing. I dragged it into my bedroom and set it up on my side of the bed.

Olivia settled right down in spite of the brightness in the room, hiccupping quietly as her eyes closed. I sat on the edge of the bed, my hands braced on the mattress beside me. My mind was back in an old farmhouse as I lay shivering on the couch, unable to get warm. I blew out a puff of air, wondering if I'd see my own breath.

I didn't.

One thing I had never experienced in this house were cold spots. Smells and sounds, yes, but never a change in temperature. But I had seen, as clear as anything, a shadowy figure standing in between me and a light switch. There were only two possibilities:

A) I had completely lost my mind and hallucinated all of it, or

B) the ghosts were waking Olivia up to get my attention.

Chapter 21

May 26, 2010

Telling Alexandra I couldn't have Olivia over again hurt me, but she agreed. Her daughter's safety had to come first.

"Will you be okay?"

"I assume so." I shrugged, trying to choke back unexpected tears. "Not that I have much choice."

She nodded, her expression serious. "If you ever need a place to stay, you know where we are."

Without thinking about it, I hugged her and Olivia. "Thank you."

"Take care."

Less than an hour later, sitting in front of my computer, I dreaded what I was about to do. I had taken Joel at face value when he'd said what I'd wanted to hear: my house wasn't haunted. But after last night, I didn't feel safe in my home. Alexandra had offered a place to stay, but their two-bedroom bungalow was a tight enough fit for the three of them without me taking up space. And temporary at best if I did. Without any other family or friends nearby, I had no choice but to stay in the house. That left me in a position of having to seriously consider my own mental state, or intensely debate whether I shared my house with spirits. Since I was pretty sure I'd get locked up if I told the VA I saw and heard things, I figured a more experienced paranormal group would be the better way to go.

I found a really promising group, well-established with a decent site. Unfortunately, the Spectral Searchers team was based up in Falmouth. Probably too far for them to want to come to me, but I used the contact form, anyway. The worst they could do was say no, right?

After I clicked Send, I sat back in my chair. "It's all you can do for now."

Pushing away from the desk, I did my best to forget everything.

A few days later, I logged in to slog my way through the mandatory participation for one of my classes. When everyone made the same mistake, it made me think I had made the mistake. Hopefully, the participation drove the grade and not my response.

Before logging off, I checked my email one more time. A new message popped up.

"Who the hell is Miranda St. John?"

I opened it, expecting a link or some ridiculous solicitation from someone wanting me to help them with their millions.

Dear Melissa,

My name is Miranda St. John, and I'm the co-founder of Preternatural Research and Investigation of Southern Maine. We're based in Limington. Lucy from Spectral Searchers forwarded me your email because her team doesn't work in your area.

I would appreciate the opportunity to come to your home and investigate. We are available this upcoming Friday night, or Friday or Saturday next weekend.

Please check out our website (link in my signature) and our bios, and let me know what you think. If you have any questions, reply to this email instead of using the form on our site.

Sincerely,

Miranda

Without thinking too much about it, I checked out their site. Neat, clean, and professional They did one or two investigations a month, and each one had its own page full of results with a summary. Nothing screamed phony to me—some of the investigations even said they were inconclusive—so I shot Miranda a reply letting her know I was at her disposal, the sooner the better. I gave her my number and let her know to call me to confirm, since I might not be on my computer again for a while.

After lunch, halfway up the stairs with a basket of clean laundry, the phone rang. I raced to the top of the stairs, dropped the basket on the floor, and caught the phone at the end of the fourth ring, right before the machine picked up.

"Hello?" Out of breath from running up the stairs, I angled the phone so I wouldn't be panting into the receiver.

"Hey, is this Melissa?"

I nodded. "It is."

"Hey Melissa, it's Miranda St. John from PRISM." She continued when I didn't say anything. "I know it's short notice, but we can come by this Friday if that works for you?"

"Yeah, that would be great."

"Excellent." She explained that she and her six-person team would be here around eight on Friday night. "We're excited to see you. We don't get to investigate new houses very often."

"Apparently, it makes my claim less valid since my house is new." I hadn't meant to sound quite so bitter.

She made an affirmative noise. "I think it's a common misconception that only older places can be haunted. We'll come in and see what we can find, or hopefully explain some of what you have been experiencing."

The tone of her voice comforted me. Like I'd made the right decision to let her and her team come in. I thanked her again.

Chapter 22

June 4, 2010

Just after dark, I met Miranda St. John. I liked her immediately. Part of the short girl club, she had a personality at least six feet tall. She said *hello*, then held up her hand to show me a digital voice recorder tucked in her palm.

"First rule of the team is to always be recording, so I started this the moment you opened the door, and everyone else is going to have theirs running while they set up. They will all be on until we all leave, okay? Second rule, once we meet in person, you get to call me Mandy. When people call me Miranda, I know they're either a doctor's office or trying to sell me something."

Smiling, I nodded, and she ushered me outside to where a tall, skinny guy and a woman with purple hair pulled equipment out of the backseat of a car. "Tall guy is Brian, and this is Jodi. She's my tech queen, and I wouldn't get anything done without her. Brian is new to the team, so he'll be floating between other groups."

Two other team members approached us, one a very petite blonde who might have been fresh out of high school and an older woman with graying hair. "Amy is newer to the team. Tonight is the first time she'll be in just a pair, and she's been great. And Laura."

The younger girl did one of those elbows tucked in at the waist half waves before she offered her assistance to Jodi, and the gray-haired woman smiled, waving her free hand at me.

The last two team members pulled even more equipment out of the back of an SUV.

"This is Sam," she indicated the very tall guy, dark hair, "and Alicia. You will see Alicia taking notes all night. She went to the Registry of Deeds in Alfred to research your house. I'm sure you already knew there was nothing to find."

Hands on hips, Mandy surveyed the crew as trunks and car doors closed one after the other. She waved to an empty-handed Sam. "Third rule of the team, we work in at least pairs, that way if something happens, it's already corroborated."

Now I really, really liked her. The first group I had worked with had been very professional, but this reached a whole new level.

Everyone headed toward the house, and Mandy nodded at me, her brown hair bouncing on her shoulders. "Let's start outside. Why don't you tell me about what's been going on."

I pointed to the woods behind the house. "I hear footsteps in the leaves. I'll hear four or five footsteps, and then nothing." My thoughts suddenly moved like pudding, and I couldn't seem to form words. "It's like, you can't walk through the woods without making noise."

"Hmm." She nodded and walked to the back corner of the house, staring into the deepening shadows.

"I also hear footsteps on the gravel sometimes, too, and it's the same thing."

She kicked some leaves out of the way with her foot. "Can you show me where the edges are?"

I did.

"Do you ever hear one immediately after the other? Footsteps on the gravel then in the leaves, or vice versa? Or maybe the footsteps are continuous?"

I shook my head.

She nodded. "What else outside?"

Feeling like an idiot, I explained how much darker the yard stayed outside the circle of the porch light. How I would never go on the back porch after dark even with the light on, and something stalked me any time I went anywhere near the back of the house, inside or out. The newly installed blinds hadn't done much to lessen the sensation. She didn't say anything, and her face didn't change. No judgment there.

"Okay, let's go inside. They should be mostly set up."

We walked past the two cameras Amy had set up on tripods in the outside corners of the living room.

She tore her attention from whatever she fiddled with and gave me a small smile. "One is night-vision, and the other one is regular."

In the kitchen, Jodi sat at my table, reaching over to plug in a laptop.

Laura and Brian waited in the living room at the end of the hallway, camera bags at their feet. Laura glanced up from her phone and slipped it into her pocket.

"Oh, sorry guys." Mandy looked at me. "What rooms would you say are the most active?"

I pointed down the hallway. "Definitely the main bedroom, last door on the left, and some stuff has happened in the room across the hall, where my niece sleeps when she comes over."

Mandy pushed open the door to my office-slash-craft room where I kept my rifle and all of my sharp, baby unsafe things. "What about in here?"

"Nothing." My mind raced for a second, and I shook my head. "I don't think anything has happened in there. Well, unless you want to count weird smells in the hallway."

"Okay." Mandy placed her palm flat on the narrow door of the hall closet and frowned. "What's going on with this?" Her fingers traced the edge of the duct tape I'd put up to hold the door closed.

"The framing wasn't done right or something, so the door opens at odd times."

Mandy sucked in her upper lip and pointed over her shoulder to the kitchen. "And I assume that's the cabinet door that doesn't stay shut?"

Sure enough, the cabinet door on the end hung open, my dishes stacked neatly inside the cupboard.

"That's a loose hinge, but I keep forgetting to fix it."

"Sounds like you've done some research on your own."

Instead of telling her about my ghost hunting experience, I nodded.

Mandy sent Laura and Brian to set up a camera in the room across from mine. It seemed empty without the pack and play.

Mandy brought me back to the moment. "What kind of activity have you noticed?"

I started with Rexy and his ball, and then explained about the toy with the brand-new battery going off for no reason, and the night Olivia woke up screaming.

Mandy shook her head, tapping her chin with her knuckles. "That's no good. I don't suppose you have the toy?"

"My sister gave me the toy and a few other ones for tonight." We headed toward the living room, where the bag of toys sat near the door. "This room has been kind of a hot spot, too,"

I offered. I explained Alexandra seeing the man twice, and the dog. "And footsteps on the porch. Sounds like someone in work boots walking around."

"Wow. It sounds like a lot has been going on. Why did it take so long for you to reach out?"

I shrugged and folded my arms. "I did, actually. I contacted a different team, and they were here for a while, but they didn't find anything." I considered mentioning my own pitiful investigation, but decided not to bother.

She nodded. "Sometimes the team can make a difference. We're going to finish setting up. If you need to get away, you can go into the extra bedroom. Wait until the door is closed before you turn any lights on, so it doesn't mess with the night vision."

One by one, the members of the team came into the living room, waiting for Mandy.

"Okay, guys. I want someone in the living room all night tonight with that camera facing the front door. You guys can rotate through the bedrooms and the basement." She pointed at the stairs. We hadn't talked about the basement.

I shook my head.

She split the group into teams of two, and assigned Brian to go with Laura.

She scanned the eager faces. "Are we ready to go lights out?"

They all chanted together, "Lights out, lights out, lights out!" before splitting off in their assigned teams.

Lights flicked off throughout the house.

Sam and Alicia headed into the basement.

Not long after, camera flashes illuminated the stairway walls.

I ran a hand through the underside of my hair and followed Mandy into the kitchen. "What do you do?"

She sat in one of the chairs and checked out the camera feeds. "I usually keep an eye on the live feed, and I get to hang out with you. If you get sick of me, I'll probably go tag along with the rest of the group." She crossed her legs and made a vague waving gesture at the screen. "It's all recorded, anyway, so it doesn't really matter."

I tried to not say anything, or to speak in a very low voice so it wouldn't interfere with the investigation.

Overall, the team carried out the investigation quietly and professionally, and Mandy didn't call it until nearly midnight. They weren't able to make Olivia's star—or any of her other toys—go off. There were some thumps here and there, and Laura and Amy saw something outside. A few times, their K-II meters went off for no discernible reason. Mandy remained very upbeat about the whole thing, or maybe she was a positive person in general, but when she and the team left, my mood had improved.

Being around people all night had wiped me out, and I wanted nothing more than a good night's sleep. Snuggling under the covers, I checked my phone. A text from Ryan, time stamped over an hour before.

I hope everything is going well.

My thumbs hovered over the keys as I pondered a reply. After checking the time, I snapped my phone shut and snuggled under the covers. Sleep found me quickly.

Chapter 23

June 18, 2010

The next two weeks passed without much of anything going on aside from my online classes. The sociology class itself bored me, but at least the professor, a man from Syria who overused the word "literally," kept things interesting. I went to dinner with Sarah and Alexandra, and spent a lot of time at the barn. My grilling education went better than expected. I didn't lose my eyebrows even once. Ryan and I spent some time together as well, often with Rexy.

Mandy called me on a Wednesday, wanting to come to my house Friday night and do the reveal—the part where they let me know what they may have found during their investigation. In the evening when everyone would be available. I said sure. Both the teams I'd worked on previously did reveals in person—Joel's abrupt phone call had actually been outside of the standard practice—and I didn't make any assumptions.

I had already invited Ryan over for dinner on Friday, so I called him to see if he wanted to eat in instead, and he could be there for the reveal. He hesitated, and didn't sound particularly enthusiastic, but agreed.

At 5:59 Friday night, I was straightening up while Ryan did dishes when Mandy knocked at the door.

She smiled and waved at me through the door, and I beckoned her in.

She poked her head in before stepping into the living room. "Hey, Melissa, how have things been?"

"Pretty quiet, actually." Aside from the cigarette odor that came and went at random and a few footsteps, things *had* been relatively quiet.

"Has anything been different?" She held the door open.

I shook my head.

Sam knocked his boots on the steps before ascending the porch, followed by Amy, then Laura. Brian brought up the rear.

I frowned. "What's going on?"

Mandy smiled at me like a cat that had gotten a mouse. Smug, in any case. "Let me set up my laptop. The team wanted to be here for this." She noticed Ryan at the sink and pink tinted her cheeks. "Oh, hello."

"This is my friend, Ryan. Ryan, Mandy."

Ryan stuck his hand out and shook hers. "Nice to meet you."

"I asked him to be here for the reveal if that's okay?"

"Of course." Mandy moved to the table and started setting up her laptop. The rest of the team had come in, wordlessly splitting into groups and dispersing through the house. Mandy glanced up and noticed me noticing. "It's one of the things our team does sometimes, check for EVPs while I do the reveal." She gestured to the chair next to her and sat in front of her laptop.

Sitting beside her, I didn't recognize the audio software she had installed to clean up the files. It appeared similar to what my first group had as far as functionality, but it wasn't something I'd ever used to know how it worked, other than it cleaned up background noise and enhanced the sound.

Ryan stood by the back door, drying his hands on a dish towel like this was the most normal thing in the world.

Mandy plugged a wired mouse into the side of the computer and opened a folder labeled "Newfield" with the investigation date. After half a second, files began appearing in the folder. She stared at me, an odd smile on her face.

My jaw dropped. Fifty-four files!

"What do you think?"

I sat back in my chair, shocked. "Wow."

"Yeah. Normally, in an active haunting, we might get two, almost never more than three." She gestured at the screen. "When we started finding all these in the audio, we thought for sure something was wrong with the equipment. But let's go over these together, just in case we have something in here that shouldn't be."

She turned the volume up and clicked the first file.

I cringed at my voice on the recording. *"It's like, you can't walk through the woods without making noise."*

I'm sorry, but it's very dark out here.

I couldn't have torn my eyes from the screen if I'd wanted to. My voice came out slightly better than a croak. "Play it again."

Mandy adjusted the sound and played it again. *"...without making noise."*

I'm sorry, but it's very dark out here. A raspy, whispery voice. Harsh.

Chills raced up my spine, and goosebumps covered my arms.

"And we caught that on two recorders, by the way." She opened the next file.

Laura spoke. *"Light up, we'll know you're here."* She paused to wait for an answer. *"You can make a noise."*

As if in response, a high-pitched yipping noise came through the speakers.

Ryan spoke up from his post next to the back door. "Coyote. There's a pretty big pack out here."

Mandy smiled at me. "See? This is why we do this." She made a note on a piece of paper at her elbow.

She clicked the mouse, and another audio file opened. "Laura got this one on the front porch."

A shiver ran up my spine at the familiar thump of work boots crossing the wooden decking. Then, what sounded like a burp and a grunt.

"Are you kidding me?" a male voice asked. Probably Brian.

More footsteps.

It took me a few tries to swallow, but I managed it. "That sounds like Brian was walking across the porch."

"No problem," Mandy said, making another note. "Pretty sure he had sneakers on, but I'll ask him."

Whoever had done the analysis had clearly erred on the side of caution, keeping things rather than risk throwing potential evidence out. At this rate, there may really be only one or two actual EVPs.

I'm sorry, but it's very dark out here.

I shivered and sat on my hands. The next two files didn't have anything I could hear.

Mandy frowned as she continued her list. She muttered something under her breath that sounded like "Laura," but I couldn't be sure, and I didn't want to ask.

"This one is when I went for a walk around the house so Jodi could take a break. In your bedroom."

The clip had been cut off at the last syllable of someone's sentence.

Mandy held up a finger, telling me to wait.

"Come sit on the bed with us."

I didn't hear anything but Mandy's voice, and shrugged.

She turned the volume up and replayed the file. A barely discernible whisper played between the cut off sentence and the invitation to sit on the bed.

My brows furrowed. "What did it say?"

Mandy shook her head. "I don't know, and I didn't want to guess." She skipped the next couple of files. "Oh, this one."

Laura and Amy were talking about seeing something. "They were at this window," Mandy explained, pointing to the one I'd had covered in newspaper before the blinds went up.

"Why don't you come over to the window so Laura can see you?"
No thanks.

Ryan's eyebrows shot up. "What did it say?"

A click and drag of the cursor raised the volume, and Mandy skipped back. *"...so Laura can see you?"*

No thanks. A whisper, but clear as a bell. And it wasn't Amy or Laura.

"What are you doing?" Ryan moved closer to the table to see what Mandy clicked on.

Without thinking, I answered his question. "She's digitally manipulating the raw data to isolate the audio, but she's doing it from the originals in this moment so we can tell that it wasn't doctored." I moved in closer to Mandy.

Her mouth opened into an 'o' of surprise and her brows furrowed, but said nothing. She clicked again to start the file.

Mandy spoke on the recording. No, Jodi.

The tall one. A breathy whisper, like the one from outside.

Mandy clicked so fast, I lost track of how many files she'd opened. I didn't comment on the ones she'd skipped over.

Two of the team members were talking, walking around.

"Laura doesn't smoke anymore." Jodi's voice.

I don't know what I'm doing here. Faint, but clear enough to say it was the same voice that had said "no thanks."

"I definitely hear the walking now."

Shivering, I hugged myself as I realized it wasn't Jodi walking around, but the owner of the breathy whisper who didn't know what they were doing. A strange numbness came over me, dulling my senses. My world had narrowed to the speaker and the strange whispers coming out of the computer.

"This is one of Brian's. He's trying to get someone to get his K-II meter to go off."

"–that if you want."

I want it, came the breathy reply.

I rubbed my face, then pressed my hand together against my mouth. What. The. Fuck. Was happening in my house?

"Uh," Mandy said, torn. "I'm not going to open this one." She made a note on her paper and glanced at me. "So far, Laura's have all been a bust. I'll give it to you on a CD, and you can listen to it later if you want." She pointed to the screen. "This is another one of mine."

Someone talking in the background. Then Mandy's voice played. *"Can you make the lights go to, like, red?"*

A *grunt* in response. Deep and guttural, but more man than animal.

"And then I was going to tag Jodi out." Mandy clicked again.

"Maybe I'll go sit in the kitchen. Do you want me to go sit in the kitchen?"

Yes. Barely half a second, and clearly a woman's voice.

Mandy clicked her tongue against her teeth as she skimmed the list, her cursor pausing to hover over the icons. She skipped a few more. "We have quite a few that are just humming." She glanced at me. "I was out with Brian on the front porch for this one."

Sam wandered into the kitchen, grinning from ear to ear, leaning with one elbow on the half wall.

The noise of boots on the porch had me shivering again.

"That was probably Brian," Mandy said, then paused expectantly.

Wait right here. Maybe the same voice that said "yes" a few files ago. She dragged out "here," the word fading into a breathy whisper.

"And we were heading back into the house a few minutes later."

The first four and a half seconds of the clip were probably the longest of my life.

Did you have to leave? The same breathy woman's voice again, but so quiet this time, Mandy had to crank the volume for me to catch it.

My hand covered my mouth, reading into the message in the context of what was happening. "The ghost wanted to talk."

Mandy nodded. "I think it did. Several of these are actually in response to you, by the way."

"Play this one." Sam pointed to the screen.

Two people laughing. My voice, *"Feel your way to the couch."*

I remembered this. Laura had stumbled into a wall in the dark, and we had laughed.

'Cause you want it. A voice so faint that it could have been anyone. Except maybe the owner of the grunt.

"Can you please come back?" Amy's voice asked.

"Have you had any activity?" Brian's voice.

Amy said, *"No."*

The irony of it, not knowing there was something with them at the moment they'd been discussing they'd had no experiences. And at least three separate voices so far. How many were there?

"This one is in response to you, too."

After a moment, I recognized this as the conversation we'd been having at the end of the night, not long after Laura had bumped into the wall.

Laura laughed. *"I know you even got on all fours, which–"* someone's laugh interrupted her voice *"—that's great."*

"I'm sure the child enjoyed it," I said, then laughed. I'd relaxed by the end of the investigation.

"Yeah," Mandy said. She'd gotten down on her hands and knees in Olivia's room to play with toys earlier in the night, hoping to get a response.

"Yeah." Laura's voice dripped with sarcasm. *"The child's like–"* a scoffing noise *"–get us, moron."*

"It's probably why they don't want to talk to me." Mandy's recorded laugh played.

Be gone. Throaty and deep, either another man or the first one.

Despite not being a praying person, I prayed it was the first one.

"Hey," Mandy said. *"If you light this light up to red, we'll go. We'll get in our cars, and we'll leave you alone."*

I didn't know how much more of this I could take. The idea of spirits wandering about willy-nilly without me knowing had me extra creeped out. I couldn't figure out what to do with my arms, so I sat on my hands again. Without noticing my discomfort, Mandy kept clicking and opening files.

Laura spoke. *"I've definitely seen it, too."*

Lo, hiyanna. Another woman, the pitch of her voice distinct from the first few files.

That made four.

"There's something right out there," Amy said.

"What the hell was that?" Ryan leaned forward, standing close behind me now as Mandy made some adjustments.

She played it again, louder.

Breathy and quiet, but not a whisper. Confident. *Lo, hiyanna.*

Ryan didn't say anything, so Mandy moved to the next file.

Amy spoke to something or someone, her voice clear, but her words indistinct.

It's all mine, a male entity replied in a velvet tenor

A fifth voice.

Amy's voice on the recording didn't change at all as she kept talking, completely unaware she wasn't alone.

Mandy's eyes sparkled with excitement like a little kid on Christmas morning, and if Sam's grin got any wider, his jaw might fall off.

"Do you want to keep going?"

I shrugged one shoulder, hoping to appear casual rather than frazzled. "It's why I called you, so yeah, go ahead." I ran my tongue over my teeth and bit my lip. I knew exactly why she was so excited, and I didn't want to squash that, but dammit, I was halfway to a meltdown over here.

Sam's recorded voice was so loud, I jumped. Mandy apologized and lowered the volume before restarting the audio file.

"Actually, if you..." Sam's voice became inaudible like he'd turned away from his mic.

My old house. A forlorn whisper, but maybe it was the woman who'd been caught before.

Please let her be the woman from the other EVPs.

"Do you know if anyone died on the property?" Sam asked, folding his arms across the top of the half wall.

Twisting in my chair to face him, I shrugged again. "No, I don't, but I doubt it. I've spoken to Ruth Ayers once or twice. She wrote *The First Families of Newfield,* and she was the person I talked to for information on this property, and she said it's always been woods."

"Figured I'd ask." He tipped his chin toward Mandy. "How many more do you have left?"

"Just a few." She grinned like this was the best day of her life. "This one I hoped you could help us with. You said you have a young niece. Does this sound like her?"

A child's whined, *I don't want to go to sleep.* The high, plaintive voice belonged to a child of maybe seven or eight.

Up to at least six.

I pressed into the back of my chair until the spindles pressed painfully into my spine. "She wasn't here the night of the investigation. And she can't string that many words together yet."

Mandy smiled, but worry etched Ryan's face.

"This is another one from when we were going around at the beginning of the investigation." Mandy clicked open another file.

My own voice came from the speakers again. *"And then, I went to check on her, and she was passed right out. The star turned itself on twice."*

That's nice.

A seventh voice, another woman. Instead of screaming I clenched my thighs together and sat straighter against the back of my chair.

The next recording took place at the end of the investigation, when we were standing around, chatting and laughing a bit. A dog barked on the recording, and my gaze went back to Mandy, then Sam. Both of them watched me, gauging my reaction. Rexy hadn't been with me that night, and my only neighbor didn't have a dog.

When I didn't react, Sam whispered to Mandy, and she rolled her eyes.

"I'm not particularly proud of this one, but I have to play it." She clicked the icon.

It was her own voice, a lilting singsong. *"I'm in here all on my lonesome."*

Bitch. Maybe yet another woman, this one with a deeper voice. Or, if there was a power in the universe that didn't hate me, one of the others had gotten irritated.

Confident the universe did hate me, I brought my tally to eight.

But I didn't trust my own ears. "Did it just–"

"Call me a bitch? Indeed, it did." Mandy sat back in her chair. Shaking her head in amazement, she navigated to a different folder. "This was really great for us, and the whole team is so excited. Like I said, there are more audio recordings, some humming or indistinct whispering or breathing, or stomping, but you haven't even seen the best part."

She clicked on an image file. A photo of my backyard popped up on the screen, She pointed out two spots of light in front of the pine trees, one purple and one bright white. "These are really incredible. See how they have their own light and appear solid? There's some controversy about orbs being paranormal or not, but I wanted to show this to you, anyway."

Several more round spots existed in the photograph. I pointed to one of them. "Is this an orb?"

"See how these two are uniform with no spot any brighter than any other?" Mandy pointed to a different one. "And these have bright outlines and dim in the middle? They're probably dust. The two we care about are the bright ones. And I saved the best for last."

This had already sucked all the energy out of me. I wiped my palm across my face. "There's still more?"

She laughed. "I only have one more thing. I know this is a lot."

She opened the second picture file, and my jaw dropped. Mandy stood next to the table, her LED flashlight and K-II meter in one hand, her digital voice recorder in the other.

"See all those wavy white lines? Those are artifacts from the LEDs."

In the photo, Sam stood on the other side of the stairs in the hallway. I had no idea what he was doing there, peering over the half-wall and down into the basement stairwell. The most interesting part of the photograph was the translucent, yellow-orange glow—fog? No, too luminous to be fog—behind Mandy, going from the floor almost up to the ceiling. I stared, trying to make sense of it.

I pointed with my finger, tracing the shape without touching the screen. I'd made a mistake. "This is between you and the camera. I thought it was behind you at first." The glow had shape, texture, almost shaped like a woman with the right imagination. The movement came through in the photo, the light twisting as it moved upward from the floor.

"It is. We have no idea what this is." She zoomed out, so the entire glow showed on the screen. "This is really amazing. It's the first real evidence we ever caught on camera. We had four other groups analyze it—definitely paranormal."

Though still sitting in my chair, I needed to sit down. I had been on dozens of investigations over the years, and had never caught anything, but forget anything like this. The quantity and quality of the EVPs, along with the photographs, were all mind-blowing. I was stunned. I half-listened as Mandy and Sam joked. They played a couple more EVPs I couldn't really pay attention to.

My house—my brand-new house—was haunted. I was relieved I wasn't going crazy. Also kind of angry. Maybe one or two other things.

Mandy said my name, and it took a moment to register.

"Is it okay if we go around the house again?"

With a sigh, I rested my forehead on my palm. My mind needed a few minutes to process. "Yeah, no problem."

"We aren't setting up the live feed or anything, just taking pictures and seeing if we can catch any more EVPs."

"Sure, go ahead." I stood up, banging my legs against the table. "I need to step out for some air."

On the porch, I leaned against the rail and took several deep breaths. The door opened and closed.

Ryan put his arm around my shoulders and squeezed. "You okay?"

"I think so." I turned to face him, half-sitting on the railing. I wanted to slide my arms around his waist and rest my head on his chest. Instead, I tightened my grip on the railing. "It's exciting yet terrifying. Validating. I don't know how I feel."

"What can I do?"

"I don't know if there's anything anyone can do." I shivered as his arm dropped from around my shoulders. Every shadow had become menacing. "I don't want to be here alone, but I don't have anywhere to go. What can I do about it?"

"It's not much, but Rexy could stay here with you tonight, if that would make you feel better." He pulled his phone out of his pocket and played with it for a minute. "But I'm his ride, so I'd have to crash on the couch, if that's okay with you."

I smiled. "Sounds good to me."

He pushed himself off the railing and stuck his phone in the front pocket of his jeans. "I'll be back in about an hour. Do you need anything while I'm out?"

"No." I shook my head. "Just come back soon."

Ryan took longer than an hour to go get Rexy, and everyone had left by the time he got back. The dog bounded across the yard from the parking area, tail wagging, and Ryan followed behind with a bag from Hannaford. I met them both at the door, hoping he didn't notice the salt I had spread across the threshold to keep spirits out.

"I brought a treat." He smiled at me. "Some assembly required."

"Okay." I sagged onto the couch, resting my elbow on the back so I could lean my face into my hand. "What would you like to do?"

Grocery bag in hand, Rexy at his heels, Ryan stepped into the kitchen. "Why don't you find something short to watch while I put all this together and we'll go from there?"

Watching him disappear around the corner, I couldn't help but smile. I loved having him in my life and in my house. Ryan was so much more than I had ever dreamed of. Clever, sweet, and I still wasn't tired of looking at him. Too bad I wasn't even on his radar. I settled in to watch whatever History Channel had on, half-listening to him moving around in the kitchen.

He emerged about ten minutes later with two bowls and a grin. "Ta dah!" He handed me an ice cream sundae built on top of a brownie. He sat next to me, one leg folded on the cushion, facing me.

I took a bite and about died. He had warmed the brownie, and my brain stopped working, I liked it so much. Around a mouthful of ice cream I said, "You can't feed me like this. It's better than sex."

My face caught fire. What had possessed me to say that?

He laughed at me. "You say that about riding your horse sometimes, too." He winked at me, and the warm tingles started.

We finished our ice cream, and he followed me into the kitchen.

"What do you think about all of it?" I glanced at him as I closed the dishwasher door.

"All of what?"

"The house being haunted."

"Ghosts aren't real." He shook his head. "I didn't want to say anything because I know you believe in it, but you asked."

It took me longer than I liked to formulate a response. "You heard the EVPs. You saw the photo."

"Cognitive bias. They couldn't find an explanation for the photo because they didn't look for one because they wanted it to be ghosts. And EVPs would be really easy to fake."

Crossing my arms over my chest, I frowned at him. "She didn't manipulate anything until after we listened to it, and even then, only adjusted it to be easier to hear."

"That's true, but do you know what she did?"

I knew where he was going with this. "I don't have to understand how the software works to know what she did was legit. I couldn't do a DNA test, but I don't question those results."

Exasperation filled his voice now and he raised his hand. "All I meant was, it could've been someone whispering into the recorder."

"They were in teams. How do you explain the ones that both people were talking, and something came up on the recorder?"

"Didn't you say there was a guy who bounced between teams so sometimes there were three?"

"One of them wasn't even in English."

"Do you know what language it was?"

"No."

"Then how do you know they weren't nonsense words?" He raised his arms in defeat. "The thing is, you don't know. And there's always a catch. They get something out of doing this, even if it's not money. You can't know what their real motivation is."

My frown deepened. Doubt nagged at me now. A legitimate group wouldn't allow that kind of thing to happen. The problem with ghost hunting groups, though, was the lack of a uniform standard. I didn't know Mandy, either. I liked her, and I liked the team, but what did that mean as far as their ethics went?

"How do you explain the photo?" I grabbed the dishcloth and wiped down the sink and counter. An hour ago, I had almost come to terms with my house being haunted, and now I'd been launched back into indecisiveness.

He shrugged. "I can't. But someone out there, some expert in photography, would probably be able to." He shook his head. "There's no such thing as ghosts. It's a scam, some kind of set up so they can sell you—"

"Magic rocks and candles?" I finished for him. The validation from Mandy evaporated and, suddenly isolated again, I struggled with what to believe.

He pulled the dishtowel off the oven to fold it neatly and put it back. "Pretty much my thought. These psychics and ghost hunters and all that. They're out for people who are gullible enough to want to shell out money to fix problems that don't exist."

I gestured at him with the wet cloth in my hand. "So, you think I'm gullible now?"

"That's not what I said." His tone was soothing. "All I'm saying is, be careful."

After Ryan settled in on the couch, I showered and climbed into bed. My bedroom door stayed open. Poor Rexy couldn't decide who he wanted to sleep with.

Lying in the darkness, Ryan's mother came to mind. She had lost four grand, and her car. If it hadn't been for Ryan, she would've lost everything. Mandy hadn't tried to sell me anything. Yet?

Staring at the ceiling, my words about magic rocks echoed over and over in my head. Eventually, I got out of bed and made my way to my dresser in the dark. I could've turned the light on, but I didn't need to. My splayed fingers traced the top until they hit the corner of a wooden box.

The lid lifted easily, and my fingers found the sharp edges of a chunk of raw obsidian Alexandra had given me on my last birthday. The weight of it in my hand reassured me. I hung my robe on the corner of my bed and slipped back between the sheets. I turned the obsidian in my hand over and over until it warmed from playing with it.

Sleep dragged at my eyelids. I slid my hand behind my head to put it under my pillow. But the last thing I wanted to do was to have to fish it out from under the bed. After some fumbling, I dropped the stone into the pocket of my robe.

My mind finally quiet, I fell asleep.

Before dawn, I woke to Rexy whining to go out. I stumbled out of bed and pulled on my robe, but stopped dead in front of the bedroom door.

Looming in front of me were three black figures, vaguely man-shaped. They huddled together, the largest one—both in height and breadth—in the middle. All three were blacker than black, like shadows within a shadow, or seeing a hole in the dark, my brain somehow discerning between the shades.

They wavered, as if breathing, or shifting their weight from side to side.

Still fuzzy with sleep, all I could do was stare. I closed my eyes and brought my hands to my cheeks, reassuring myself I was awake, and this was real. When I reopened my eyes, they were still there.

Waiting.

Staring at me.

Waiting.

"Ryan, they won't let me leave."

Silence. The shadows continued their weird shimmering and swaying.

"Ryan?" No response. "Rexy?"

My breathing stopped, and I couldn't force myself to exhale. I reached out to grasp the edge of my dresser, and a weight in the pocket of my robe bumped into my leg. The obsidian. I slipped my hand into the pocket and touched the cool angles.

The shadows shuddered, agitated. The edges of the obsidian dug into my palm as my grip tightened. My other hand searched for the box of crystals and tumbled stones. I groped around on the dresser, unable to tear my eyes away from the hulking black entities. I found the box and plunged my hand in. I hoped that whatever I grabbed might be useful.

The shadows turned toward the dresser in unison, and then recoiled away. They fled into the corner near the bed. The two shadows on the sides fell sideways into the walls, while the tallest one in the center stretched up to the ceiling and leaped over me.

The stones dropped and pattered on the carpet like rain. I pressed my hands to my face with my feet rooted to the floor. My breath came in shuddering gasps, and the blood pounding in my ears deafened me.

Eventually, I straightened and walked down the hallway.

The reason for Ryan's silence was obvious. He had already left.

Wiping my face with my hand, I walked into the kitchen for a drink of water. A hastily scribbled note protruded from under the handle of the microwave.

Had an emergency call at 3 a.m. and had to go. Didn't want to wake you. R.

I crumpled the paper in my hand and threw it toward the trash can.

Then, I froze. Rexy was gone, too.

What had woken me up?

I didn't tell Ryan about the shadow men stopping me from going out the door that morning, but I told Alexandra. We were sitting at lunch, and she picked the tomatoes out of her salad.

"Seriously, all I asked for was no tomatoes. Is it really that difficult to not add them in?" She physically recoiled when she spotted a mushroom. "My God, what kind of world am I living in?" Alexandra picked through the rest of her salad with her fork, searching for any additional objectionable vegetables.

Her mission complete, she turned her attention on me. "You okay?"

"I'm not sure." I told her about the reveal, the photo, and the ridiculous number of EVPs. She chewed slowly, reserving judgment for the end of the story.

"How did Ryan take it?"

I shoved my own salad around with my fork, not really wanting it. "He said it was all crap. Paraphrasing, naturally. That EVPs are fake, and ghosts aren't real."

She took a drink of her water. "Fine. Tell him to figure out what the 'real' explanation is." Shaking her head, she stabbed some lettuce so hard, the fork skittered across the plate. "That makes me so mad. He doesn't see it or feel it or experience it, so it's not real, you know? Such crap."

"I don't think it's like that." Even as I defended him, I didn't know why. I was angry with him for dismissing my experiences, even after hearing all the EVPs and seeing the pictures for himself. "Do you think my house is haunted?"

Alexandra didn't even finish chewing to answer. "Uh, yeah. I'm the one who climbed into your bed in the middle of the night because I saw your ghosts, remember? Twice."

Honestly not in the mood for salad, I pushed my plate away. "I didn't think it would happen again."

"You mean, after Rebecca's?"

"You remember that?"

"I was too much of a coward to stay the night there, so I made you do it, and they practically chased you out. Of course, I remember."

I sighed. "I wish I could forget."

Chapter 24

June 30, 2010

Scared by everything that had happened, I emailed Mandy rather than waiting for her to call me. I kept it short, sweet, and to the point, just asking if she caught anything.

I rode Tori, or tried to. It seemed like every time I wanted her to zig, she decided to zag. The height of her head and neck mirrored my frustration. Once she braced those huge muscles, I had a fight on my hands I couldn't win. Another one.

I tried so hard to do what my trainer had taught me, but why was it so hard when I was on my own? Tori flung her head up and spooked, and then Jan called my name. I sagged in my saddle in defeat as she strode up to me.

She placed her weathered hands over mine and squeezed them. "You need to let go." Jan shook my hands in hers to force me to release the reins. As soon as I did, Tori let out a deep breath and dropped her head, chewing on her bits.

"I'm sorry, I don't know what's going on with me today."

"I can see you struggling, and you can talk to me. If you need help, all you have to do is ask."

I nodded and rubbed Tori's mane with two fingers. Asking was far too difficult.

After apologizing profusely to my wonderful horse that I clearly did not deserve, I decided to do some research when I got home.

Out of habit, I opened my email as soon as my computer started up.

Hi Melissa,

I hope you had a good week. I'm sorry I haven't gotten back sooner. I had surgery Friday and took the weekend to try to catch up on much needed rest! We did catch some more interesting things on both audio and video this time. Again, nothing threatening. Even without any recorded evidence, the investigation was quite active! Would it be okay if Sam and I came up this Wednesday around 8:30 to do the reveal?

Mandy

My mouse hovered over the reply, but I wanted to do my search first. I started with the Newfield Historical Society site (always the best place to start searching), and puttered around on the Registry of Deeds before finally giving up and replying.

Hello Mandy,

I would love to hear about it.

I did some sleuthing, and there were two houses on my road that were burned down in the 1947 fires. Sixteen people died in the fires, but I haven't had a chance to see who or where the deaths were at this point.

It's funny, but I was worried you wouldn't catch anything. I thought the most recent investigation was going to be a dud! Lol.
Melissa

Not quite ready to set it down yet, I did some more searching about the 1947 fires. How I had grown up in Southern Maine and never heard about this tragedy before was beyond me. Known as "The Year Maine Burned," in 1947, fires wiped out nine towns and Millionaire's Row in Bar Harbor, along with half of Acadia. So much acreage burned that if laid end to end, the two-mile-wide swathe would go from Kittery to Fort Kent. Most of the homes in Waterboro and neighboring Shapleigh were also burned, which explained why all the houses were newer. Digging into Newfield specifically, I read a story about a doctor trying to escape the fires, and the harness burned off his horse. I didn't want to read anymore after that.

As I went to put my computer to sleep, my new email icon popped up.

The fires may explain a lot about some of those EVPs that came from your house, like the "I don't know why I'm here." Even if we hadn't caught anything this time around, it wouldn't have changed our opinion on whether your house is haunted or not. With everything we caught the first time around, plus the K-II activity, there is no way that everything has a plausible explanation. I hope you're okay with all of this.
Talk to you soon!

Several times, I read over her email. On the one hand, it was very validating to have her reiterate how much activity they'd caught and remind me there weren't plausible explanations, no matter what Ryan said. But I definitely wasn't okay with any of the things that had been happening.

I spent some time tidying up, and just as dusk fell, as I turned on every light in the house, Mandy arrived on my front porch, a large hard case tucked under her arm. She waved at me through the glass, and then pointed at the door handle on her side. I gave an exaggerated nod, and she stepped in.

This was the third time I'd met Mandy, and she was probably one of the most genuine people I'd ever met. Something about her energy instantly lifted my spirits—no pun intended—and I enjoyed being around her.

"So, how have things been?" She panted, setting the case on my dining room table. She glanced at me as she undid the latches and frowned. Probably the first time I'd seen anything like it on her face. "What's wrong?"

I crossed my arms and shrugged. This was the part where I wanted her to tell me she could fix it. That they had a piece of equipment that would take all these ghosts away from my house and out of my life, and things would be normal. Maybe she had a proton pack in her car. I should've told her about the three shadows, and how they fled when I grabbed my stones, but I didn't seem able to.

She sat and pulled out the chair next to her. "So, we caught some more stuff, even though we were only here for a couple hours last time." Her smile had returned full force. "This has to be the most haunted place we've ever been. It's fantastic."

I didn't say anything as I watched the files populate. I counted them and waited for more to appear. None did.

"Only eighteen?"

She laughed, a high, musical sound. "'Only.' Remember what I said about very active hauntings might only have three?" Her face sobered as she pointed to the time stamp on the first file, then the last. "We were here for an hour and forty-eight minutes, and got eighteen. That's a lot. Before we get started,

I extended the clips, so you'll have a better idea of the conversation. There were a few that were totally random."

She clicked the top icon. Laura's voice said, *"...and I shut off the flashlight."*

Indistinct. A moaning sound.

Mandy made an adjustment.

"...the flashlight."

MmmHmm. So quiet that I still almost missed it. A woman's voice, maybe younger? Without reviewing all the files from last time, I didn't know if I needed to add another spirit to my list or if the group had already caught her.

Shivering, I rubbed my upper arms to try to settle the goosebumps. This all had taken on an entirely different meaning now.

Second file.

Sam's voice. *"Remind me, you guys got the other one over there? So, yeah."*

A loud sigh, with just enough voice that I thought it might be a woman. Was there some kind of ghost sorority in my basement?

"That could've been anything." I sat back in my chair, tucking my hands under my thighs.

Mandy shrugged. "It was my recorder that picked it up, the breath was very close, and it wasn't me. But we don't have to count it if you don't want to."

Shaking my head, I leaned forward as she clicked the third file.

Mandy's voice emerged from the speaker. *"Are you alone?"*

Thud. Like a paperback book being dropped on a bed.

The silence stretched so long, I wondered if Mandy had missed her cue to cut it off.

Amy's voice. *"Did anyone else hear that?"*

Mandy replied, *"That bump?"*

The .wav file ended with a beep

I swallowed. "I mean, it's a bump. It could have been any-thing, right?"

The corners of her mouth twitched downward, and her eyes narrowed a smidge. "Of course. We don't have to count that one, either."

I worried that I'd offended her with my criticism. I loved her, and I loved her team, and I had no doubt in my mind they'd done their due diligence and hadn't included EVPs that could be easily explained. But my life was so full of the paranormal right now—even more than when I had been going on inves-tigations on a regular basis—which I didn't want any more of. If there was something I could dismiss, I would do it. We went through several more, finding reasons to discard them.

Before clicking the next file, she reached out but stopped an inch or so shy of touching my arm. "So you know, this was outside. Sam and I were out there, so you have to listen." She clicked.

The sounds of the night came through, muffled and distort-ed. Quiet, but not silent. Nothing I could identify clearly, just the sounds my backyard made after dark. The recorder moved as whoever held it moved their body.

Then, so low I almost missed it, a woman hummed. Three beats, nothing musical about it. Like listening to someone talk through several walls. Something must've shown on my face because she went to the next file without saying anything.

"This next one was recorded in your niece's room while we were setting up."

The voices reminded me of when the group had been wan-dering around, kind of socializing after Mandy had packed up her laptop after the first reveal. The indistinct chatter was cheer-ful, upbeat.

Then my own voice: *"Right?"*

In a moment of perfect timing, a dog barked, sharp and clear. Happy if not excited, and in the same room as the recorder. The talking continued without acknowledging the sound.

My chest tightened and I fought to take a breath. Rexy hadn't been there that night. Ryan had gone to get him while the team investigated.

I ignored Mandy staring at me. "What's next?"

Mandy made some adjustments and the recording played with a fuzzy crackle.

We had been talking. Mandy said something like, "so probably."

Then my voice.

Someone responded.

Here, kitty, kitty, kiiiiiiitty. Loud and clear as a bell, even through the fuzz, over the talking that continued in the background as if no one had heard it. Because they hadn't.

My eyes widened and my heart pounded as I turned my wide-eyed gaze to Mandy. "That was my voice, but that wasn't me. I didn't say that."

Her lips pursed and her brow furrowed as she nodded. "I know."

She moved to the next one.

"If you can make these lights light up, we can talk to you," Laura's fuzzy voice said.

Thank you. A distant voice, but this one had a different dialect or affectation from the others. I couldn't tell the gender of the speaker.

I shivered, wondering if the polite voice was one of the ones that had tormented my niece.

"So, in this next one, Amy and Brian were playing with their K-II meters." She held up a hand, feigning a grimace. "I know I said it wasn't a real investigation. They got a little excited and brought it in to see if they could get any responses."

"Thank you!" Amy said.

I jumped at the loud thumping coming through the speaker.

"That was me," she clarified on the recording. *"Can you do it again for me? Thank you so much!"*

Brian's voice was indistinct. *"...sit on the floor. What a good job!"*

We're sorry. Loud enough that it must have been close to the recorder, it belonged to a woman with a deep voice. Hadn't there been one in the last set of recordings?

Tears welled as Amy kept talking to the spirit that she had no idea was in the room with her. How many times had one of these entities apologized to me, to us, and I hadn't heard them? My mind tore in several directions, between compassion and anger, waffling from fear to curiosity.

Mandy clicked. "This one isn't much, but I wanted you to hear, anyway."

Indistinct talking came through the speakers. I couldn't even tell who the voice belonged to. Then, a single syllable whisper, closer to the recorder than any of the voices.

Mandy played it a few times, fiddling with the sound, but nothing came out but an indecipherable sound, like a breath into the mic.

She skipped to a file near the bottom of the list. "This was from closer to the end of the investigation."

Several people were talking, but I couldn't identify who.

"You got here quick, though," Sam said.

"That one to me sounded like 'here we are'." It sounded like Mandy, but could have been Jodi.

"What does that mean, considering the context?" Sam asked.

My own voice startled me. I hadn't realized I'd been recorded. *"I heard the whisper–"*

Hello. Thank you. Another distinct voice, like a teenage boy whose voice hadn't changed yet.

"–I just didn't hear what it said."

"That's why we keep our recorders going," Sam said.

Mandy touched my hand, and I twitched as I tore my gaze away from the screen and the jumping lines showing audio levels.

"I don't want you to freak out." She gave my arm a short squeeze.

Ha. Freaking out was a long time ago. It might not have been showing on my face, but I had passed freaking out. I don't know when it had happened, but it was definitely way before this moment.

I nodded.

My voice came out over the speaker again, and I fought the urge to cringe, hating the sound of it over a recording. *"Do you want to be here?"* I asked.

Yes, I do. A slow and deliberate statement from yet another woman's voice. Then a staccato like rain pouring on a metal roof, *Yes, I do.*

Oh, freaking out was so, so long ago.

Chapter 25

July 1, 2010

After Mandy's second reveal, Ryan asked me to watch Rexy for him again, and I was so happy to not be alone in the house, I didn't care he didn't give me a reason. He picked the dog up the next day. On his way out, with one hand on the doorframe, he invited me out to dinner, citing the number of meals I'd made for him. We'd agreed on Calhoun's tonight.

In spite of my previous bad experience there, I still loved the place. Was this a date? I wondered, and kept trying to tamp the idea down, reminding myself men like Ryan didn't date women like me. But I agreed to go, anyway, needing some time away from my house that wasn't a classroom or the barn. I didn't bother dressing up any more than usual, but I added a dash of makeup. For my own pride, I did make sure my hair looked nice. Nothing made me feel more uncomfortable than being out in public with weird hair.

The hostess at Calhoun's tried to seat me in the same booth I'd been in before, so I asked to sit in a different section. She led me to the other side of the dining room. "Do you need a corner?"

I shook my head, and she gestured to a booth on the wall. Browsing the menu and waiting for him, I wondered whether he'd show up. It wouldn't be the first time a guy friend asked me somewhere and then didn't show up or call.

The server stopped by, and I ordered Sangria.

My heart leaped when Ryan came through the door. I only had a few seconds to ogle him while he scanned the dining area for me. I drank him in, from his favorite Red Sox cap, to his sinfully fitted jeans, down to the hiking boots he wore everywhere.

Spotting me, he waved at the hostess and headed over, sliding into the booth across from me. "Have you been waiting long?"

On the inside, I sighed. "A few minutes."

"Sorry, got caught up talking to my dad as I walked out the door." He took off his cap and dropped it into the corner of the booth.

My mother would have approved.

"Have you been here before?" He glanced at both sides of the menu before opening it to scan the inside.

"I have a couple of times." I set my menu down on the table, smoothing my hands over it. Where was that drink?

"I haven't. What's good?"

"Depends on what you're into. For steak and potatoes, they make a good ribeye, and their mashed is great. If you want something lighter, they can do a salad as an entrée. No matter what you get, I can't recommend their chipotle ranch enough."

He pursed his lips and nodded, his brown eyes moving across the page. "Good to know, good to know." He dragged out the last syllables, his head bobbing with each one. "What are you getting?"

"I haven't decided yet," I lied. I'd known what I wanted for at least ten minutes, but I picked my menu back up, anyway. "Do you know what you want?"

"Yeah, these burgers look good."

The server stopped by with the waters, and he ordered a Sam Adams. He thanked her, and she walked away.

"Do you want an appetizer or anything?"

The server came back with his bottled beer and smiled at Ryan.

He smiled back. Polite, not flirty. "How about the pretzel bun with queso as a starter. I'll have the fully loaded burger with fries. And I need something to put some chipotle ranch on."

I grinned at that, and then the server turned to me, her smile fading a bit.

For half a second, I thought about the salad, but said, "I'd like the prime rib dip with au jus and fries."

"Sure thing, hon!" She finished jotting on her pad and grabbed our menus. Tucking them under her arm, she strode toward the kitchen. My favorite thing about this place, aside from the home-style food, was definitely the service.

Ryan leaned back, his full attention on me. "So."

"So." I fought not to squirm. "You never told me how you know Sarah, and when I asked Alexandra, she told me I'd have to ask you."

He chuckled.

Warmth flooded through me, and I took a sip of ice water to try to cool off. Where the hell was that drink? I should have been over the blushing and stammering by now. Apparently not. Sitting across from Ryan in a restaurant was somehow different from sitting in my kitchen, where we would have a game or food between us. Or the living room, where we'd eat from the coffee table while we watched a movie.

"I met Sarah backpacking on Chocorua."

I'd figured him for the outdoorsy type with those well-worn hiking boots. I didn't know he liked mountains.

"I think it was six, no, seven years ago." He shrugged one shoulder. "We met on the mountain."

I took another sip of water. "Do people usually meet each other on mountains? It seems like it would be a solo thing, or a group thing."

Red tinted his neck. I'd hit a nerve. "I was in some trouble, and she helped me out."

My gaze didn't leave him, hoping he'd tell me the rest of the story.

His color deepened. "You can either hike on the trail or you can go up the rocks on the side. I was up on the rocks, and I slipped and fell."

Saying nothing, my eyes widened. I'd seen the James Franco movie as soon as it came out on DVD.

"Sarah happened to be hiking the trail, and she helped me out."

In my mind's eye, I envisioned Sarah, standing at barely five-feet, two inches and quiet, dwarfed by Ryan's height. "How did she help you?"

He let go of a breath. "Frankly, she kicked my ass." He chuckled and shook his head. "Threatened to toss me over her shoulder or drag me by the other ankle. She basically had to pull me out of the rocks, splinted my leg, and we limped down the mountain together."

"She made you go back up with her later, didn't she?"

He laughed, showing off perfectly even white teeth. "She did. How did you know?"

Now my face heated. "She and Alexandra were talking about hiking Chocorua, and she told me about some jackass who fell and broke his ankle the first time she went up, and how she had to—" I made air quotes with my fingers again "—rescue him."

He shook his head. "She and Alex are quite the couple."

I looked him in the eye and, deadly serious, I said, "Don't ever let her hear you call her Alex. I told you she hates it, and why."

"Yeah, she's pretty feisty."

"That's a new way to describe it." My face relaxed into a smile. Safer ground. "I think Sarah has brought some calming influence to the table."

"I didn't know her before, but they seem happy together. Sarah's good people."

The pretzel came out from the kitchen, and my mouth started to water.

He cut it in half and took a piece, then tore a chunk off to dip into the queso. "You can have the other half if you want."

I reached out as he reached for his beer, and our hands brushed.

I snatched mine away like I'd been burned. "Sorry."

The expression that crossed his face didn't quite register with me. "It's all good. You're more nervous than a long-tailed cat."

"In a room full of rockers." I took a deep breath. "Sorry, I don't know what's gotten into me tonight. A little on edge, I guess."

"Me, too, actually." He sank back into the booth, resting his arm along the top. "Part of the reason I invited you out is to explain what's been going on now that it's more or less resolved." He shifted to steeple his hands and let a breath out. "You know I was married before."

"Yes."

"And I told you the divorce was ugly."

Had he? I didn't remember him talking about his divorce, but I wasn't surprised. I knew how bad marriages could be. "Yes."

"Part of the reason it was so ugly is she's a train wreck with finances. She maxed out eight credit cards, and then tried to make me pay for it as—" he made air quotes "—marital debt."

I wasn't sure where this conversation would end up, or why he needed to drag it out. I clasped my hands under the table. "Okay."

"Part of the issue had to do with a car."

The bell on the front door clanged as it was yanked open, and a tall redhead in a halter top and painted-on white pants stormed in.

The hostess greeted her with a smile and got snapped at for her trouble.

Stunned and staring now, I found the woman causing the disturbance beautiful in a very classical way, except for the scowl on her flawlessly made-up face.

Ryan turned to see what had captured my attention, and swore under his breath.

"What is it?" I asked, my attention torn from the scene and back to him.

His profile, anyway, since he didn't so much as glance away from the door. He pushed himself to his feet.

The redhead stalked over to our table—impressive, given the height of the heel on her sandals. "You are such a fucking asshole, you know that?" She rummaged around in her bag.

I'm pretty oblivious to things, but even I recognized the Coach logo.

"How about we don't do this here, Kirstie."

Ah, the ex-wife.

Ryan braced his palm on the table and moved toward her so he could leave the booth.

"No, we're doing this now. I can't believe you took my fucking car." She threw a fat white envelope down on the table with enough force, it skidded the entire length of the tabletop and hit the wall. Taken out by the impact, the saltshaker rolled and fell to the floor.

Ryan's jaw set and he didn't acknowledge the envelope, instead focusing all his attention on the titian beauty. He wasn't alone. The diners around us gawked. "Kirstie, let's go outside."

She crossed her arms and put all her weight on one shapely leg, the impeccably pedicured toes of her other foot turned out. She glared at him, her brown eyes practically spitting sparks. "Why? Because you're on a date?" She glared down at me—and here I thought looking down your nose at someone was just an expression—and her lips tightened. "I don't care. I want my car."

"Kirstie, let's take this outside. I'm not talking about it in here." He grabbed his ball cap and pulled it on. "Let me up so we can go outside and talk."

The sound Kirstie made came out halfway between a grunt and a growl. I half expected her to stomp her foot, too.

"Fine, whatever." She backed up toward me, too far into my space for my comfort. She sneered at me again, her lined lip lifting. "I know you said farm girls were hot, but I didn't realize you meant the dairy farm. Or the cows."

My right eyebrow dropped, and I shook my head. "Jesus, I get why she's your ex."

His eyes watered as he coughed into his fist, and a blush bloomed on Kirstie's cheeks.

"How about you keep your dumb bitch mouth shut." She slapped the plate with the bread, and it skidded toward me. The cup with the queso tipped, and I flailed to catch it. "There, shove that in there."

Oh. My. God.

My cheeks heated furiously as people at the bar turned around to gape at us. My hands shook as I righted the dishes on the table, but I met her gaze. "Does being hateful to strangers make you feel better about yourself?" I asked. "It's sad that you think a person's worth is all about their appearance."

Flipping her perfectly curled hair over her shoulder, she stalked out after Ryan, who waited for her with the door held open. His face a stone mask, color still rose in his cheeks as she stormed by him. Although the attention followed her out the door, my face flamed with embarrassment.

As soon as the door closed behind them, I got up and went to the ladies' room.

Convincing myself I wasn't hiding, I stood in a stall and took deep breaths. I had been treated rudely in public before, but usually just stares. Even Josh hadn't gone so far as to compare me to livestock in a crowded room. It may have affected me less if Kirstie had been some random stranger, rather than Ryan's ex. Or maybe if she was closer to a six than a ten.

I didn't like the realization I'd fooled myself about Ryan. How stupid could I be?

I took some time washing my hands before finally emerging. No one spared a glance in my direction as I made my way to our table where Ryan sat, playing with the bottle of beer in front of him. He watched as I slipped into my seat.

I panicked, and my gaze searched the table. "Oh, no. What happened to the envelope?"

He held it up from his lap. "It's fine."

"I'm sorry. I should have thought—"

"Don't be sorry. Wasn't your fault." He sighed. "That is the situation I was going to tell you about. I cosigned a loan for a car she bought. When we got divorced, I had to give her a certain amount of time to get a new loan to get my name off of it, but her credit was bad because of the maxed-out cards.

She kept making the payments, so I let it slide. It wasn't worth going to court again since she was current. She missed a couple of payments, and my credit took a hit. That's what all the texting was about, me trying to explain to her that she needed to get caught up because it was impacting my credit."

I couldn't stop my eyebrows from furrowing. "What texting?"

"Remember the day I went to your house and I, uh, startled you?"

My mind searched for what he meant. I remembered him scaring the bejesus out of me, but texting?

"While you were watching Rexy for me this weekend, a buddy of mine and I went to her house and took the car."

I finally remembered him scowling at his phone while I'd made dinner. It left me more confused. "Wasn't that more than a month ago?" I pressed my finger into the tabletop like an imaginary calendar. "And you took until this weekend to pick it up?"

"She promised to get caught up. She promised a lot of things, and I wanted to give her a chance to follow through." He shrugged. "I keep hoping maybe she'll straighten herself out, so I give her chances, and she keeps disappointing me."

Biting my lower lip, I nodded and sagged into the booth. "And the envelope that she threw at you?"

"It's the money to pay off the car. She probably got it from her parents. Tomorrow, I'm going to get the loan squared away, and she gets her car." He grinned. "And that's it. The car was the last thing connecting us, and now she can go live her life, and I can live mine."

Not knowing what to say, I nodded.

Ryan reached across the table to cover my hand with his, and his brow furrowed as he stared into my eyes. "Are you okay?"

His thumb brushed across my knuckles, and I couldn't breathe. Maintaining eye contact became impossible, and I wanted to hide from the concern in his dark brown depths.

"Yeah, I'm fine."

"I'm sorry about what she said."

"I don't want to talk about it."

He nodded. "Okay."

Our food came, and we ate more or less in silence. Half of my dinner would come home with me to eat later. Being called a cow in a crowded room had killed my appetite.

"Do you want to get dessert?" he asked as the server cleared our plates.

Staring down at the scarred tabletop, I shook my head. "It's getting late, and we've been taking up this table for a while."

"You're right." He stood and waited for me.

Sliding out of the booth, I hesitated to put weight on my left foot, as it had gone completely numb from mid-calf down. Naturally, the moment I tried to take a step, my ankle rolled. I fell right into him, and he caught me by my elbows. It was like falling into my horse. Solid muscle. My face flamed to the roots of my hair.

"You okay?" The sides of his mouth twitched, but he didn't actually smile. Just almost. His gaze searched mine, and then moved down.

I regained my feet. "Yes, just embarrassed." Humiliated, more like it. "Let's go outside so I can get some air, please."

The brisk breeze across the parking did a lot to cool off my face, and I released a pent-up breath. The lights marching across the parking lot around us obscured all but the brightest stars.

He cleared his throat, attracting my attention How was it possible for him to look even more appealing? He tucked his hands into the pockets of his jeans as we walked, and he watched his feet.

"I had a question for you, if you don't mind."

I nodded, tensing my muscles to suppress a shiver. The cool breeze forewarned of an impending storm. "I reserve the right to not answer."

"Sarah and Alex—I mean, Alexandra—said you swore off relationships."

"That isn't a question."

"Why did you swear off?"

I couldn't look at him and answer this particular question. We walked in the general direction of my car and I took my time, staring at the ground. After what had happened tonight, I didn't have anything to lose by answering honestly.

"I got married to someone I barely knew, and spent a lot of time trying to make it work. It never did. I convinced myself that if I could figure out what thing I was doing wrong, it would work out. We fought all the time. He spent a lot of time telling me I wasn't good enough and how flawed I was." I crossed my arms under my breasts. "When I started gaining weight, it gave him more ammo, and it spiraled downward after that." I tipped my chin to meet his gaze, defiant. He'd asked. It's not like I had decided to bring this up out of the blue. "I don't want to get into detail, but let's just say that him beating me up is probably the easiest part to talk about."

A car drove by, filling the silence between us. He didn't say anything. Waiting for me to finish, I realized.

I started walking again, and he fell into step beside me. We stopped behind my car. I glanced at him, but his gaze scanned the parking lot. In for a penny, in for a pound, so might as well tell him the whole story.

"I don't talk about it, but when he died in Afghanistan, I felt more relieved than anything else." I flipped a rock to the side with my toe. "I mean, I was sad, and I loved him, but at the same time, I could finally breathe again.

"I learned to accept condolences, but every time someone said 'I'm sorry for your loss,' I wanted to scream. No one wanted to hear anything other than my hero husband had died for his country. The ultimate sacrifice. His mother insisted on a funeral with full military honors, and she shot death glares at me over his casket when I couldn't shed a single tear." I waited for the horror at my confession to contort Ryan's features, but his expression remained as impassive as before.

Shrugging, I kept talking. "I felt really guilty for a long time, not being sad enough. And the what-if thinking, like maybe he would have been different when he came home. I struggled with that, and every time I tried to do something about my weight, I ended up gaining more, so it was tough for me to get back out there. When I finally did, I was treated like I was less than. I wasn't treated like I would've been if I was smaller—and I know what that's like because I used to be fit and in great shape. I was in the Air Force, for fuck's sake." The words came out harder than I'd intended, but I couldn't stop now. I told him about what Josh had said, and how he'd taken a call and disappeared. "I wasn't disappointed, either, because he was obviously a jerk, but it stung to be so blatantly rejected like that. I didn't know how to respond, you know?"

I paused for breath.

He had that unfamiliar expression again. I shifted under his gaze.

"Sarah told me the last guy you went out with was a jerk, but I didn't realize how much of one."

"That's one way to put it." My heart sank. "I gave up after that, sick of guys who were total jerks, or creeps, or being some kind of weird fetish for them. Asking me if I'd be open to being friends with benefits, because apparently, I'm good enough to fuck, but not good enough to date." I shuddered, only partly from the brisk wind that had kicked up. "I deserve better than that, and I'd rather be alone, honestly."

He stuck his hands deeper into his pockets. "I'm sorry you went through that."

"Thanks?" Still stinging from Kirstie's comment, and now raw from reliving a dark chapter of my all-too-recent history, I mumbled a goodnight and reached for my door handle.

His hand covered mine, and my gaze flew to his, confused.

"Do you mind if I follow you home?"

My brows rose. "You mean back to the dairy farm?"

He shook his head. "Please don't let what she said get to you."

"Kind of hard." I shrugged and tried to swallow around the painful knot occupying the back of my throat. "Words hurt, and I guess something let what she said hurt more than it would have normally. Maybe because she was right. Guys who look like—" I gestured to him "—don't go out with girls like—" I gestured at myself. "It's just, every time I think I'm okay with it, something happens to remind me I'm considered less than a person because of my weight. And do you know what? I may not meet the—" I made air quotes with my fingers "—standard of beauty because of my size, but I tried all the diets and all the fads, and I realized I could be okay with who I am, and I really am at this point." My traitorous lower lip trembled into a frown at the lie and tears burned behind my eyelids but I refused to cry in front of him.

His hands went to my shoulders, and his gaze absorbed my features. "You're funny, and kind, and a good person. I'd rather be with someone like that than a supermodel any day."

My heart thudded, and the lump in my throat threatened to cut off my air. I clenched my teeth and tightened my lips to stop the damned quivering of my lips, straightening my frown. Someone like me. Not me. I'd already known, but the confirmation stung. I pulled out of his grip and cleared my throat as

I unlocked my door. In a minute, I'd be out of here, and he wouldn't see the tears welling.

I had to clear my throat again to speak as I sank into the driver's seat. "I'm really tired, so I think I'm going to go home and go to bed."

I yanked my seatbelt too hard. Of course, it locked. Precious moments wasted releasing it. A tear escaped as I pulled it, slowly this time, across my torso.

He leaned on my open car door and ducked down. "Really, you shouldn't listen to her."

"Thank you for dinner, Ryan. Have a good night."

I slammed my door a little harder than I'd intended to, but at least I made it out of the parking lot before I started crying.

Chapter 26

July 1, 2010

My front porch light beckoned from the road, but the house cast shadows across parking area. I fell out of my car and hurried to get into the glow spilling onto the ground. After being in the dark last night, and my skin already prickling from an unseen gaze, I didn't want to be out here by myself. There was nothing there—there never was—but I couldn't make the feeling go away, so I'd avoid it.

I calmed myself down a bit by the time I stepped through the front door and turned the overhead light on. My hand still on the switch, both light bulbs went out with two loud *pops* in rapid succession.

I flipped the last switch, and the lamp in the corner turned on. I waited, I'm not sure for what, my hand resting on the plate. Finally, I let my arm drop to my side, and I wrote it off as coincidence. I was sure if I researched, I would find that CFLs always popped when they burned out. Why they would do so after only a couple of months, though, I didn't know.

Taking off my shoes, I had a bad case of the creeps, like someone watched me from the rear porch. I walked to the kitchen for a glass of water, turning on lights as I went until even the porch light glowed. I couldn't turn my back to the door, so I leaned against the counter and faced it instead.

My phone rang as I finished loading the dishwasher. Ryan's number appeared on the screen.

"Hello?" I sounded wary.

"I wanted to make sure you're okay."

I crossed my arm over my stomach and tucked my hand under my other elbow. "I'm about as good as I'm going to be. I've had a long day."

"Do you want to talk about it?"

I released a deep breath. "Mandy was back last week, a day or so before I watched Rexy for you. They found more EVPs."

He hesitated. "Why did you have them come back out?"

I sighed again. "There's been a lot of weird stuff going on that I can't explain. And Alexandra has been here twice, and both times, she saw something."

"I'm sure there's a rational explanation for it."

"If there is, I can't figure it out." I wiped my face with my hand. "Don't you believe me?"

"I'd like to. You're what I would consider an intelligent and rational person." The weight of his pause came across the line. "Maybe Alexandra was dreaming?"

"While she was wide awake?" I hesitated. "Rexy saw something, too."

"My dog saw a ghost?"

"Kind of." I explained how Rexy had gone to the exact spot where the ghost dog had disappeared. I went on about how Rexy had chased something around the corner and into the woods, and kept dropping his ball in front of the wall. "The first time we were watching TV, and he tracked something across the room, too."

"Could be a coincidence."

"It could be." I found myself not wanting to talk about this with him. Not that he was judging me, or didn't believe me, I didn't have the energy to try to convince him about my experiences. "Thank you for calling to check up on me. I'm fine. I'm just really tired."

"Okay. Have a good night."

I flipped my phone shut and stared at it, not sure about anything anymore.

Knowing sleep would be elusive, I forced myself to follow my bedtime routine anyway, and got into bed. Lying there in the dark, my mind raced. Too much had happened in the last few days. I was overwhelmed, and that didn't even include dealing with summer classes. The summer sessions were short, the same fourteen-week classes crammed into four weeks. I already had finals looming on the horizon. My life was skidding out of control, and I couldn't stop it.

My eyes finally started to drift closed when the lights appeared on the ceiling. First one, then two. Bright, as if a flashlight was being bounced around outside. Too bad the blinds were closed.

I froze, not wanting to breathe. Afraid to move.

Lightning struck outside, and I jumped. The loud rumble of thunder had me up and out of bed. I wasn't going to sleep right now, and there was no point in trying. Figuring I'd watch some TV to try to shut my brain off, I headed down the hallway. My hands hit the open closet door.

Something welled up inside me I couldn't name. I grabbed my small hammer and a screwdriver out of my junk drawer. Within seconds, I had pulled the hinge pins. For good measure,

I put the closet door flat on the floor in my craft room and closed the door firmly behind me.

"Not going to open anymore now, are you?"

Nothing on TV interested me, so after fifteen minutes of flipping through channels, I shut it off. In the semi-darkness of the living room, I draped one arm over my eyes. Maybe I'd sleep better out here.

Footsteps thudded on the front porch. My heart leaped and my eyes flew open. If I sat up a few inches, I'd be able to see who was there.

My brain chose that moment to replay one of Mandy's EVPs.

Sorry, but it's very dark out here.

"Nope." Pushing myself off the couch, I went into my craft room. The closet door on the floor gave me the creeps, so I rearranged the bedroom closet and shoved it in there. I used an old USB cord to tie the doors shut.

I twitched my mouse to wake up the computer, and squinted at the monitor as I sat down in my chair.

Hi Mandy,

Sorry to bother you, but I just had a quick question. Is it typical for there to be an increase in activity after you've done an investigation? After you left, I saw lights on the bedroom wall again with nothing outside to create them (unless we have a 50-watt lightning bug outside). I seem to notice an increase after you've visited.

Again, sorry to bother you, it's not a big deal, I'm just curious.
Mel

I spent more time than I should have messing around on my computer, playing Angry Birds, and finding more of my high school classmates on Facebook. My email pinged.

Hey there,

It definitely could happen that the activity increases after our visit. They know you are "aware" of them. How long were the lights there? Did they move in any specific pattern? Don't think that you're bugging me at all. I'm here to answer any questions you may have, whenever you need me!

My computer shut down, and I crept back into bed. I think I may have dozed, but when dawn's light slipped under the bedroom door, I hadn't slept at all. Tired of tossing and turning, I got up and spent some time on my computer, breezing through my online final. Getting through multiple-choice tests was one of the many skills I'd gotten from my time in the Air Force.

Out of habit, I opened my email client and frowned at an email from Laura. I scanned it, and my frown deepened. She'd left PRISM to form her own group, and wanted to bring her new team up to do an investigation.

I wavered. Some of the EVPs Mandy and I decided had natural causes were from Laura.

Without responding, I shot an email off to Mandy, asking her why Laura would be emailing me, then pushed myself away from my computer. I needed to get out of the house.

Chapter 27

July 3, 2010

At this point in time, I had more or less resigned myself to my house being haunted, regardless of what Ryan thought about it. It was a lot like when I'd been trapped in my marriage, but at least in this situation, I felt slightly less weird about asking for help.

Today was one of the first real scorchers of the summer with heat hitting the upper eighties.

I took my first shower of the day to cool off and sat at my computer wrapped in a towel, my wet hair brushed away from my face and dripping onto my shoulders. Without much interest, I did some more research about the house and the general area, and came up with a lot more nothing. I'd emailed a couple of places who might have a lead on the unknown phrase. The one person who bothered to respond confirmed in a very terse email that it belonged to the Algonquin language family, but refused to translate.

At the bottom of my new messages, Mandy had emailed in response to my communication the other night. I snorted at the length of the message—practically a novel coming from her.

Melissa,

Laura decided to form her own group for a few different reasons, the main one being a disagreement on team dynamics. She had her opinions on how a group should be led, which didn't coincide with ours. You are not the first person to contact me, confused about why Laura has reached out, and we told her we are aware of her doing this and have asked her to stop. I'm very sorry she did this. I'm not sure when she contacted you, but hopefully after our email to her, she won't do it again.

Be assured, if you had them up there, you wouldn't be causing any trouble for our groups. We have wished Laura the best of luck for her crowd, despite everything that has happened. We can't, though, in good faith, say any evidence that she collects is accurate, which you experienced firsthand.

On a different note, I wanted to let you know I was recently made aware of a new group that has formed in the area. Their name is "Southern Maine Extreme Ghost Hunters Society." I may have spoken to the founder once, but I'm not exactly sure of what their investigation techniques involve or how professional they are. I do know you're looking for a group which operates more on the spiritual side, and I believe that hers does. As I said before, though, I can't really tell you much other than that. If you want to contact her, I'll paste the web address below. Her name is Debbie.

Where I'm not too familiar with her group, it is best I hear things from you as well as anything they share with me. That way, nothing gets missed or miscommunicated.

I had talked with Debbie briefly about a week or so ago, she was having problems with her site, and I was trying to help her out. I mentioned your house to her, but didn't go into much detail, as I wanted to talk to you about it first. Hopefully, they are on the level and can help you out. If they can get some specifics, then it may help to produce more targeted evidence when we come out. I'm not sure if she has my contact info, but feel free to give it to her if you both decide I should be contacted.

Talk to you soon, stay cool, and take care! If you have any more questions, email me any time!

Mandy

P.S. - if you're up for it, we'd like to do an overnight investigation at your house. Let me know what you think!

I shot her a quick reply.

Thanks for the lead! Also, I just wanted to let you know my research into the "unknown phrase" has hit a dead end. It has been confirmed the language is Native American, it is most likely Passamaquoddy, but the shamans and other individuals that have knowledge of the language don't even want to discuss it because it's a message from the spirit world.

The group Mandy directed me to didn't have a great site (and what an awful name), but they had people on the team who might be able to help. My eyebrows went up at the size of the team as I scrolled through everyone's description, but I focused on the bios at the end. A spiritual healer and two sensitives. I shrugged. Not sure what they'd be able to do—and not sure I fully believed in them, anyway—I used the contact button and sent a brief message about what had been going on. Mandy had done so much to help me throughout (and all volunteer) that I mentioned her by name, as well as her group.

As I got ready to log off my email pinged.

P.P.S.- I know you had mentioned something earlier about something keeping your niece awake at night. When you have a chance to speak with anyone from Southern Maine Extreme Ghost Hunters Society (that's a mouthful, isn't it?) this would definitely be good information to let them in on. It doesn't sound like anything is trying to harm or scare anyone, but it's still very bothersome and unnerving, nonetheless! I was thinking if you are up for it, maybe we could do this:
You have SMEGHS up to see if they can get specifics (i.e. names, dates, etc.) and then have them debrief us on what they were able to get. Our team can then come back there and have a more focused investigation, asking certain questions that pertain to what info they may have gotten. From what we have so far, we definitely know there's a man, a woman, and a dog, but maybe the sensitives on SMEGHS can find out more.
I hope that all goes well with Debbie's group. If you need me to contact them and fill them in with everything, I will be more than happy to do so! Definitely keep me in the loop, and we will plan to come out, if it works for you, after their investigation.

As I hit reply, my notification pinged again, and I groaned.

P.P.P.S.- Would you mind if I posted that EVP up on a few boards to see if I can get any information? I would of course keep your name and location confidential. I want to see what others can get from it. It's interesting that no one wants to translate this for you. I can't imagine how frustrating that must be! Have you seen anything else unusual lately?

Another ping.

P.P.P.P.S.- In the meantime, if you're searching on your own, please watch out for scam artists who rely on "smoke and mirrors" in order to create a name for themselves. There are so many out there who claim to have a gift, but cannot provide actual proof of it. If you do end up finding someone on your own, let me know who they are so I can ask around about them to see if anyone might be able to vouch for their validity. I will be on the lookout!

I hesitated now to respond because I might get yet another message, so I replied to her most recent one with a simple, "Thanks."

The smoke and mirrors comment made me think of Ryan's mother. It might be better for me to not say anything to him about psychics visiting my house.

With a few days before the start of the second summer session, I found myself without much to do. After getting dressed, I aimlessly drifted around my house, cleaning things that didn't need to be cleaned before I finally set up on the couch with a cross-stitch kit and turned on a History Channel documentary marathon.

This particular kit had been a gift from Alexandra, two white wolves in birch trees on black fabric. I'd started it a long time ago, but I hadn't had the motivation to sit and work on it for a while.

As I pulled the fabric and folded pattern out of their plastic bag, something clattered to the floor. Thinking my embroidery scissors had slipped out of the bag, I bent down to pick them up.

My missing sapphire and diamond wedding band lay glittering on the floor.

In disbelief, I picked it up, staring as I turned it over in my hand. Inside the bag, my engagement ring winked back at me. Alexandra had given me this kit long after I had stored the rings in my jewelry box. Even if they hadn't been collecting dust in the box, I couldn't come up with a single reason why the rings would be in with the kit.

Sitting on the couch, I absorbed myself in the project, putting the rings out of my mind.

Ryan texted not long after, letting me know he had a property catastrophe he had to deal with, so he wouldn't be coming over tonight. With long hours of being alone stretching in front of me, I decided to at least pretend to be productive. Except for folding, doing laundry was probably the laziest of the chores, and at least it would give me a reason to get up and stretch now and again. With the basket balanced on my hip, I headed down the basement stairs with one hand trailing on the banister.

Halfway down, something solid hit me in the back, right between the shoulder blades. My upper body jerked forward. I dropped the basket and caught the railing with my other hand. I swung forward and landed on the next step, hard. My bad knee buckled, and only my white-knuckled grip on the rail stopped me from going the rest of the way to the concrete below.

The air around me crackled, and the hairs on my neck and arms stood upright. I shivered as a cold gust of wind swept past me.

Leaving the basket lying where it had fallen and clothes scattered on the bottom steps, I took the stairs up two at a time. Without even thinking, I snatched my keys and ran out the front door to my car. I backed all the way out of my driveway so fast, the rear end fishtailed. I didn't stop at the end of the drive and backed right into the road. I slammed the car into Drive and hit the gas so hard, my tires squealed for several seconds before my car lurched forward.

My brain finally engaged when I got to the stop sign at the end of the road. I gasped for air and unrolled the window, suddenly suffocating in the confines of my car.

I only had one place to go, so put on my blinker and headed for Alexandra's.

No one was home when I got there, so I sat on the side porch and waited. My cell phone had been abandoned in my house, and I realized I had no idea what time it was, or when—if—someone would be home.

Alexandra's electric-blue jeep pulled into the drive, and I waved. Standing, I waited for her to come up the walkway. In leggings and a tank top with her hair pulled back into a ponytail, she must have come from the gym.

"How's it going?" I wiped my sweating palms on my jeans.

"By the look on your face, I'm going to say better than you." She sorted at her keys as she walked up and isolated the one for the back door. "What happened?"

My hesitation lasted for less than the space of a breath. "Something pushed me down the stairs."

She nodded, as if she had already known. She passed me and put her key into the lock. "I was worried this would happen." She glanced at me over her shoulder. "Are you okay?"

"I guess so." Following her into the house, I was immediately overwhelmed by the acrid odor of burned cinnamon.

Alexandra read my face loud and clear, and half-rolled her eyes. "We had a housekeeper come in today, and Sarah freaked out that the house stank because of the diapers, so she put some cinnamon or something in the oven. The whole house reeks of it." She dropped her keys on the counter and picked up the mail. "Come with me." She strode out of the room and I followed like a lost puppy.

We went into her bedroom, and she booted up her computer. "I've been doing some research. I think you need some actual help instead of someone pointing out the obvious."

"What do you mean?"

"I mean, you need an exterminator, not someone to tell you there are mice in your walls. You already know that."

She opened her bookmarks menu and clicked a page for a local paranormal investigation group. "I had no idea there were so many of these groups." She clicked a few more times, and her printer whirred.

She pulled the page off the tray and held it against her chest, concern in her blue eyes.

"Mel, I love you. You're in over your head. When it was just bumps in the night, that's not a big deal. Now you have spirits who are hurting you—and tried to hurt my daughter—because they want attention. You need to figure this out." Her speech complete, she handed me the paper.

Nothing she'd said was wrong, so I nodded my agreement as my gaze scanned the page. This was the same group Mandy had recommended. I had already reached out to them, which calmed me for some reason.

"You can stay here as long as you want, and feel free to use my computer to contact these guys. But definitely contact them."

Chapter 28

July 16, 2010

I cursed myself for being late, still dressed in my riding clothes that didn't fit, but were better than nothing, and grimy with a layer of dust sticking to my glow from the humidity. I took a few deep breaths on my way up the driveway to calm my nerves. Six other cars were parked next to the house, so I pulled off to the side and onto the sparse grass I called a lawn.

Kicking the dirt off my riding boots against the steps, I tried to see into the house with no luck. A veritable mountain of soft cases for cameras and laptops cluttered the porch next to the door. Taking another deep breath, I stepped into my home.

Taken aback by the crowd of people, I had to ground myself by ignoring the mob in the kitchen and checking out the four people standing in my living room. Ryan, here to meet them for me, wore baggy shorts and flip-flops instead of his jeans and hiking boots for once. A pale woman of medium height with short blonde hair and an expression I could only describe as pinched. A heavier-set woman with her naturally curly hair pulled away from her face with skinny side braids. And an older gentleman with lined, tawny skin, large ears, and a broad nose. The curly haired woman wore a floral blouse and flowy pants, but everyone else had dressed simply in shorts and t-shirts.

All eyes in the living room—the people in the kitchen mustn't have seen me—turned on me as I entered, and my face heated. My riding tights were bunching at the knees and slipping over my hips in addition to me being grungy.

"Give me a minute to clean up and change, please? I'll be right back." Ducking my head, I excused myself and headed down the hallway.

Behind me, the small group chatted about the weather.

I rushed through washing up and threw on the first thing my hands touched. I ran my fingers through my short, sweat-soaked hair a few times and called it good.

Walking back out, I felt much better. I stuck my hand out to the closest person, the woman in the floral blouse. "I'm Melissa."

She smiled at me, making no move to shake my hand.

Embarrassed, I started to drop my arm, but she grabbed it.

"I'm Ruth Keene. No relation to the author of *Nancy Drew*."

I laughed because that's where my mind had immediately gone. "Nice to meet you. I hope you don't mind, but I love your highlights."

Ruth smiled and patted her mahogany curls. She introduced me to Alan Bouchard. "We're old friends. He's a Penobscot Elder." She gestured to the blonde woman. "Debbie Michaud is our team leader and the group founder."

Nodding, I wondered about the people in the kitchen, or where the other spiritual investigator was. "Very nice to meet you all."

"We have two more investigators coming," Debbie said. "They should be here any minute."

My eyes widened, but I didn't say anything. This team was massive. A quick scan told me the total group would come up to thirteen people. Paranormal groups were usually eight or less for a reason. I was already not a huge fan of crowds, and Debbie also gave off a nervous energy that put me on edge. I couldn't help but sag with relief when she went outside to meet the late arrivals.

Ruth smiled at me. A knowing smile that made me uncomfortable. "Do you know what you are?"

"I don't think I know what you mean?" I had a dozen sarcastic responses lined up. Pat on the back for me for not saying a single one of them.

"Do you ever feel really tired after being around people?" She tipped her head forward and sideways. The gold hoops dangling from her ears gleamed.

Ryan emerged from the kitchen, a bottle of beer in his hand. He leaned against the doorway, watching me.

"I figured that's because I'm kind of introverted."

Ruth's curls bounced against her shoulders as she shook her head. "You have it backward. You avoid people because they make you tired." She looked at Alan, then back at me. Her russet eyes stared through me. "You're a filter."

Ryan coughed behind his hand, and Ruth glared at him.

"You take in the negativity from the people around you. They leave feeling better, but you get loaded down with their crap, for lack of a better word. That's why some people are more exhausting than others." She glanced at Ryan again, and her smile became forced. "Where is your restroom?"

I directed her down the hall.

Alan hadn't spoken yet, and something about him made me edgy. Like I'd done something wrong, and he was waiting to scold me.

His eyes narrowed, and he put his hands behind his back. "How long have you lived here?"

Easy question. "Since spring."

He nodded as if he'd expected that exact answer.

Ryan leaned against the wall, ankles crossed, beer poised at his lips. His expression blended wry amusement and disdain.

"Thank you so much for coming out here to meet everyone. When Debbie called and said they were on their way, I was really in a bind."

He shrugged and sipped his beer.

"I know this isn't really your cup of tea, so if you want to go, that's fine."

Ryan stuck his lower lip out and shook his head. "Nah, I'll stay. I might learn something."

My eyebrows raised.

Debbie popped her head in the front door, saving Ryan from the comment I wanted to make. I was pretty sure I'd never get used to strangers coming and going without knocking.

Debbie jerked her chin at me. "We're ready. Can you come outside while the team sets up cameras?"

Two women stood on the walkway holding voice recorders, and Debbie started talking to them. With her back to me, I was excluded from the conversation, but I gathered their names were Michaela and Kristin.

Standing on the lawn just off the stone walkway, I watched as the pile of equipment disappeared into the house. Even if I'd been introduced to everyone on the team, there was no way for me to remember everyone's name. We walked around the house, and I explained some of the activity that had been going on. No one responded, so I fell into an awkward silence.

All four of us went through the back door. The living room had emptied except for several cameras.

Debbie adjusted something on the recorder in her hand. "I'm going to head into the basement. I'll be right back."

My gaze followed her down the stairs, but I hesitated at the top. Someone had picked up my clothes and put them back in the basket, which sat in the middle of the floor. I still couldn't bring myself to go down the stairs after a week. I had done my laundry at Alexandra's.

A young man appeared in the hallway with spiked, blond-tipped hair, long in front and shaved in the back. He flipped the strands out of his face without breaking eye contact.

"Where are Ruth and Alan?" one of the investigators asked.

Michaela answered from behind me before I had a chance. "I don't know, but it's not fair that all they do is tag along and don't have to do any actual work."

The two of them launched into a conversation about the unfairness of it all while they made their way back outside as if I wasn't there.

Shaking my head, I walked down the hall, searching for someone else in the group.

Alan stood in my office, gazing out the window. "There's a horse here."

My eyes rolled, but only on the inside. Great. I had pictures of my bay pinto mare all over the house and on the walls. He must have seen them.

"Oh, yeah?"

He nodded. "Yes. It's staying here with you."

I resisted the urge to cross my arms over my chest. "What does it look like?" I struggled to keep my face neutral, but he was about to expose himself as a fraud.

His brow furrowed. "Tall, reddish brown." He touched his forehead and dragged his index and middle fingers together down to his chin. "A wide, white marking in the middle of his face."

My jaw dropped. I'd had the horse, a gelding exactly like Alan had described, euthanized so long ago, I'd put him from my mind.

Alan nodded, watching my reaction. "He said he is at peace, and he says thank you."

Tears came, and I dashed them away with the back of my hand. I still struggled sometimes with the decision I'd made. Hearing this man tell me the horse was okay did something for me, like a weight off my soul. I clung to it.

Clearing my throat, I bumped my mouse to take my computer out of sleep mode. "If you don't mind, there's an EVP I'd like you to listen to."

He nodded and stood behind me, staring over my shoulder at the screen.

"...definitely seen it, too."

Lo, hiyanna

He stepped forward with his gaze focused on the media player. "Play it again."

I played it several more times at his request, then started replaying automatically. I lost count of the number of times I'd hit the circle arrow before he had me stop.

"I don't know what it says, but it sounds like Algonquin. I'll ask the Clan Grandmother." He nodded toward the screen. "Play a couple more?"

He didn't say anything, nor did his expression change as we went through the list of files. He didn't take any interest in the other ones until he got to the one with the spirit apologizing.

"Play it again."

"...without making noise."

I'm sorry, but it's very dark out here.

Nodding like he understood, he gestured for me to follow him.

We went out the front door to a white Ford Focus. He pulled out two pieces of wire bent into an L shape. The short side of the L rested inside a hollow white tube handle while the long side swung freely.

Holding one in each fist, the wires swung outward, away from each other. "These are dowsing rods."

I nodded like I had a clue what he meant.

He walked slowly in an ever-widening circle. When he got near my well cap, the rods crossed. They crossed again in the yard behind the dining room window. He went to the parking area, and the rods crossed. Then again in the small, wooded area between my house and the road. Over and over again, the rods crossed, and the more the rods crossed, the more Alan frowned.

"What's wrong?"

He twitched as if he had forgotten my presence and I'd startled him. "I'm not sure yet. Oh."

I followed his line of sight to two women emerging from around the back of the house. An impossibly tall woman with dark hair smiled, while her red-haired companion stood more my height.

Alan waved me over. "This is Rosa and this is Leigh."

My hand came up in a half wave.

Two more investigators walked through the leaves behind my house in the rapidly falling darkness, distracting me.

"Rosa is a Reiki healer, and Leigh is the other sensitive on the team with Ruth."

Ah. "How are things going so far?"

Leigh shrugged a shoulder, her expression bored. "Hard to tell yet."

Rosa's eyes bored into me, and I shifted my weight.

Ruth stepped onto the front porch, waving Alan over, and Leigh went with him, leaving me alone with Rosa. She asked me a few questions about the house, which I had already gone over ad nauseam with Debbie before she'd even set up the investigation. How did this information not get shared with the team?

Rosa nodded in all the right places, but I could tell she wasn't really interested. Her gaze slipped over my shoulder, and she smiled.

Turning to see what had caught her attention, it turned out to be Ryan walking around the side of the house with the spikey-haired investigator.

"Well, hello," Rosa purred, sticking out her hand to shake Ryan's.

He took it automatically with a nod. "Ryan."

She bit her lower lip as she examined him from his feet to his eyes and then back to his chest. When she actually batted her lashes at him, I wanted to slap her. "Rosa. Very, very nice to meet you."

To his credit, Ryan's tone didn't change as he gave her a neutral response.

Three people walked past me—people I had no clue who they were—and I had to excuse myself.

Stalking into the house, the door hit a camera bag on the floor behind it. Without pausing, I headed to my bedroom and closed the door behind me. I didn't turn on the light—I had no idea what someone might have set up in here—and pressed my forehead against the cool wood to take a deep breath.

"Hello."

I jumped about a foot in the air, spinning to find the owner of the voice behind me. Someone I recognized, at least. "Hi, Leigh."

"I'm glad I got to catch you alone."

The way she said it set my skin crawling. Maybe I was just wound up from all the people and the chaos. I wanted to be alone, but definitely not with her.

"I know who's in your house," she whispered, leaning toward me.

"Oh, yeah?" I remembered Mandy's analysis of a man, a woman, and a dog. I wished I knew what Mandy had told Debbie, and what Debbie, in turn, had shared with the rest of the team.

"Yes. A woman. And she died here."

I hoped her sight in the dark wasn't good enough for her to see the wince on my face. What a cliché. And obviously, Debbie hadn't passed on the fact I was the only owner or occupant of this house since it had been built.

"She was pregnant and had a drug problem. Drunk one night, she fell down the stairs, leaving her kids alone for two days before someone found them."

Now I really didn't want to be alone with her. What a nut. I made an appropriate noise and slipped out the door into the hallway.

Even with all the lights off, the house wasn't completely dark with dusk lingering outside. I stepped across the hall into Olivia's room and checked to make sure I was alone before shutting myself in. Pressing my shoulders against the door, I took several deep breaths.

Someone turned the knob and tried to push it open. My tolerance wearing thin, I squeezed my eyes shut and clenched my teeth.

Tap, tap, tap. "Is there a spirit holding the door closed right now?" an unfamiliar voice asked from the hall.

Out of patience, I flung the door open. The two investigators in the hall jumped.

"Excuse me," I said, pushing between them. I needed to get outside, to go get some air. I didn't know if Ryan was still out there with Rosa or not.

Half a dozen people stood between me and the front door, so probably for the first time in months, I slipped out the back door, not caring it was after dark, or that the light was off. Darkness had finally staked its claim on the landscape, but I didn't hesitate as I walked down the gravel path around the corner of the house into the parking area. Giving my eyes a few minutes to adjust, I not only realized I was alone outside, but half of the cars were gone.

As I wandered around the front of the house, several investigators carried equipment to cars. Not believing my own eyes, I watched them leave. If I'd had my phone on me, I would have checked the time.

Debbie emerged from my front door with two investigators close behind. She waved at me and headed for one of the few remaining vehicles.

"Are you leaving?" I didn't need to know the exact time to be confident she and her team hadn't even been here for an hour. Two women got into a car without a word to me and backed out, and I waited for them to pass before I walked over to Debbie. "You're going?"

"Yeah, we didn't get anything. We'll call you if anything shows up on the EVPs." Without another word, she got into her car and left, leaving me dumbstruck in the driveway.

The front porch lights came on, and I squinted against the brightness.

Alan emerged on the porch.

From behind me, Ruth said my name, and I jumped.

She put a hand on my shoulder. "You okay?"

"Yeah, just jumpy. Sorry."

She shook her head. "No need to apologize." Raising her arm, she flagged Alan down. "We're going to head out, too. Alan and I will confer and see what we come up with." From a pocket, she produced a business card.

An address in Sanford. I didn't recognize the street name, but that wasn't saying much.

"I did a little cleanse in the house. Not much, but it should help."

I had a thousand questions and didn't know what to say.

Alan tapped me on the shoulder and held his hand out to me.

I gave him Ruth's card.

He scrawled a phone number on the back with a tiny golf pencil. "You should hear from us by next weekend. If anything happens again, you can call either one of us."

He watched as Ruth got into her car, and then nodded at me. "Before I leave, I wanted to let you know I think I know what is happening here."

I had nothing left in me. My shoulders sagged. "Yeah?"

He nodded, his gaze toward the trees at the edge of the driveway instead of me. "There are three in the house." His expression softened. "One of them is a grandmother. She's here with the dog. It's–"

Ruth beeped the horn, and Alan waved at her. Turning back to me with penetrating eyes, he nodded toward the card in my hand. "Call me."

"I will. Thanks." I tucked the card into my back pocket as he walked away.

Ryan stood on the porch, leaning on the railing. I joined him and waved as the last car left the driveway and disappeared down the road.

His arm slid around my shoulder. "How are you feeling?"

Shrugging out from under his arm, I reached for the door. "I don't know how I feel about psychics and shamans, but

Alan knew something I don't know how he would've known." Before he could say anything else, I turned to him. "I don't think I want to talk about this right now. I'm still kind of freaked out."

"What can I do?"

My face heating, I asked him to walk down to the basement in front of me.

With a shrug, he trotted down the stairs. At the bottom, he flipped on the light. He turned, and stared up at me with one foot on the bottom step and his hand on the rail.

I followed behind slowly with my hand tightly gripping the railing. Nothing tried to push me down the stairs this time, at least.

I picked up the laundry basket. "I should get this started." My calm voice didn't hint at how hard my heart pounded in my chest.

He nodded, his expression unreadable. "Do you want me to wait down here?"

"No, I'm okay."

I wasn't sure which emotion would win the battle inside me, fear or stupidity. Loading my laundry into the machine, I had to force myself to not look over my shoulder. That I struggled made me feel like an idiot. The fight continued even as I went up the stairs as quickly as I could without running.

Ryan stood in the middle of the living room on his phone. He glanced up at me. "What do you want to do tonight?"

"I would really, really like to get out of here."

"Where do you want to go?

I sagged with exhaustion. "Literally anywhere but here."

Chapter 29

July 19, 2010

Unlike after Mandy and her team investigated, my house remained still and silent after Debbie's group left. For days, there were no slamming or opening doors, no footsteps, and no unexplained music. I cherished the quiet, not knowing how long it might last.

After finishing up my assignment, I opened my email client. I deleted a couple of obvious spam emails and unsubscribed from two lists. I also had an email from Mandy.

Hi Melissa,

I saw some pictures of the investigation posted on Debbie's My-space account...you had quite a full house! How did everything go? I'm assuming by her posting pictures on public sites she must have already done a reveal with you. Were they able to get anything? I'm not sure what their plans are, but if you would like, we could

come out for the overnight sometime in the next few weeks, if you would be available. I hope everything is going well for you!
Take Care,
Mandy

A full signature, complete with a phone number, followed her name. That was new. I logged into my MySpace account and searched for Debbie. Sure enough, picture after picture of my house had been posted on her page, including a full frontal showing the house number.

Rereading her email, I wondered if Mandy already knew Debbie hadn't followed up with me and she was passive-aggressively pointing it out. It could go either way.

Mandy,
I actually haven't heard from Debbie yet, so I guess I need to follow up with her. There was a Penobscot Spiritual Healer, a Reiki person, and two sensitives. Not happy that Debbie posted this, and

My fingers paused over the keys. I liked Mandy, and I didn't want her to get the wrong idea, but...

I wasn't impressed with one of her investigators flirting with Ryan right in front of me! I'll get back to you on the overnight.
Mel

Perturbed about Debbie posting photos before she talked to me, and the fact they hadn't really investigated anything, I didn't want to reach out to her about it quite yet. I logged off and went to the barn to ride Tori.

Part of my class assignments included following up on a class message board, so I got back online before I wanted to be. Only one other person had completed the assignment, so I commented on their post and reopened my email. Mandy had already replied.

I was going to say, wow, that was a quick reveal. I was definitely surprised to see pictures up already. Did either of the sensitives pick up on anything while they were there? I know it has only been a few days, but do things seem to be any less active? I know you wrote that things were quiet after they left, but I wasn't sure if you were referring to the paranormal activity or activity of the "living" realm, lol.

I hope whatever they did will help clear some of the activity from your land and you can finally stop having to deal with this burden. At the least, hopefully things will quiet down. Just let us know when you would like us back out, and we can definitely come to see if we can pick anything up! Until then, please, don't hesitate to keep me informed, and let me know if you have any questions or concerns. Talk to you soon!

I sat back in my chair, reading and rereading Mandy's email. The kindness and support from her meant the world to me. Alexandra was obviously there for me, but also my sister, and—despite being only one day older—took the "I'm the big sister and know everything" approach. She might tell me the house was haunted to appease me, and her know-it-all approach to spirits got my hackles up. But Mandy's more compassionate, yet no-nonsense, approach validated me. And what did she have to gain from telling me my house was haunted? It was her own time being wasted.

The phone rang, and I came back to reality. "Hello?"

"Melissa, it's Debbie." Birds chirped in the background.

My good mood soured. "Debbie, I was going to email you in a little bit about my investigation."

"Well, we didn't find anything."

My eyes rolled. Of course, she didn't find anything. Half of the hot minute the team spent at my house was setting up and breaking down. "So, why do you have pictures on your MySpace page?"

She stammered for a moment, making an excuse about getting the team name out there, even when they don't find anything.

"Aren't I supposed to sign a release for you to post the findings online?" I'd signed one for Mandy, conditional on my photo and identifying features of the house not being shown.

"Oh." A long pause. A bird shrieked. "No one has ever complained before."

Sitting up straight, I shook my head. "Well, I'm complaining now. Please take the pictures down."

"Fine." The line went dead.

Still shaking my head, I replaced the receiver.

Chapter 30

July 24, 2010

Alexandra pulled a navy blue dress off the store rack and frowned, shoving it back. "I don't like any of these."

"Clothes for someone my size aren't going to look like the clothes you buy for you." I took a deep breath, trying to quell the nausea rising in my throat.

I grabbed another peppermint out of my pocketbook and popped it in my mouth. The queasiness got worse. I'd been dealing with low grade stomach upset for days, and throwing up for the last several hours. A shooting pain went through my ribs, and I winced. I'd been through these symptoms on and off for years, and all I could do was wait it out.

Her frown didn't change when she sighed, pulling a purple dress off the rack. She held it out in front of her. "This is so blah. I wish it at least had some sparkle or something. Maybe a belt?"

"We have plenty of time to find something. And today should be about your dress, not mine." The room didn't quite spin, but at least wobbled around me.

"It's fun to shop for other people and spend their money." She glanced up at me, and then stuffed the dress back on the rack. She rushed to my side, grabbing my elbow. "Mel? Are you okay?"

I nodded. "Yeah, I'm fine. Just not feeling all that great." Another pain had me halfway to doubled over before I stopped myself and straightened.

"You are really, really pale, Mel." She pulled me into a nearby dressing room. She sat me down on the bench and bent to examine my face. "You don't look good. What did you eat last?"

"I had some crackers for breakfast, but I threw up." I tried to take a deep breath, but the my churning stomach wouldn't let me. Sharp pain shot through my ribs again.

The back of her hand chilled my forehead. "You're warm."

I shoved her hand away and stood up. The room spun, and I stumbled back onto the bench. "I'm fine."

"You are not fine, Mel. Why didn't you say something?" She dug through her pocketbook for her phone.

Forcing myself to stand, I braced myself on the wall, trying to ignore the pain ripping through me. "I wanted to help you find a dress."

"You need to go to the ER."

"I can't." I pressed the side of my fist against my mouth and forced air in through my nose. Bile rose in my throat.

She shook her head, setting her silver drop earrings swinging. "What do you mean, you can't?"

"VA healthcare, remember?" Grunting, I leaned forward. "I can only go to the local ER if it's life, limb, or sight, otherwise I have to go to Togus." I laughed. "Or I have to pay the bill. I can't afford it."

She chewed her lower lip. "Is there someone you can call for permission?"

I shook my head and closed my eyes to combat the resulting spinning. "Not on a Saturday."

"At least let me get you home."

"That sounds like a good idea."

In the car, she kept stealing glances at me. I didn't pay much attention to her because the pain took up all of my attention.

"I really think you should go to the ER."

"Alexandra—"

"The VA is stupid," she snapped. "How are you going to know if it's life, limb, or sight when you aren't a medical professional and you don't know what's wrong?"

She had me there. I leaned forward, trying to ease some of the pain in my abdomen. I ignored the pain in my shoulder. I'd been living with that for years, too, but never this bad.

"I'm taking you to the ER."

Part of me wanted to argue with her. Part of me wanted to fight about the cost. The rest of me was scared. I didn't say anything because I didn't want to die, and feared I might.

She took Exit 7 and pulled into York. At the light, she drummed her fingers on the steering wheel. "I'm glad we decided to go to Portsmouth instead of Portland."

I didn't reply. I couldn't, and she talked to herself to keep her anxiety in check.

She gunned the car down Route 1, and hit the gas to make it through a yellow light before it changed. Barely slowing, she cut the two turns into the hospital parking lot. "Do you want me to drop you off or do you want to walk?"

"I can walk." Why was my brain telling me to stop being dramatic? I tried to silence it but couldn't concentrate through the pain in my guts.

She parked as close as she could to the ER entrance. She walked around the back of the car to come help me out.

"I'm fine," I protested, leaning on her arm as I stood from the car.

"You are not fine." She held me up across the parking lot. "Remember when you told me I get to make medical decisions for you? This is me making a medical decision."

"Only if I was plugged in and unresponsive. I'm still coherent."

"Yeah, and you still make dumb decisions when it comes to taking care of yourself." She held my elbow and walked with me through the ER entrance.

A woman behind the desk with short, curly reddish hair smiled at us. "How can we help you today?"

Alexandra didn't miss a beat. "This is my girlfriend. She's been having abdominal pain and cramping. Low grade fever, lightheaded, and dizzy. Nausea since this morning."

The woman nodded and handed Alexandra a clipboard. "Fill this out for us, please, and someone will be right out."

Alexandra shoved me into a chair in the waiting room across from an enormous fish tank and took the seat next to me. She filled the form out so fast, I don't think she read any of it. She shoved the clipboard at me, pressing a pen into my left hand. "Sign this."

My usually neat signature wobbled across the page, trailing into a scribble somewhere beneath the line. The brain fog made concentrating difficult. The clipboard disappeared, and Alexandra took it back to the front desk.

Someone appeared in front of me. They were talking to Alexandra, but I couldn't understand what they were saying. Two people floated in front of me. Hazy, indistinct.

The world spun, and everything went black.

I didn't understand what was happening around me. I was lying down, but I was moving over a bumpy road. There were bright lights and voices floating around me. I sucked in a deep breath and shivered.

"It hurts," I mumbled.

I fell into oblivion.

When I woke, I couldn't focus on the person at my feet. They did something, and I jerked my foot away. More gibberish. Bright lights reflected off shiny doors behind them. Maybe I'd been abducted by aliens. But he wore green scrubs. A woman in a white cap stood behind him in the corner.

My eyes drifted closed, and the pain started in my feet again.

"Stop it," I mumbled and turned my face away from the bright lights.

"Can you hear me, Mel?" the voice asked.

"I want to sleep."

"We're taking you back to your room so you can sleep, okay?"

The doors slid open, and I was wheeled into a hallway.

I drifted in and out until I jerked to a halt in a dark room. I patted around me for my phone.

"What do you need?" the concerned voice asked.

"Where's my phone? I have to call Alexandra."

"She'll be here in a bit."

"I need my phone." I kept groping for it. When did I get into bed? My feet started sweating, but I shivered from cold.

"Alexandra has your phone. She'll be here in a minute."

"But I can't call her without my phone." I surrendered and lay back on the pillows. My eyelids had turned to concrete, and it was too much effort to keep them open.

When I woke again, I was alone. Bright fluorescent lights from the hallway spilled into the dark room. I squinted and swallowed a few times. My experience in hospitals was enough that I recognized where I was, but not why.

A woman in a short-sleeved white dress walked past the doorway and glanced in. Her hand stopped on the frame, and she backed up a step. Curly blonde hair spilled from beneath her white cap.

"How are you feeling?"

"I'm really thirsty." I went from warm to shivering in under a second. My teeth chattered like machine gun fire in the quiet of the room. Squinting into the bright hall, I tried to see her feet, but my vision wasn't right. I sagged and tucked my trembling arms closer to my sides. "Why are you dressed like you walked off the set of *Pearl Harbor?*"

She ignored my question and moved closer to the doorjamb than should have been possible. "How's your stomach?"

"I'm not sure."

"I'll get you some ice chips instead of water so you don't chuck up." She took a step forward, but seemed to think better of it and backed completely out of the room. "I'll get you a blanket, too. I'll be back before you sack out again."

She disappeared into the hall, and I slid my arms beneath the blankets. My shivering quieted, and I warmed back up. Despite her promise, I fell asleep again before she returned.

Chapter 31

July 24, 2010

My tongue stuck to the roof of my mouth, and a thousand spiders danced on my face with tiny tap shoes. Arachnid Riverdance. I squinted against daylight flooding through the large windows.

Sarah patted my hand. "How are you feeling?"

"I'm not sure." Swallowing, I tried to make sense of my surroundings. I lay in a bed with thick plastic rails. Sarah sat next to me, holding my hand. I lifted my free hand to rub my the spiders away, but the pinching of an IV needle taped to the back of my hand stopped me. "What happened?"

The door opened a crack, and Alexandra stepped in with two cans of ginger ale stacked in her arms and a package in her other hand. She smiled at Sarah, then set her burden down on a small side table and kissed my forehead. "Oh, honey, you scared me so bad."

"What happened?"

"You fainted in the waiting room." She put her fingers over mine, unable to take my hand because of the IV. "How are you feeling? I hope you don't mind I called Sarah."

"Really confused." My hand went to my abdomen. "At least my stomach doesn't hurt anymore. And thirsty. The nurse never brought me the ice chips she promised."

They exchanged a glance. "What nurse?"

Weights had attached to my eyelids and holding them up took Herculean effort. "Last night. She stopped by to check in on me."

"Keith is your nurse, and was the only one on the floor last night." Alexandra cleared her throat. "They gave you Dilaudid, honey."

Even in my current state, something inside me thrilled at the endearment. "For what?"

"The pain, of course." She moved closer and put one hand on my shoulder. "The doctor said you needed surgery. He couldn't believe you walked in here." She perched on the edge of my bed.

Wincing, I tried to push myself into a more upright position. "Why did he tell you that?"

"Because I'm your power of attorney, remember?" She smiled at me like she would at her daughter. "I keep it in my purse in case you fall off of a horse, or decide to do something dumb, like be all stoic and not take care of yourself until you land in the ER."

"You're hilarious."

"I do my best." She stroked my hair away from my forehead, then my ear. "They took you in for emergency surgery, and your gallbladder ruptured while you were on the table. If I had taken you home, you probably would've died."

"I guess that means I was right to give you permission to boss me around."

"I'm going to call Ryan to give him an update. He's very worried about you. I promised to call him when you woke up."

I wiped my face again to make the spiders go away. "Why does Ryan know?"

Sarah sighed beside me. "Someday, you're going to have to come to terms with people caring about you, Mel. He called your phone after you passed out. Alexandra filled him in."

"You'll be fine now, though." Alexandra grabbed my other hand and squeezed it.

I didn't know what to say. I went to my default. "I'm sorry."

"Don't be. You're okay and that's what matters." She touched my hair again.

Sarah and Olivia were so lucky to have her. I was lucky, too, but didn't deserve any of them. Tears clogged my throat and threatened to spill out of my eyes. She slipped out of the room, closing the curtain behind her.

Sarah squeezed my hand. "You scared the hell out of her, just so you know." Her smile was amused, but her eyes were worried.

I patted her arm as my eyes drifted closed. Suddenly, I was so tired. "I'll try not to do it again."

Chapter 32

July 29, 2010

Recovery kind of sucked. Following three days in the hospital, I stayed with Alexandra and Sarah, and tried to stay out of the way. I mostly slept. But after only two days with the four of us crammed into their tiny two-bedroom house, I assured Alexandra and Sarah I was fine to be on my own. It was complete and utter boloney, but my presence there burdened them, and disrupted their routine. I had to go home, and that's when I realized I really, really didn't want to.

Me being me, I didn't say anything, just thanked Alexandra for everything when she dropped me off. I pretended to search for something in my bag while she pulled out of the driveway, and I waved when she pulled onto the road. Once her car disappeared from sight, I studied the house. So innocent. The purplish siding and the bright white trim were homey, almost cheerful. The dark windows, however, watched me. Waiting. I stood there for several minutes, my small bag in my hands, not wanting to go in. Not wanting to be there.

If I procrastinated any more, I'd end up going into the house in the dark, so I dislodged my feet.

The silence in my house when I walked in wasn't like the woods on a winter day, or the kind of silence when the snow falls in big, fat flakes, their whispers absorbing all the sound. Or even like walking out of my apartment late at night after the traffic had died, and the empty streets longed for the bustle of the day. My house had been waiting for me and trying to hide. Lurking. The hair on the back of my neck stood up as I turned on the lights and tossed my bag on the couch. I hadn't been here in almost a week, and something was very unhappy with me about it. Watching me.

My chest constricted as I moved in precise, measured movements that brought me physical pain as my muscles tensed and screamed at me to leave the house. My incisions hurt, forcing me to a near standstill.

Turning lights on as I went, I got a drink of water from the kitchen sink. My unseen stalker had moved to the window and stared so intently, I had to leave the room. Heading back into the living room, a shadow crossed the front porch. I jumped, spilling half of the contents of my glass all over myself and the floor. I stepped back, hitting the corner of the half wall. I was trapped between something watching me from the backyard and whatever waited on the porch.

Tap. Tap. Tap.

The shadow came closer.

Ruth tapped again on my front door with long acrylic nails, leaning close so I could see her. Her hair floated around her oval face.

I barked a laugh, tears pricked my eyelids, and I opened the door.

She smiled at me as she stepped into the house. "I'm sorry for dropping by unannounced. I lost your phone number."

"I don't think I ever gave it to you." I gestured at my soaked shirt. "Let me go change, and I'll be right back. Can I get you something to drink?"

Her russet eyes missed nothing as she studied me. "I'm good, thank you."

My cup safely on the coffee table, I rushed to my bedroom to change into a dry shirt.

Ruth was sitting on my couch when I got back, browsing through one of my Dressage Today magazines. She set it down and folded her hands on her lap as I settled on the other end of the couch.

"Again, I'm sorry for dropping in unannounced, but I felt the need to speak to you." She smiled. "In my line of work, you don't ignore things like that."

"I haven't been home for a little while because of a medical emergency." Suddenly exhausted, I sank onto the couch next to her. "I hope you haven't been trying to catch me long."

"Not at all." She glanced around the living room, and her gaze settled on something behind me. I fought the urge to see what it was. "We didn't have a chance to talk. Your boyfriend wasn't in a particularly receptive mood, and it shook me."

"He's a bit of a skeptic." I chewed the inside of my lip. "I kind of am, too, to be completely honest. And we're just friends."

Her expression told me she didn't have time for my denial. "You tell yourself that you're a skeptic, but I know that you know better." Ruth turned her face in such a way that she was almost looking down her nose at me while tipping her head to the side. On someone else, like Kirstie, it seemed condescending, but on her, the expression leaned more regal. Like an eagle staring at its prey. "I needed to tell you what is happening here."

My face, always great at expressing every thought in my head, couldn't stay impassive. "You know?"

She nodded, curls bouncing. She smoothed some strands behind her ear, showing off dangling turquoise earrings. "How much do you know about spirits?"

"I'm going to say I know nothing, and you can explain the whole thing to me."

Again, she nodded. "Each spirit has its own light. Imagine a candle."

I nodded.

She cupped her hands together, as if she would conjure a flame between her palms. "In the darkness, other spirits can see this light, and are attracted to it. Which makes the light brighter."

I didn't like where this was going.

Her hands dropped to her lap. "When you moved here, you had three spirits. I know Alan told you about them. There's a young boy, a woman who Alan will tell you about, and a man." She held my gaze, waiting for me to say something. When I didn't, she continued. "You said the child that comes over is your niece? The young boy likes her toys. The man is in his mid-forties, and he stays downstairs. In that space you created like a small living room. He sits on the couch. I don't know what he's watching, but that's what he does. Very friendly."

"What about the woman?" I shifted my position on the couch.

She pursed her lips. "Alan will have to talk to you more about her, but she's an older woman, here to protect you and your niece from the other spirits."

"But isn't her light attracting others?"

"No." She shook her head, the curls escaping from behind her ears. "She's different, that's why Alan needs to speak to you." She reached for me, seemed to think better of it, and put her hand back in her lap. "The problem is, as you start collecting these spirits, you're bound to get some bad apples."

I wiped my face with my hand. "Why are they even here?"

She shrugged. "It gets boring on their side of the veil. They're restless, wandering the earth seeking whatever it is that's holding them here. Some of them don't know."

"So, if they're wandering, why are they staying here? I can't help them."

"But you can hear them." She shifted, sitting up straighter. "You may not consciously hear them, but you do hear them. You're someone for them to chat with. Give them something to do. Spooking the living is entertaining for them."

Of course. I took a sip of my water like we weren't talking about invisible people wandering around my house and scaring the daylights out of me. "How are they getting here? Are they all just wandering around the world and happen to be congregating here?"

She sighed, the sound of a person getting ready to do or say something they didn't want to do. "Part of what Alan did was search for vortexes on your property."

"Vortexes?"

"It's a cross-point in the earth's energy fields, sometimes at intersecting ley lines."

"And a ley line is?"

One slender finger pressed on the side of the bridge of her nose as she closed her eyes and inhaled slowly. Exasperated with my ignorance already. "You know what longitude and latitude lines are?"

"Of course." I'd learned in the fourth grade.

"Like those lines, ley lines crisscross around the globe. In the 1920s, an archaeologist named Alfred Watkins noticed ancient sites–the Pyramids of Giza, Stonehenge, et cetera–are aligned." Her hands made a gesture in the air like pulling string between her fingers. "Some of the sites are natural, others manmade. Ley lines are the connection between these sites around the world, because they're lines of supernatural energy. Like rivers."

I frowned. "Can't you make a straight line pretty much any-where? How does the Mercator projection affect it?"

She scowled at me, her eyes hardening. "Does the Mercator projection help you with your ghosts?"

My face heated. "No."

"When you're dealing with science, ask scientific questions," she said. "When you're dealing with spirits and hauntings, sci-ence won't help you."

"Yes—" I snapped my mouth shut before I could add ma'am.

"Anyway." Her brows rose as she gave me a moment to open my mouth and shove my foot in. "Each vortex where the ley lines cross creates a kind of doorway for the spirits. Imagine it like a subway station in New York City. You have seven of these vortexes on your property, one of which is in your basement. The house was built on top of it."

How was I supposed to react? Stunned silence seemed to be working for me, so I went with it.

Ruth wasn't a fan. "Melissa, you have seven of these subway openings next door and no locks on your doors that can keep these spirits out."

"What do I do?"

Her hand covered mine, the deep color of her skin a contrast to my own pale complexion. "Give Alan a call, and he'll come out and help you. Because of some of the spirits in the house and on the land, you need Alan. Call him. My cleanse of the house helped, but it will only last so long until these vortexes are dealt with."

I didn't say anything. This was too much to take in.

Ruth shook her hand, jarring mine, and my gaze went to her face. Her gaze intensified. "Call him tomorrow."

Disagreeing with her would be pointless. She wasn't going to leave until I said what she wanted to hear. "I'll call him tomorrow."

Sitting back, she smiled and brought her hand back to her own lap. "Great." She stood, brushing the front of her blouse, this one a pink so pale, it was almost white. "I'm going to run. Do you still have my card?"

I nodded, still absorbing the information she'd given me. I hadn't felt safe here in a while. My mind conjured an image of an endless line of ghosts emerging from a subway, and I shivered.

She put her hands on my arms, her gaze meeting mine. "It's going to be okay."

My head bobbed again.

She let me go, but her gaze was unwavering. "You are a filter for negativity, but there is more to it than that. You have a gift."

"Like I'm a psychic?" I didn't mean to scoff, but it came out in my voice. I cringed.

Her nostrils flared as she took a deep breath in. "Like you have a gift, and you shouldn't be ignoring it. Have you done Tarot before?"

My face heated again. "I actually used to do readings for people."

"And what did they say?"

"That I was very accurate."

She nodded, one slender brow rising. "Spirit speaks to you. You should try listening sometime." Her eyes closed, and she became still. When her eyes opened again, her gaze went through me. "You have a lot of fear within you. It swirls around your heart, closing you off, making you hard." She shook her head, and her features softened, became sympathetic. "But you aren't a hard person, but you want people to think that. Just because your ex-husband, and others, abused you, doesn't mean everyone will." She patted my hand. "You have someone in your life who is very special to you, and you love them very much. You need to let them in."

Ryan's face came to mind. Of course, she'd assume we were together after he met the team here with me. "He doesn't like me like that."

Her curls bounced around her face as she shook her head. "You are so afraid of being hurt that you're blind to what's in front of you. Not him." Her eyes closed again, and she grabbed my hand. Her brows drew together as if she was deep in thought. "It's a woman. You've loved her for a very long time." The russet eyes bored through me again. "You love her so much, you never told her how you feel because you were afraid it would make her unhappy. And you were right." Her eyes closed yet again, and she drew herself up. "You're like sisters now."

My jaw dropped and I pulled my hand from hers. I had never, ever told anyone about my crush on Alexandra. Ever. Not even my therapist knew. It was locked away tight with my darkest secrets.

"How did you know that?"

She smiled at me. Gently, like I was a child. "Because Spirit speaks to me, Melisandre. And I listen."

I sat stunned on the couch as Ruth closed the door behind herself. After I managed to shake myself out of my stupor, I jumped up and flipped the porch light on so she could see on the way to her car. My heart raced, and I couldn't catch my breath. I had never told her my full name, but she could have found that. But how she knew about Alexandra...

The house seemed a little emptier now that she'd left. Once my nerves settled a bit, I realized it was also a little calmer, less hostile. Although, I couldn't explain why. She'd given me a lot to think about, but despite her reassurance things would be okay, I didn't like the idea of my unlocked door outside the subway entrances. For ghosts.

When I went to bed, I left my bedroom light on. And the hallway light. And the bathroom light.

Chapter 33

July 30, 2010

Catching up with my online classes had been easier than expected, only taking a couple of hours to complete my assignments. As one of the last students posting, there were plenty of people to give feedback to on the message board, so I did the mandatory two, and then two more for some extra credit.

Riding wasn't possible at the moment, so I put Tori into a program with my trainer to keep her active while I finished recovering. I could still brush her, though, so I groomed her today ahead of her ride, and then went into the tack room for her equipment.

My trainer poked her head in. "Hey, Mel. How are you doing?"

Smiling, I pulled my saddle off the rack and onto my hip. A twinge in my belly, easy to ignore. "Good."

"Tori is a bit wound up today."

I nodded and grabbed her bridle. "I figured she would be."

Jan stepped into the tack room, already wearing her tall boots over hot pink breeches. "You aren't doing the brave thing with me, right? You'd tell me if you weren't feeling well?"

I'd never tell anyone that. "I'm okay, I guess."

My favorite thing about Tori, or horses in general, was their magic in clearing my head. Someone explained to me once that the motion of the horse and the entire body being involved affected brain chemistry or something, and some people would get high from riding. I happened to be one of those people. My high would last from three days to a week, and if I waited too long, I would get antsy, needing to ride. Watching Jan ride Tori had a similar effect as riding Tori myself. Sitting on the bench on the short side of the indoor arena, my hands reacted as if they were on the reins and my legs twitched as Tori moved.

I took my time walking Tori around the ring to cool her out, and then drying her off. Eventually, I ran out of things to do and had to go home. I wasn't even out of the farm's driveway when dread about returning to my house filled me. And I realized the stress of my house made me depressed.

With no traffic whatsoever, the drive home sped by in a blur, suddenly slowing when I took the turn down my road.

I pulled into my driveway just far enough that my rear end wasn't in the road. I shifted into Park, but left the engine running. In the late afternoon light, the house seemed unassuming and quiet. The windows didn't reflect light the right way, as if the sunlight couldn't make it into the house. Then again, most of the windows on the front of the house were under the farmer's porch.

I was at war with myself, the victim of my own gaslighting about what was going on inside. Saying things to myself like the farmer's porch was the reason for the odd darkness inside on such a bright day and ignoring that all the windows were identical. I had spent months trying to convince myself I wasn't seeing anything, I was overreacting, or my imagination was playing tricks on me.

Anger welled up inside me, and I didn't pause to question it. I pulled the car into gear with enough force, I slipped out of Drive and had to adjust the shifter before I could make it up the driveway. Slamming the transmission back into Park, I practically ripped the keys out of the ignition and shoved the car door open. My riding boots stomped on the stone walkway.

The key didn't seem to want to work. I didn't jiggle the lock as much as I slammed it. The door finally opened, and I flung my keys into the center of the room.

"Listen up, assholes!" I put my hands on my hips, my feet spread apart as I yelled at the empty air. "This is *my* house, and you do *not* belong here. I'm telling you right now, get out, or I will make you get out! I've had enough of your nonsense and your games. I don't want you here, and it's time for you to leave. *All* of you!"

Breathing heavily, I stayed in the same position for several minutes, glaring in the direction of any noises. Finally, I relaxed my posture, but my muscles refused to let go of the tension, and my lungs couldn't seem to draw in enough air. I needed something to do, anything that would make my body move and hopefully let go of the tension. Aside from a single cereal bowl, there were no dishes to wash. I rinsed it and dropped the bowl into the dishwasher. Despite the unit being half empty, I ran it anyway.

I rubbed my face with my hands, cursing my tidy house, which had been freshly vacuumed. I considered doing windows, but the logical part of my brain whispered that my shoulders would regret it in the morning. You know, after I had calmed down.

Several deep breaths later, my muscles still screamed for release. My phone rang, and I jumped. Checking the caller ID, it wasn't anyone I wanted to talk to, so I let it go to voicemail. In my heightened state right now, every ring made things worse.

Eventually, I gave up. If a walk was all I could manage, it was all I could manage. I went to the end of the road and back, not realizing how long the road actually ran, especially when my foolish, reckless brain decided continuing down the unpaved portion would be a good idea. By the time I turned around, I remembered the sneakers on my feet were months overdue to be replaced, which is why I never wore them.

I got home, sweat dribbling down my back, and my heels raw from the pace I had set. I fought to not limp up the driveway, the muscles at the front of my hips screaming at the slope. The walk had worked, though. I didn't care my house was haunted, or that it was almost dark.

Chapter 34

July 31, 2010

The night passed quietly, which surprised me after my outburst. Not really hungry but trying to force myself to eat something, I stared into the refrigerator as if it had all the answers. I was supposed to be on a low-fat diet without a gallbladder, and nothing I had that appealed to me complied with the list the hospital had given me.

Closing the door knocked an overloaded magnet onto the floor. Picking everything up, I lifted Ruth's business card in my hand. Turning it over, I read Alan's scrawled phone number. Shivering, I imagined Ruth had something to do with the card falling to the floor, reminding me of my promise to call Alan today. I dialed and prayed it would go to voicemail. I'd rather leave a message than have an awkward conversation about who I was and why I was calling.

"Alan here." His gravelly voice sounded annoyed.

The speech I'd rehearsed for his voicemail flew out of my head. "Hi Alan, it's Melisandre—Melissa. Mel. You came to my house a while ago with Ruth and Debbie's team?"

"Ah." The gruff voice relaxed a bit. "Ruth said you'd be calling, I just expected you sooner. Anything been going on?"

I hadn't realized he'd been waiting to hear from me. I explained my conversation with Ruth.

"When do you have time?"

I glanced around the corner to the clock on the stove. It was Saturday, I had all day. At least, what was left of it. "I'm free to talk now."

He chuckled. "I meant for me to come up to the house."

"I still have today."

"That doesn't work for me. I can come out on Thursday."

I bit the inside of my lip. "Any chance you can come by any sooner?" Now that a solution might be on the horizon, I was desperate to end this. Hello, anxiety at being demanding and presumptuous.

"Not until Thursday. Does around four work?"

"That works—"

A loud squeal like metal on metal ripped through the line and into my ear.

Startled, I dropped the receiver to the floor. I scrambled to pick it up.

"Alan?"

Silence. I pulled the phone away from my ear. The digital screen that normally showed the number and time was blank. I set it back down on the cradle and nothing happened. The little charging indicator didn't light up, either. I picked the phone up and set it back down to see if the connection might be the issue.

I sighed. It was dead. My cell phone seemed to be working fine. It must have been an issue with the unit, or the landline.

I made a mental note to find a replacement and put it out of my mind.

Chapter 35

August 4, 2010

More or less, I managed to drift through life over the next few days. Dealing with assignments, watching Jan ride Tori. On Wednesday, the night before Alan was due to come out, Ryan and I were lying on my bed together, Rexy between us with his head on Ryan's thigh. The small fan in the window had been replaced with an air conditioner in deference more to the humidity than the heat. It hummed now, filling the silence between us. We were "testing" it, he said.

"I'd hate to leave and then have you find out it doesn't work."

He'd dozed off within minutes, and I was just so *comfortable*. Ryan jumped out of bed.

My eyes, heavy with sleep, jerked open. When had the sun gone down? I sluggishly thought as I pushed myself to a sitting position.

Ryan and Rexy ran together out of the room, leaving me very confused.

Some of my tension left, and I sank into the pillows, waiting.

Rexy barking outside kept me from relaxing.

The front door opened and closed, and Ryan's footsteps padded down the hall. He didn't say anything as he closed the bedroom door behind him.

I waited until he lay back on the bed and adjusted his pillow. "What the hell was that?"

He didn't answer me for so long, he might have fallen asleep. "I heard something."

"What did you hear?" I frowned at him.

"Footsteps."

The air conditioner filled the silence with its steady hum.

"You heard footsteps?"

He pushed the pillow farther underneath his head. "Yeah. On the porch."

"What was Rexy barking at?"

There was that pause again. "I don't know. There wasn't anything there."

His words hung in the air, echoing in my mind until I fell asleep.

I don't know what time it was or how long I'd been sleeping when I snapped awake. Ryan was sitting up in bed, his hand on my shoulder, shaking me, and saying my name.

Why was I sitting up? The green light from the smoke detector through the open bedroom door—hadn't he closed it?—cast his face in an eerie glow.

"What?" I shrugged away from him, cranky at being woken up.

His hand shook me again. "Wake up."

"I am awake." I pulled out of his grip and lay back down, facing the window.

"Are you sure?"

My eyes rolled and I sighed, pressing my face into my pillow. "That's a dumb question since I'm lying here talking to you."

His hand found me again, sans the gripping and shaking. "Yeah, well, two minutes ago, you were sitting there talking to someone else. I think you had been for a while."

I rolled to my back. "What are you talking about?"

"You were yelling at someone, having a conversation."

My heart pounded. "No, I wasn't."

"Yes, you were."

Rather than rolling toward him like I wanted, I sat up. "I must've been sleepwalking. Didn't I warn you about that?"

He shook his head. "I don't know, you were pretty clear."

"I always am." I lay down on my side with my back to him. My heart thudded in my chest as I stared toward the window. "I want to go back to sleep."

He didn't say anything, but lay back down, as well. I could practically hear him thinking.

"Can you?"

"Eventually. I'm a little freaked out right now." His arm draped over my hip. "Do you remember anything?"

"Not until you woke me up." His breath caressed my ear. I squeezed my eyes shut and fought to stay still when my body craved his warmth.

His hand rubbed my hip. "You were talking to someone, and I think I saw a shadow at the end of the bed."

That got my attention. I rolled over. "A shadow?"

"Yeah, like a weird, flowy, shimmery green shadow. Which doesn't make any sense because shadows are black, but it's the only way I can think of to describe it." He stared at me. "You were talking to it."

At this rate, my heart was going to give out, the way it pounded. I had nightmares, a lot, about things I might do while sleepwalking. Somehow, talking to ghosts hadn't factored in, but it was one of the more terrifying possibilities. The memory of Rebecca's place invaded—the scream, the ghosts realizing I could talk to them and coming after me, trying to communicate.

With a jolt, I remembered a nightmare I'd had before I moved in. The hallway that had been so unfamiliar in the dream was in my house.

This was my worst nightmare—one of them, anyway—coming true. Suddenly, I couldn't breathe. Was my mother haunting me? Was the dream, as Ruth said, Spirit speaking to me? Warning me?

"I don't know if I can go back to sleep," I said. What I meant was, 'I don't know if I want to go back to sleep.'

"We can just lie here," he suggested, his hand finding mine. "I won't fall asleep."

"Yeah, let's try that."

Despite his words to the contrary, Ryan's soft snores started within minutes.

Chapter 36

August 5, 2010

Thursday finally arrived, and my stomach did somersaults, not knowing what to expect.

Alan's Focus pulled into the drive, and he parked next to the house. Hands on the front porch rail, I waited for him to come up. He didn't resemble what I'd imagined a shaman would, wearing jeans and gym shoes, a Korean War Veteran hat, and a small leather bag hanging from a cord around his neck. He had a small pouch in one hand as he made his way to the porch, staring at the ground.

He nodded to me, doing a small bow as his head came forward. All business. "How have things been?"

I shrugged. "Not bad. Some footsteps. The smells are gone, and no one has seen anything since Ruth did her cleansing." My mouth moved to tell him about the shadowy figure Ryan had encountered last night, but before I could, he nodded as if he'd gotten the answer he'd expected.

The following silence made me uncomfortable. "Ruth said I needed to talk to you about one of the spirits, and said you were the only one who could move them?"

Nodding again, he came up the front porch steps. He tipped his head toward my front door. "Come with me."

I followed him into my house, and we walked straight through to the back door. Standing in the kitchen, he gestured to encompass all the land behind my house.

"All of this land used to be part of the Newichawannock Abenaki tribe." His faded blue eyes focused on me, one hundred percent a teacher in this moment. "This was their hunting ground. All across your hill—" he waved the flat of his hand at the hill behind my house "—you have warriors. Braves. Twelve of them."

My jaw dropped.

"They don't want you here. You need to make peace with them."

I started to say I didn't do anything, but snapped my mouth shut rather than let the ignorant words out.

"And you have three spirits in your home. I'm going to talk to them." He set his sack on the table, pulling out a canister of Shaw's brand cornmeal and a folded square of paper. Last out of the sack was a bundle of white sage and a very large flight feather, probably from a turkey.

The folded paper held loose tobacco, an offering for the native spirits outside, along with the cornmeal that he sprinkled liberally without explaining anything to me. I followed and watched him say prayers I didn't understand outside, and like a puppy, trailed behind him when he went back in. He smudged the inside of the house with sage in a very specific pattern, saying more prayers in what I assume was Penobscot.

After he packed up his sack, he stopped me. "I have made peace with the warriors on your hill. They won't look in your windows anymore, and I've asked them to protect the land, you, and your family from anyone who won't pass on this land in peace."

"I really was being watched?" All the nights of slinking around my house, avoiding the windows. I'd been right all along. I wasn't crazy.

He nodded again. "You still have three spirits in the house with you." Very matter of fact, no questions to be asked. "I told them if they would stay here in peace and harmony that they could stay. If they wouldn't stay in peace in harmony, they had to leave."

He paused. If it had been anyone else, I would've accused them of trying to create a dramatic effect. For him, I wondered if he was listening to messages from the spirit world I wasn't privy to. "Ruth told you there is a man downstairs, and a boy. I asked her to not tell you about the woman."

"Right. She told me to talk to you."

Another deep nod. "She's a tribal grandmother. She was the one you heard on the recording."

My heart stopped. "The Algonquin?"

"The Clan Grandmother confirmed, it's part of a sweat lodge chant." Before I could ask him what it meant, he held a hand up to stop me. "Even I am not allowed to know what it is, other than it was part of a communication with the spirit world." He jabbed his index finger at me. "Stop playing the recording. Don't play it anymore."

I took a step back, surprised by the intensity. I didn't know how to reply. "Ruth said she came here to protect us?"

Nodding appeared to be a primary means of communication for Alan. "She is. She is here to protect you from the spirits coming through the vortexes." He held his hand about hip high.

"She has a wolf, her familiar." His gaze bored through my soul. "What's important is the spirits are out of your house, and I have put a shield over it so they can't get back in." He jabbed a finger at me again. "Don't do something stupid and invite them back into the house."

I squirmed under his gaze, thinking about my outburst when I demanded they leave. "Is it bad I acknowledge them? Speak to them?"

His eyebrows went up and his lips turned into a thin line. "The more attention you pay to them, the more they want." His eyes narrowed. "But you know that already, don't you?"

Was he accusing me of doing this on purpose?

Walking to the door, I made an offhand comment about Debbie.

Pulling up short, his thunderous glare killed the words in my mouth mid-sentence. "Don't talk to me about Debbie. And don't say anything to Ruth about her, either."

How many times had I apparently offended him today? Compared to everything else, though, this seemed easy enough to fix. "What happened?"

He explained, leaving me speechless. I hadn't been a huge fan of Debbie's, but the behavior he'd just described to me was the kind of ignorant thing my mother would've done.

Horrified, I shook my head and walked him out.

Once he left, I changed out of my riding clothes. Ryan and I had made plans, and I'd hoped to make something special for dinner.

I didn't want to think about ghosts anymore today.

Chapter 37

August 5, 2010

Later that night, after Ryan had left, I snuck into my office to give Mandy an update.

Mandy,
The Native American Spiritual Healer, Alan, finished a blessing on my house this afternoon. The entire feel of the house is different, even Ryan noticed it the moment he walked in the door.
This next bit I would prefer to stay between you and Sam. I'm not interested in damaging anyone's reputation or causing trouble, just wanted to give you an FYI. Debbie lost 6 people from her group after making accusations of black magic, spells, and mind control towards Ruth and Alan! The owner of her website is one of the people that left, so her site is down, including the e-mail addresses, so you can't get in touch with her via the internet site as of this time.

In a little while, I'll check in and let you know if things stay settled down, and we can decide if you still want to come out.

My hands hovered over the keyboard. So much more I wanted to say, but I couldn't adequately express in something as insignificant as an email. I thanked her again for all her time and attention. Without her, I had no idea where I'd be. I shuddered, imagining trying to walk this path alone. The next time an entity pushed me down the stairs, I might not be so lucky.

The next morning, I had a quiz to take for one of my classes. A simple twenty question multiple choice that I finished in less than four minutes.

I opened my email, and smiled when Mandy's name popped up.

I'm glad to hear Alan has been able to help you out. Hopefully, things will calm down and you can get some peace and quiet for once! We are definitely still interested in coming out if and when you decide it would be convenient for you. It would be interesting to see if there is a decrease in documentable activity.

I just found out about the SMEGHS website yesterday. Unbelievable. In retrospect, she must be kicking herself in the rear for the things she said. It will always be a mystery to me why some people seem to actually strive to surround themselves in drama, no matter who ends up affected. I hope you haven't been dragged into the middle of this in any way. If you need any assistance, please let me know. If I do happen to speak with Debbie again, I promise that nothing that you wrote me about will be mentioned.

As I said before, we are definitely interested in coming out again, if you are okay with it. I hope everything stays peaceful for you and everyone is able to get some uninterrupted sleep! Regardless of whether or not you want us back out, always remember we're here to help you as best we can, whenever you need it!

Take care,
Mandy

Having learned from experience, I waited a few minutes before responding. I smiled when another email popped up from Mandy, this one much more in line with my own thinking about Debbie and her group.

P.S.- She shouldn't have brought that many people into the investigation to begin with. When I saw the pictures, I was shocked by the crowd that was there. Not only does that set the stage for disagreement, but how can you get solid audio evidence when you can barely keep track of who was where at what time? When I saw the number of people on her team, I knew something was going to happen, whether it be a clash of egos or general mismanagement. I can't believe one of the investigators flirted with Ryan. Talk about a lack of professionalism. I have to say, though, after looking at the screenshots on the website, it seems professionalism isn't exactly the first priority to a few people from the team. I was absolutely SHOCKED when I read her inquiry to that man who is doing the Pagan documentary, asking if she could be in his "witches video." Talk about being completely politically incorrect. At least you got to meet Alan and Ruth, so something good came out of it.

I'll let everyone know we are able to go back and see what works best, then I'll shoot you an email, and you and Ryan can talk it over. We really look forward to getting back out there!

I enjoyed a little bit of cattiness every now and again, and this was no exception. Mandy was right, and reflected a lot of my own opinions on what had happened with Debbie and her group. I didn't see a need to reply (and Mandy wouldn't get upset if I didn't), so I shut my computer down.

Taking a deep breath, I tried to feel some of the negativity, some of the weight I'd become accustomed to since I bought my house. There was nothing there.

With a smile, I pushed myself out of my chair, ready to conquer tomorrow.

Chapter 38

August 20, 2010

Despite Alan's warning to leave things alone, I needed Mandy's team to confirm for me that my haunting troubles were over. The atmosphere on Mandy's next investigation couldn't have been more different from the first two. Lighthearted and happy, I joked with Mandy and Sam, and toward the end of the investigation, those who weren't driving home enjoyed a beer with Ryan. The activity had dwindled to almost nothing. No more apparitions, no more banging or opening doors in the house. No more cigarette stink, even though I'd occasionally catch a random whiff of cookies.

Even when Mandy came by to do the reveal, alone with just her laptop case, the mood stayed light. I really liked her, and I was almost disappointed I wouldn't have a reason to see her again.

"No Ryan tonight?" she asked, plugging in her laptop.

"He has an overflowing toilet flooding the apartment below it, so he won't be around tonight." I held up the glass of water I'd just filled at the sink. "Would you like something to drink?"

"No, I'm good." She clicked through her folders to pull up the files she wanted as I scooted in my chair. She pointed at the open window on her screen. "Look! Only nine!"

I couldn't help but smile. I don't think she'd ever let me live that down. "What do we have?"

She grinned. "You know we were all being a little goofy. We all felt a huge difference in the house, so the EVPs are a little different for this session."

She clicked the first file. A faint tapping noise came through the speaker.

A low hum. *Mmhmm.* Short, a man agreeing to something, but no one had asked a question.

Mandy's voice: *"Is that a normal house noise?"*

She smiled. "Not a reaction to the humming, just me asking about the tapping."

The second .wav only took four seconds to play. A breathy whisper I couldn't decipher.

It seemed like nothing, and didn't bother me. I knew who had taken up residence in my house, and they weren't there to hurt me.

"Was this in response to a question?"

"Nope, silence on both sides." She pulled up the third file, and she grimaced. "This one is pretty bad. Most of these are from the end of the night when we were all fooling around in the living room in the dark."

Laughter came from the speaker. Sam's voice said, *"...more awesome if you said it with a German accent!"*

Hmm. A woman joining in on the joking.

Mandy laughed on the recording. *"Make those lights light up 'cause we're being silly!"*

She held her breath, staring at me, as if gauging my reaction.

"So, lots of humming, apparently," I said.

Her cursor hovered over the next file. "This one's me, and I'm not proud of it."

"Come on," her voice said. She'd been doing her best bedroom voice to the ghosts. *"You can sit next to Sam—"*

Please hurry. A young woman's voice, maybe just entering her teenage years, pleading with someone to hurry.

"—and next to Laura."

My eyebrows went up at that one. "Do my ghosts have a sense of humor and really wanted to sit next to Sam, or is 'please hurry' out of context?"

Mandy laughed. "The world may never know. As you can tell, these are so much more innocuous. This one is when we were trying to see if the refrigerator would set off the K-II meter. This is you talking." She clicked the file.

"You can hold the fridge door open for a minute or two and see if you can get it to turn on, if that makes a difference."

Go. The voice may have been the girl from the last file.

A K2 meter trilled and the file stopped.

My lighthearted mood faded a bit, struggling to find some inflection or tone in that single, hoarsely whispered syllable. Was it a suggestion? An order? A plea?

The next few files consisted of more humming, a sigh, and more indistinct whispering. Considering how loud and ridiculous we were being in the background, it was obvious no one on the team had been whispering.

Mandy explained that six recorders were going in the living room, but the whisper was only caught on the recorder on the coffee table next to the K-II meter.

"What's the last one?" I asked, pointing.

Mandy didn't say anything, and opened the file.

Laughter, maybe Sam's. Ryan's voice, *"Yup!"*

My voice came out of the speakers. *"I personally think that's funny."*

Before I finished speaking, a voice spoke over me, and the words sent a chill running down my spine like an icicle had dripped down my shirt.

A woman whispered, *Let me in.*

Chapter 39

August 20, 2010

Ryan came by late that night. Rexy banged into the door a moment before Ryan opened it. The dog barged into the house, tail wagging. I smiled and rubbed his side as he leaned against me.

"Sorry I'm late," he said, wiping his Sox cap off his head. "It was supposed to be a small issue, and it cascaded into a nightmare."

"Don't worry about it." I jerked my head toward the kitchen. "I saved you a plate."

"Great, thanks."

Without meaning to, I sighed as the microwave door clicked closed.

"Are you okay?" He dug into dinner, shoveling food into his mouth like he was starving.

Tears suddenly rushed up. Since Alan had left, I'd been living like my problem had been solved and my house wasn't the most terrifying thing in my life anymore. The reveal with Mandy, that last EVP, told me the peace and quiet were all an illusion. Words didn't come out, just a hiccupping cry as tears spilled down my face.

"Melissa, are you okay?" He set his plate on the counter, and then rubbed my arms. "Hey, it's okay."

I put my face in my hands. "No. I can't do this anymore."

He tipped his head. "Do what?"

I gestured at the room, my house. Everything. "This. I can't with the ghosts and the house anymore."

He stepped backward and dropped his hands. "Melissa, your house isn't haunted. Ghosts aren't real."

My jaw clenched. Anger sustained me. I felt less like a scared kid already. I shook my head, but what I wanted to do was stomp my foot. Childish, I know.

"Ryan, you've seen these things, heard them. Explain it to me. You tell me what's happening in this house right now that explains everything that's happened."

He crossed his arms and shrugged one shoulder. "I can't, but that doesn't mean it's ghosts." He shook his head and shrugged. "Lack of an explanation shouldn't, by default, be paranormal. It's ridiculous."

My heart leaped into my throat. "So, you think I'm ridiculous, too, then?"

His silence spoke volumes.

"What you've experienced is just a drop in the bucket, Ryan," I bit out. "I've been living this for months, and I can't do it anymore. I need to leave this house."

"Are you kidding me?" He crossed his arms over his chest, and his voice was incredulous. "You would give up your house over a bunch of recordings?"

I chose not to remind him of the photos. "Something tried to push me down the stairs. And the night when Olivia kept getting woken up. Two nights, if you think about it."

He rubbed his face with one hand. "People trip down the stairs, Melissa. Babies cry. People are losing their homes left and right, and you want to walk away because someone told you it's haunted? You realize you might not even be able to get out from under your mortgage right now?"

"I don't care." I hugged myself.

He froze. "What?"

"I don't owe you an explanation. I'll walk away with whatever I can and find something else."

He threw his hands up in the air and spun to face the wall before turning back to me. "Seems to me like whenever you don't like something, your solution is to leave. With dating, with this house, with your own fucking family." He shook his head again, his mouth drawn in a tight line. "Unbelievable."

Around the giant knot of anger in my throat, I couldn't get out the words I wanted to say, the nasty biting response to his cheap shot about my family when he didn't know them. But I couldn't choke out the words I should say, either. That if he couldn't support me, if he couldn't believe me, even if he didn't believe in ghosts, maybe we shouldn't be friends.

"I think you should go."

His jaw clenched. He released a breath from his nose. "Fine."

"Fine." I prided myself in the fact my voice didn't tremble like the way I quaked on the inside.

He shrugged again, turned on his heel, and left without another word. The lock turned before he closed the door, and a lump formed in my throat.

When his truck pulled away, tears fell.

I went to bed, shutting lights off as I went. Flopping diago-nally across the bed, I clutched the pillow he'd used to my chest and cried myself to sleep.

Chapter 40

August 21, 2010

The next day, I woke up with a massive headache, like I'd walked face first into a wall. I spent the next few days keeping up with my classes, and Jan rode Tori in the mornings before it got too hot.

I missed Ryan. We exchanged a couple of very neutral texts, but no plans were made to see each other. Terrified of rejection, I was too afraid to ask.

I wanted to email Mandy to let her know the inside of the house had settled completely, but I decided against it. The outside still had the footsteps on the porch and the lights still wouldn't penetrate the darkness surrounding the house. She'd done as much as she could for me already. It occurred to me to reach out to Alan or Ruth, but what more could they do than what they'd already done? Alexandra was worried about me, but

I couldn't impose on her again. She'd say it wasn't, but it would be a lie.

Ryan's words echoed in my head, stopping me from calling my realtor to find out how much the house would be worth if I put it on the market.

I finally went around my house and put electrical tape over all the lights that would interrupt my sleep. The smoke detector in the hall had been a big one. I taped a folded square of paper over the lights of the A/C so I could flip up to use the controls. Sitting on the bed, I decided to tape some cardboard over the windows to stop the strange lights from coming in to bounce around on the ceiling. Ignorance being bliss and all.

That night, I settled into my bed on my side, loving the depth of the darkness surrounding me. With a loud beep, the air conditioner behind me shut off. I couldn't be sure, but I think the power to the entire house had gone out.

Without the hum, I could hear it.

Footsteps.

Heavy boots on the porch.

Not just on the porch, but on the driveway on the other side of the exterior wall next to my head.

Crunching in the layers of leaves in the woods behind the house.

The footsteps had always been a few and stop, never more than five or six. Now a small army of people marched through my yard, across the porch. Someone climbed the stairs onto the back porch.

If I got up to investigate, there wouldn't be anything there. Nothing I could see.

I squeezed my eyes shut and tried to breathe. On the wall behind my head, something knocked on the exterior siding.

Tap.

Tap.

Tap.

The tapping moved toward the back of the house. Slowly. Dragging in between taps.

Let me in, the EVP echoed in my head. *Let me in.*

Me, asking if they wanted to be here. *Yes, I do.*

The recorder, left alone in the bedroom. *Did you have to leave?*

We're sorry.

Like a little kid, I pulled the blankets up over my head, which didn't do anything to block the sound of the window screens tearing. I jumped at rapping on my bedroom window.

More than one pair of footsteps stalked the front porch now.

Let me in.

Tapping and scraping on the siding next to the front windows.

Let me in.

Without knowing why, my eyes flew open. Barely moving, I pulled the blankets off my face.

I stared at the bedroom door, not breathing. Light seeped in from under the door. The ethereal blue, glowing fog rolled across the floor like something out of a movie.

As the light intensified, it also penetrated between the door and the frame, creating bright fingers of light into the room and casting shadows on the far wall.

The doorknob latch clicked out of the strike plate, and my entire body jerked.

The door swung open, inch by inch. My chest constricted and I couldn't breathe. I couldn't move. Nothing stood in the doorway, and the air was perfectly still in the house. There was no logical reason for that door to be opening, but logic had gone out the window the moment I'd heard the first recorded whisper.

The light brightened further, becoming more white than blue. The deep gasp of air I took in filled the unreal silence. The same silence as snow falling that absorbed the tapping on my windows. Or had it all stopped?

Let me in.

An invisible weight sat on my chest, pressing me into the mattress. My breaths came deep and fast, but I couldn't move my upper body.

I squinted against the still increasing light. Like an oncoming car with its brights on, eventually I had to squeeze my eyes closed or be blinded. Through my lids, the light burned my eyes.

The temperature in the room dropped, chilling me through my blankets, and I wouldn't have opened my eyes at that point even if I could. The bed trembled and then shook. I screamed, the unfamiliar sound shrill to my own ears. I gasped for air and kept screaming, the bed shuddering beneath me. I wanted to leap out of bed, to get out of the house, but the pressure on my chest held me firm.

When the bed stopped shaking, my screaming stopped, too.

A heavy hand touched my shoulder, and I screamed again, my eyes flying open.

The weight lifted off of my chest, taking some of my fear with it. A woman stood beside my bed, her face weathered and worn. Like the shadow men who had been darker than the dark, her form was brighter and lighter than the light surrounding her. I understood now why so many people described ghosts as wearing white. The ethereal light washed out the colors. She could only be the tribal Grandmother who had taken up residence in my house to protect me.

Not that it mattered in that moment, but she must have been beautiful in her youth. Her downturned brown eyes, almost the same color as Ruth's, were over prominent round cheekbones in a square face. Deep crow's feet lined them, and her forehead creased above heavy, furrowed brows.

She didn't move at all, but her hand on my shoulder cast my fear and anxiety away in ripples. As if in a dream, I swung my legs over the bed and stood, completely unashamed by my nakedness in front of this ghostly woman. Without speaking, she told me to close my eyes.

A sharp blow, not quite enough to hurt, right between my eyes made them pop open again. With no source, the room was illuminated as brightly as daylight, but I was no longer blinded by it.

The woman in front of me in her strapless buckskin dress had a beaded choker around her throat. Jet-black hair stood out from her umber skin and the tan of her dress. Every bead of the finely worked details on her clothes stood out in sharp contrast to the deerskin.

As if the volume on a TV was being turned up, distinct voices rose from nothing and crowded around me. A shiver of fear ran through me, and the Grandmother raised her hand to me. As quickly as it had come, fear disappeared to be replaced with calm resolve.

She turned and disappeared into the hallway.

I followed her, my feet numb on the carpet.

She glided into the living room and checked over her shoulder before turning the corner to face the front door. She pointed toward it with one hand, beckoning me with the other.

I hesitated halfway down the hallway where the solid wall to my right dropped into the half wall, exposing me to the windows behind the house. Like a splash of cool water on a hot day, peace washed through me, and I strode forward.

Emerging into the living room, I stood alone. The Grandmother had disappeared.

A shadow crossed by the front door, and I sucked in a breath. A crowd of shadows skipped and danced in the front yard. As I concentrated, I could make out faces. So many faces, clothes from many time periods.

They seemed to catch me watching them. They rushed to the front door and the window beside it at once. Hands clawed at the glass. Faces pressed against the panes as they fought for position in front of the crowd.

Let us in.

Behind me, I sensed another presence. I didn't dare to turn around. It was him. The man in the flannel who had scared Alexandra.

We're sorry.

I'm sorry, but it's very dark out here.

Something welled up inside me. A feeling. Not love, or confidence, but close enough.

Power.

The blue-white light glowed in my hands, turning my beige skin as white as snow in the moonlight. The light swept toward the front door, turning the spirits clawing at the door and window a sickly gray.

Let us in.

Light filled the room, casting sharp black shadows behind every piece of furniture and every frame on the wall. More power filled me, and I raised my hands, asking for more without knowing how. My hands heated and tingled.

A few of the spirits howled at the brightness and disappeared from the door, making room for others to take their place. From the shadows on the porch, an even darker shadow reared up. It pressed against the door, obscuring the faces of the spirits trying to force their way in. I faltered, and the front door rattled on its hinges, opening a crack.

Throwing my hands in front of me, I screamed. Not fear. A battle cry.

The light from my hands burst forward with a force of its own, throwing the door closed against the shadow pressing against the other side. With a shriek, the shadow disappeared into the night. The floor below me rumbled as the light in my hands grew even brighter, creeping up my arms now. My hands were on fire.

A spirit, a woman, with bedraggled wet hair, pressed her gray face against the glass.

Bitch, let me in.

Neither an echo nor a memory this time. She screamed at me the same way I'd heard the Grandmother tell me to close my eyes. A shiver ran down my spine, pulling the electricity even farther up my arms and into my shoulders. A familiar ache returned to both my damaged rotator cuff and my bad knee before the scalding power of the light in my hands burned it away.

The floor below me shifted and then shook. The air spun around me, lifting me. My feet came up off the carpet, and I closed my eyes against the now blinding light. I had expected only gray behind my eyelids. Instead, the ghosts appeared in infinite detail. I didn't need to have my eyes open.

The power reached my chest and burned its way down my back along my spine. The foundation rattled as the vortex under the house broke into pieces and swallowed itself.

I dared to open my eyes just a slit. My body hovered in midair, my head near the ceiling. The power from my hands connected in the center of my body. The resulting jolt arched me backward.

My mouth opened as a wail forced itself from my throat.

The wet-haired woman fled.

The wail grew louder and louder. Pushing my hands forward, I threw all the energy I had behind the howl flowing from my mouth.

Ghosts scattered from the porch like leaves in a strong wind. A few remained, clawing at the door.

Let us in.

I want it.

From behind me, *hurry.*

The sound from my throat grew into a scream. All the energy that had built up inside me exploded. A shock wave blew out around me, catching any residual ghosts with it, and scattering them to the four winds.

The vortexes on the property slammed shut in a whirlpool of sand and leaves under the force of the blast and collapsed.

The screaming from my throat stopped as I sank to the floor. Unable to stand, I fell to my knees, my hands pressed to my throat as I gasped for air. The sound I'd made wasn't for mere humans, and I would pay the price.

After a few minutes, or a few hours, I looked up. Outside, the half-moon cast soft shadows across the lawn. A bat flew across the yard.

I was alone.

Chapter 41

June 25, 2011

In the backyard of someone's house, I sat in the front row of rented plastic chairs as my best friend married the love of her life. Olivia sat on my knee, with one of Sarah's friends next to me, a Moby wrap over her dress with a sleeping baby Emma tucked inside.

Alexandra had decided to buck tradition entirely, wearing an emerald green, vintage 1920s evening dress with a mermaid skirt. Floral lace with beads and sequins, the capped sleeves set off the shape and pale skin of her neck to perfection. Every time she turned, I spotted my malachite necklace she'd borrowed, and the sight of it had me choking back tears. In tall heels with her mass of thick ebony hair piled high on her head, she towered over her diminutive wife. Sarah, in an A-line gown of ivory satin, stole the show. The simplicity of her dress and her blonde hair hanging loose in gentle curls across her shoulders allowed her natural beauty to shine through.

Their firm, clear voices speaking their vows—sweet, simple, and to the point—reached every person there in all ways. When it came time to kiss the bride, Sarah, always uncomfortable with public displays of affection, turned pink. Alexandra hesitated. Without warning, Sarah threw her arms around Alexandra's neck and pulled her down for a kiss.

Everyone cheered. Excited by the crowd, Olivia—now three—joined in and clapped.

Once the ceremony finished, everyone rushed to Sarah and Alexandra to congratulate them. I stood to get ahead of the crowd, bringing a still cheering Olivia to her mamas. She reached for Sarah, who took her from me and balanced the squirming toddler on her hip.

The infectious ear to ear smile on Sarah's face would have me smiling so hard all night that my face would hurt. I congratulated them both, and then stepped aside for everyone else to share their well wishes, more than content to bask in the pure joy around me. This had been a long, hard fight for both of them, and they deserved every iota of happiness they could get on this day.

"Hey."

The familiar voice sent a warm tingle up my spine. I turned toward Ryan. My heart leaped into my throat.

"Hey, yourself." I had forgotten how tall he was. In my flats, I barely came up to his collarbone.

"So, how are you?" He moved one hand to tuck it into a pocket that didn't exist in his charcoal gray trousers. He dropped it to his side instead.

I stepped back so I could take him in. He had already rolled up the sleeves of his blindingly white shirt. The open collar revealed his tanned chest, the fabric pulled taut across his shoulders and skimmed the muscles in his upper arms. He'd even abandoned his usual hiking boots for shiny dress shoes. My heart twinged. I had missed him.

My smile didn't need to be faked. Not today. "I'm actually really good." It faded. "I'm really sorry about your dad. Alexandra told me he passed away just after Christmas."

He shrugged. "He was ready to go and tired of being sick." The silence stretched until he released a pent-up breath. "Can I buy you a drink?"

I smiled again, and blamed the atmosphere. "Sure, that would be really nice."

We walked together to the food tent. Tables laden with food everyone had brought to share lined the walls. In the corner, a separate table practically sagged under the weight of over a dozen bottles of wine and a glass jar of homemade lemonade.

Ryan reached into the cooler underneath the table and pulled out a bottle of beer. "What can I get for you?"

Pursing my lips, I perused my choices. I finally settled on the lemonade.

He handed me a plastic cup nearly filled to the brim. I took a sip, not sure what to say, but happy to have something to do with my hands.

"So." I took another sip, not quite looking at him, but also not *not* looking at him. I decided I was okay with letting him sweat a little.

"So."

People came up behind us, searching for drinks, and Ryan steered me through the back of the tent with his hand on my elbow.

I kept my mouth shut, determined to let him say something first.

His gaze scanned me from head to toe, starting at my face. He grinned. "You look amazing."

That wasn't what I'd been expecting. I smoothed my short hair behind my ear, my fingers trailing over the back of my drop earrings. While shopping for her wedding dress, Alexandra had found what I wore—a dark purple dress with an empire waist and a hem that hit perfectly at the knee. I felt good, and it felt good to be noticed.

"Thanks."

He released a long breath. "Listen, I'm sorry for what happened. I wanted to text you or call about a thousand times, but I couldn't think of what to say to make up for being such a tool."

I shrugged. "I didn't call or text you, either." The part where I assumed he didn't want to hear from me remained unsaid.

Wiping the condensation off his bottle with his thumb consumed his attention, and his brows furrowed. "Well, I'm sorry. For not calling and, well, for not believing, to be honest. Did you end up moving?"

"Nope. I was able to fix the issue with the house."

He kept avoiding me. "Something happened when my dad died, and I think I was wrong to be so cavalier about your ghosts." Ryan's brown eyes met mine, searching. "I think I could benefit from being a little more open-minded."

Sympathy welled inside me, and I squeezed my lemonade cup so I wouldn't reach out to touch him. "Oh?"

He frowned. "I'd hate to be a buzzkill talking about this here."

The music changed from gentle classical to an upbeat pop song. Someone plugged in the strings of white Christmas lights draped under the tent, and they bathed everything underneath in white light even as the sky turned purple around us. A dance floor had been set up, and Alexandra and Sarah were dancing together with Olivia. Their broad smiles did something to my heart and tears welled up. Alexandra spun Sarah under her arm, and Olivia giggled. There was that joy again.

Smiling, I tipped my lemonade toward Ryan. "How about this. I'm here alone, and you're..." I left the end a question.

"Also alone." He grinned.

"So, we're here together alone. That's good, because there's something I've been wanting to ask you." I glanced over my shoulder at the happy couple again before turning back to Ryan. "Do you want to go out sometime? Like on a real date?"

He grinned. "I think we can do that."

We joined my family on the dance floor.

Sarah winked at her wife, and Alexandra gave me a knowing smile.

She broke away from Sarah and grabbed my arm. "I'll bring her right back!" she promised Ryan before propelling me out of the tent. She made a show of making sure no one was listening.

"I saw you guys smiling. Did you finally pull your heads out of your respective asses?"

"What are you talking about?" I wanted to scowl at her, but the mood around us and my success with Ryan had me too giddy.

She scoffed at me. "Do you seriously think I picked some random guy friend to help you move? And sending to him to your house on errands? Please." She rolled her blue eyes. "It takes you way too long to figure things out sometimes."

I gave her the most appropriate response I could think of. I stuck my tongue out at her. "Don't you need to get back to your wife?" I asked, unable to keep the smile off my face.

She grinned at me and started backing toward the dance floor. "I most definitely do, but the day wouldn't be complete if I didn't give my little sister a hard time."

She half-danced, half-ran back underneath the tent. She spun, the bottom of her skirt flaring around her, and then swooped a giggling Olivia up over her head.

Ryan caught my gaze and headed toward me.

I could not stop smiling.

No matter what happened tomorrow, tonight, I was finally home.

CHECK OUT THESE OTHER GREAT READS FROM ROWAN PROSE:

Brigid Barry is a lifelong resident of Maine. A disabled Air Force veteran and blessed parent of twins, she lives on a small hobby farm with her favorite husband and too many animals. "Straw Girl" is her debut book.